"If you do not let me pass this instant, I shall scream and accuse you of behavior most unbecoming to a gentleman."

Elise clung to her indignation in the hope that it might subdue her rising panic.

"Indeed?" He sounded bored. "And I shall accuse you of behavior most unbecoming to a lady. But I think we both know you are not a lady."

As she backed away from him, darting glances to and fro, Alex swept back his jacket to plunge his fists on his hips. He was tied between impatience and intrigue. Novice Jezebel maybe, but she had perfected the persona of a prim maiden, and it was definitely not the reaction he was used to arousing when he was stranded with a woman in the dark.

"Are you saying you aren't Lady Lonesome?" he demanded.

"Do I look as though I might adopt such a ridiculous sobriquet?"

* * *

A Date with Dishonor
Harlequin® Historical #1157—October 2013

Author Note

Most young women dream of finding a perfect mate. In reality, the quest for "the one" is rarely easy, and never more so than in Regency England's polite society, where etiquette and social class presented barriers to ill-starred lovers.

In *A Date with Dishonor,* Elise Dewey would sooner forgo marriage than endure the sort of mésalliance that caused her warring parents such unhappiness. But she is persuaded to move to town to assist her sister's search for a husband despite her misgivings that Beatrice is going about things in a hazardous way. When her sister's unorthodox methods of attracting a man cause a calamity to befall them, it is innocent Elise who bears the brunt of the disgrace. Alex Blackthorne is a womanizing rogue—just the sort of fellow Elise has tried to avoid—yet now she is at his mercy, sensually enslaved by the charismatic viscount, despite their families having tangled tragically in the past....

The second novel in the series will feature Beatrice as the heroine. She has been unlucky in love, and has been taught a hard lesson about taking risks with her reputation and virtue. At the age of twenty-five, she seems content to live quietly in the countryside with her beloved papa. Then an old flame turns up out of the blue, reigniting in Beatrice a yearning she believed she'd conquered long ago.

I hope you enjoy reading about the Dewey sisters' tears and laughter while looking for love as much as I have liked writing the stories for you.

A Date with Dishonor

Mary Brendan

HARLEQUIN®HISTORICAL

Recycling programs
for this product may
not exist in your area.

ISBN-13: 978-0-373-29757-3

A DATE WITH DISHONOR

Copyright © 2013 by Mary Brendan

Printed in U.S.A.

MARY BRENDAN

was born in north London, but now lives in rural Suffolk. She has always had a fascination with bygone days, and enjoys the research involved in writing historical fiction. When not at her word processor, she can be found trying to bring order to a large overgrown garden, or browsing local fairs and junk shops for that elusive bargain.

Chapter One

'Hell's teeth, give it up, man. Can't you see how vulgar it all is?'

The weary censure had been directed at a gentleman who gave no more response than to deepen the furrow in his brow. He leaned forwards, resting his chin in his cupped hands, absorbed in his reading.

Viscount Blackthorne adjusted his neckcloth with nimble fingers but, when his friend continued frowning at the newsprint spread on the table, he turned impatiently from his reflection to whip the offending paper out from under the fellow's elbows. Having efficiently folded the gazette, his lordship tossed it on to a wing chair.

Hugh Kendrick huffed in indignation, lolling back in his seat with a sulky expression. 'Well, something's got to be done, Alex. If I don't offer to pay Whittiker soon, the odious skinflint will dun me. Then everybody else will pitch in. Only needs one of 'em to start the ball rolling and my desk will be groaning under the weight of writs.' His glum face again sought the support of his hands. 'If I end in the Fleet my mother will have a fit, and Toby…' the mention of his older brother caused his mouth to twist in a grimace '…no doubt Toby will demand a dawn appointment on Clapham Common because I've sullied the family name.'

'Don't be so damned melodramatic.' Alex Blackthorne's lack of sympathy held a hint of amusement. A moment later he was once more contemplating his appearance, long patrician fingers dusting an immaculate broad shoulder encased in charcoal superfine. 'You're not the first man to have let a woman make a fool of him and bring him close to ruin.'

'You wouldn't let it happen to you.' A look of begrudging admiration shaped Hugh's features.

'No…I wouldn't.' Alex grinned lopsidedly at the glass, but decided not to rub salt into his old friend's smarting wound by elaborating. He'd already given him his opinion, on numerous occasions, on the subject of idiots who allowed courtesans to fleece them.

Hugh sprung to his feet, snatching up the gazette. 'I reckon it's a sound idea and I'd found one that seemed just the ticket. Here, I'll read it to you…'

A protracted muttering accompanied Alex raising his deep-brown eyes heavenwards.

Ignoring his friend's weary cursing, Hugh began, 'Lady Lonesome, desperate to free herself from the constraints of a cruel guardian, seeks kind gentleman to offer protection from…'

A snort of laughter curtailed Hugh's recitation. 'Methinks the lonesome lady is keener on a plump wallet than a kind gentleman.' Alex quirked an eyebrow. 'You should suit each other well. She's after the same thing you are.'

'Ah…ha!' Hugh exclaimed in triumph. 'Well, that's where you're wrong. Had you let me finish…' He shook the paper in emphasis, then resumed, '…she seeks a kind gentleman to offer protection…' a dramatic pause preceded '…from fortune hunters as an income of two thousand pounds per annum is available to an applicant able to convince her he is in possession of sincerity and a desire and capability to be a caring husband and father.' Hugh looked up with an expectant smile. 'She sounds rather sweet and—'

'And she sounds rather pregnant.'

Hugh's jaw sagged. 'You think…because she requires the fellow to be a good father…?'

Alex shrugged. 'It wouldn't be the first time desperate parents attempted to buy back a girl's sullied virtue by getting a ring on her finger.' He chuckled at the astonished look his comment had provoked. 'Come on, Hugh,' the Viscount ribbed gently. 'If anyone should know that, it's you.' Alex watched his friend colouring miserably, but felt unremorseful. Hugh was a good friend, but it was high time he toughened up. Alex knew he might not always be around to save the fellow from his niceness and naivety.

A year ago Hugh Kendrick had been burdened with the task, and the cost, of salvaging his sister's reputation when she'd allowed a callous charmer to compromise her. Toby, her brother and legal guardian, had refused to chip in a penny piece to protect their widowed mother from the shame that would have besmirched them all had his sister's disgrace become common knowledge.

'Never mind, Lady Lonesome's cash will come in handy.' Alex patted his friend's shoulder. Despite his mockery, he was beginning to find it all quite intriguing. He relieved Hugh of the paper and read for himself her requirements in a mate.

'Why in heaven's name would she need to advertise for a husband if she's a modest heiress?' He shot his friend a darkly humorous glance. 'If she's not a fallen woman, perhaps she's way past her prime and has ample girth and greying hair.'

'I don't think I care overmuch either way,' Hugh responded mordantly. 'She can be as fat or faded as she likes. It's the colour of her money I'm interested in.'

'You and a hundred other fellows with pockets to let who've read that.' Alex returned the paper to his friend. 'You know I've said I'll lend you the money.' His tone quietened, growing serious. 'You've not yet come to such a sorry pass that you'll need to rear another man's bastard, or risk getting leg-shackled to an old crone with a few pounds in the bank.'

'And I've said I won't take your money…not again.' Hugh turned his head to conceal his florid cheeks. Alex had paid off his debts once before. On that occasion he had been blameless for the mess he'd been in: a victim of his sister's folly. Sarah had since settled with a husband in Cheshire and Hugh thought his money… Alex's money, he mentally corrected himself…very well spent. But he'd sworn never again to take advantage of his friend's wealth or generosity, and he didn't intend to go back on his word.

Besides, he was twenty-nine, and for some while had been contemplating the benefits of settling down with a wife. He was the youngest son of a baronet and had few prospects and fewer responsibilities. For some months he had been feeling the lack and wondering whether a wife and children might fill a gap in his life.

'She *might* be personable and sincere,' Hugh insisted optimistically, having again studied the advertisement. Instead of considering a wife as a pretty appendage, he was beginning to properly value an advantageous match and a lifelong companion.

'True…and I might be the Prince Regent…' Viscount Blackthorne intoned repressively.

Elise Dewey's complexion drained of blood till it resembled the colour of the parchment on which she'd been writing. She was used to her older sister's harebrained schemes to get rich or get wed, but so far Beatrice had put none into action. Whilst writing to her friend, Verity, Elise had been listening with scant attention to her older sibling's chatter. But then Bea had waved at her the proof that this plot was no idle boast.

'You are joking, of course,' Elise finally burst out in a hushed tone. She gazed aghast at the gazette that Beatrice had been flapping in the air.

'No, I'm not!' Bea retorted, dropping the newspaper back to the table. 'It's the only way to get away from here. It's not my fault our parents have got us in such a mess. I'm twenty-three soon and I want a husband before I get any longer in the tooth. With no portion, and no means for a social life in this dreary neck of the woods, it's the only way to do it. How are we ever to meet gentlemen if we can't afford to go out?'

'And how are you to explain away the fact you've not got two thousand pounds or even two hundred to offer any fellow?' Elise had jumped to her feet and marched over to Beatrice. Her eyes widened as she scanned the notice. 'You're mad! Utterly insane!' Her tawny gaze sprang to her sister's profile. 'Have you any idea what sort of villains or perverts you might entice to our door?'

'I'm not daft enough to give out our direction. Of course, any fellow who replies to the box number will be advised we are to meet somewhere.' Bea avoided her sister's angry stare and carelessly twirled a pearly ringlet about a finger in order to prove she was quite relaxed about what she'd done.

Elise could tell Beatrice wasn't as insouciant as she'd like to appear. 'And how does *Lady Lonesome* think such hardened fortune hunters will react when they find out she's lied and has nothing to offer?'

That comment prompted Bea to rise from her chair and peer at her face in the mantelpiece mirror. 'I wouldn't say I've *nothing* to offer.' She cocked her head. 'When he sees me he might forget about the money...' She smiled, proudly tilting her chin.

Elise allowed Bea her conceit. Her sister might be what society classed as *past her prime*, but still she was lovely to look at. Her eyes were cornflower blue, lushly fringed with long inky lashes, and her pale blonde curls always sat in perfect array about her heart-shaped face, whereas Elise's own darker blonde mop tended to resist any maid's attempts to style it. Of course...now there were no maids, and only Mr and Mrs Francis, their faithful old retainers, remained with the Dewey family and acted as general staff to the best of their ability.

'If only Mama had taken me to live with her in London, I'd be married now.' Beatrice sighed. 'Some fellow would have offered for me. I wouldn't care who he was…he could be old and ugly so long as he had enough standing to let me live a little before I die.'

'But she didn't take you,' Elise returned shortly. 'Mama didn't want us. She wanted her lover, and now she is dead,' she concluded, a catch to her voice. 'Papa has his faults, but at least he didn't abandon us.'

'I wish he had,' Beatrice hissed, spinning away from her reflection. 'I didn't want to be dragged to the sticks to moulder away and expire as a spinster. I'd rather have thrown myself on some rich fellow's mercy.'

'I don't think you mean that,' Elise replied, annoyed by her sister's hint that she'd rather be a gentleman's mistress than endure boredom.

Beatrice blushed, but her lips slanted mutinously, letting Elise know that she wasn't about to take back her outrageous comment.

'You'd better hope Papa doesn't find out what you're doing or saying!' Elise warned, her vivid eyes widening in emphasis. 'If he gets to know you've put in print he's a cruel guardian, and that you're touting yourself about, you really will end in a convent.' Mr Dewey's pet threat when exasperated by his daughters' behaviour was to send them to take vows.

'Even that might be better than living here,' Bea declared theatrically.

'Don't be ridiculous!' Elise swept up the gazette and with no further ado tossed it on to the flickering fire that had burned very low in the grate for want of fuel to nourish it.

Bea gawped at the blackening paper for no more

than a few seconds before plunging downwards to try and retrieve it.

'Don't be so daft.' Elise pulled her sister back from the hearth as Bea sucked a scorched digit. 'At least we'll get some benefit from it if it burns for a while and keeps us warm.'

'You'll get every penny I owe you.'

'Oh, yes, indeed I will.' James Whittiker stalked about the card table his low-lidded eyes on the pot of money at its centre. 'I'll take it out of your hide else, Kendrick.' It was an unconvincing threat. Despite being in his mid-twenties James Whittiker was overweight and unfit, whereas Hugh Kendrick was a fine figure of a man, known to regularly attend the gymnasium. Unless Whittiker intended setting someone else on his debtor he would come off worst in a scrap. The assembly knew it and a few rumbles of mirth increased the redness veining Whittiker's cheeks.

'What I want to know is, when will you hand over what you owe?' James flicked a finger at the stake money. 'Is there any chance some of that will be yours? If so, I'll just hover in the vicinity and relieve you of it in a while, shall I?' His sarcasm drew another ripple of amusement; those who had been observing the play knew that Hugh was losing.

'You sound desperate, James.' Alex Blackthorne discarded a card on to the baize. He stretched his booted feet out under the table and settled his powerful shoulders against the chair back. 'Having a spot of trouble selling Grantham Place, are you?' He raised lazy brown eyes to a pink, jowly face. 'My offer is still on the table.'

'Take it back. I've no use for such a derisory sum,' James sneered.

'It's the best of the six you've had,' Alex answered evenly. 'That should tell you something about your expectations where the estate is concerned.'

'It tells me you're a cheat and a fraudster, just like your father before you.' Immediately Whittiker regretted having let seething frustration make him recklessly incautious. He glanced about to see a score or more pairs of eyes had swivelled his way, some viciously amused.

The clientele of White's Club were used to overhearing heated exchanges between its members; they were also used to the possible outcome if traded insults escalated and led to a dawn meeting in a misty glade. Several gentlemen no longer patronised this establishment, or any other, because they had fled abroad to escape arrest. They were the fortunate ones; other duellists no longer drew breath following an unsuccessful fight to protect their honour.

James knew that if Alex Blackthorne now got to his feet and challenged him to name his seconds a grovelling apology was his only option. The viscount was an excellent shot and his fencing skill had been likened to that of a professional. James wasn't prepared to risk being killed or maimed because of a moment of madness. He stabbed a poisonous stare at Hugh Kendrick. It was his fault. The viscount had only chipped in that comment about Grantham to take pressure off his blasted impecunious friend.

Alex was aware of the fomenting excitement in the room. Gentlemen reacted to a hint of a duel like a pack of hyenas scenting a carcase. He sensed several had already quit their tables to stealthily, determinedly, approach and gather behind his chair. Ancient Lord Brentley had seemed to be snoozing behind a newspaper on a sagging sofa. Now he was on his feet in a sprightly shove and ambling over.

Alex folded his hand and skimmed the cards over the baize before leisurely getting to his feet. He approached Whittiker and laid a large hand on one of his fat shoulders. The fellow's nervous quivering was quite tangible through wool. 'I don't think you meant to say that, did you, James?'

Whittiker licked his parched lips. The viscount was giving him a way out, but to take it would brand him ever more as a coward prepared to dishonour his family name to save his skin.

From his superior height Alex inclined his dark head to listen for Whittiker's response. The hushed atmosphere within the room seemed to extend into eternity.

Abruptly the sound of shattering glass splintered the silence. A steward had speeded into the room carrying a tray of decanters and crashed into a table whilst craning his neck to see what had made the club members congregate close to the fireplace.

'I apologise, Blackthorne; mouth ran away with me,' Whittiker muttered, using the ensuing confusion to drown out his words.

Alex was aware of the fellow's insincerity. Whittiker hadn't even met his eyes whilst speaking. Nevertheless, he gave his shoulder a pat before turning away.

Aware of a score or more pairs of despising eyes on him, James shoved through the throng of gentlemen towards the exit.

Chapter Two

'I shan't beg an invitation from the Chapmans, so please don't nag about it.'

'But why will you not?' Bea gestured in exasperation. 'Verity constantly invites you to stay with her in London, yet you rarely go. She always comes here instead and costs Papa her keep, which he can ill afford. Just a hint from you that we would love to see her and soon we would be booking our places on the mail coach.'

Privately Elise agreed with her sister's calculation; Verity would immediately issue an invitation should she imply she would like one. Verity was a dear friend from schooldays and hadn't shunned her when her parents' disgrace became common knowledge. Neither had Mr and Mrs Chapman turned their backs on them all. 'You know why I will not do it.' Elise sighed. 'Last time we were there you embarrassed us both by insisting we outstay our welcome. We were invited to be house-guests for two weeks yet you wangled for a longer stay, although you know Mr and Mrs Chapman are not well off. I practically had to drag you home.'

'Mr Vaughan had started paying me attention. It would have been silly to leave at such a time.' Beatrice had the grace to blush despite her forceful excuse.

'Mr Vaughan knew full well where you lived in Hertfordshire. I recall you telling him several times,' Elise responded drily. 'He would have come after you had his intentions been as serious as you'd imagined them to be.'

'He *did* like me.' Bea's obstinate tone couldn't conceal an undercurrent of hurt.

'Yes, I know,' Elise concurred softly. 'Unfortunately his fiancée had a firm grip on him. And now they are married.'

'He told me if Papa had even a little to offer to ease his financial situation he'd propose in an instant. He only got betrothed to *her* because cash was dangled by her father.'

'It tends to make a big difference,' Elise agreed on a sigh. 'That's why I'm amazed you think this harebrained scheme of yours will work. Mr Vaughan liked you very much, yet he was unable to wed a woman without good connections or a dowry to recommend her.' She frowned as Bea continued staring dreamily into space.

'Will you write and ask Verity if we may stay for just one week?' Beatrice was acting as though she'd not attended to a single sensible word Elise had uttered.

'Tell me truthfully,' Elise demanded. 'Have you received replies to your advert? Is that why you want to go to town—to meet fortune hunters on neutral ground?' From the moment Beatrice had started pestering her to get them to London Elise had feared her sister was planning to disgrace herself—perhaps them all—by risking secretly meeting a gentleman.

Beatrice hesitated just a fraction too long before issuing a denial.

'I knew it!' Elise gasped. 'You've made an assignation with a stranger to beg him to marry you!'

'I won't need to beg,' Bea said airily. 'I've had a dozen or more replies, but only two seem worth considering.' She grinned at Elise. 'Some have sworn that the money is not a temptation and they simply have fallen a little in love with me after reading my sweet prose.' She chuckled. 'What piffle! I can spot a liar a mile off.'

'Do you think these two gentlemen you are pinning your hopes on aren't able to do the same?' Elise choked a mirthless laugh. 'Your respondents are doubtless not as gullible or upstanding as you hope they'll be.'

'Neither am I gullible,' Beatrice asserted. 'I want a fellow who's honest enough to admit my money was a lure. Of course, he'll also need to have sufficient income of his own and to like me well enough to propose when he finds out I have nothing. We must then both try hard to make a go of it. But I can forgo luxuries.' She continued sourly, 'I am well used to doing so.'

'Nevertheless, I think you want too much,' her sister told her. 'Your chosen two might suspect you are a doxy touting for business, then you'll be in grave trouble as they won't have falling in love or marriage on their minds.'

'They don't need to fall in love with me. I just want a kind husband and a little family.' Beatrice hung her head, concealing her yearning expression with a curtain of blonde locks. 'Is that too much to ask?'

A surge of emotion overwhelmed Elise on hearing her sister's plaintive wail. A hiccup of breath caught in her throat, bringing a salty sting to her eyes. Of course, she knew it was not too much to want! How often had she daydreamed about something similar for herself? But painful memories of her parents' miserable life had damaged her ideal of romantic love. She'd seen there was a dark side to desire that was selfish and cruel.

'Why are you acting so silly?' Elise demanded in frustration. 'You might bring disaster down on all our heads if you carry on with this.' She quickly approached her sister, clasping her hands. 'I will talk to Papa and ask him to arrange for Aunt Dolly to give us board and lodging in Hammersmith. She knows a few good families, and if she arranges some social outings you might meet a gentleman in the customary way instead of resorting to this daft—'

'I have already asked Papa,' Bea interrupted despondently. 'He insists he can't afford frivolities like trips to town to see Aunt Dolly. He says his sister is a tightfist who will want a pretty penny to feed us mutton and cabbage.' She glowered at Elise. 'He's right, too. She served up scraps last time we went there. Papa said why don't I ask you if we can arrange a trip to stay with your friend Verity Chapman, for it will be more pleasant and economic.'

Elise turned away, her brow puckered in thought. Her sister was not to be dissuaded from her pursuit of a husband. Beatrice's need to be away from the dreary life in the countryside was making her very depressed at times.

For almost seven years they had shared a bedcham-

ber in the cottage their father continued to rent. As the
time had progressed Elise had been woken at night by
the sound of her sister weeping softly into her pillow.
Bea's melancholy was now overtaking her during the
daytime too and Elise didn't want to see her sister seriously ill.

Walter Dewey surfaced from his papers and led-
gers on occasions to notice what went on in his household and had more than once enquired of Elise what
ailed his eldest daughter. On hearing the truth he tended
to become impatient. He would then impress on them
both—usually as they ate their dinner, and with much
tapping of cutlery on china for emphasis—that the fearful plight of those less fortunate made him proud that,
as a fellow abandoned by a weak woman, he was able
to keep his two daughters in adequate fashion, despite
the constant trial of it all.

Elise glanced at her sister's miserable countenance.
If they went to stay with Verity, perhaps it might be
possible to put Beatrice in the path of a decent bachelor
who might fall for her and propose. Their papa would
have his oldest child settled and the financial burden
on him would be eased.

'I'll write to Verity on one condition,' Elise said.
'You must promise not to contact any of these ne'er-
do-wells who have replied to your advert.' Having received Bea's brisk nod and breathy affirmative, Elise
continued, 'But I won't badger for an invitation if I receive an ambiguous reply. You know they are not much
better off than are we, and now that Fiona has a beau
Mr Chapman might soon have the expense of her wedding to pay for.'

Verity had written recently to let Elise know that her older sister was at last being courted. Fiona was a pleasant-looking young woman who had seemed content to let romance pass her by. Even during her début she'd seemed happier at home drawing landscapes than seeking a husband. Elise gathered from her friend's amusing prose that neither the fellow's appearance nor his character was attractive, and that Verity was of the opinion her older sibling should have stuck to her watercolours.

Elise became aware that Beatrice was waiting expectantly for her to continue. 'I will try to get you your wish…' Elise squealed as Beatrice rushed to thank her with a hug before she'd finished speaking.

'Ah…Mr Chapman is here!' Elise exclaimed in relief. She urged her sister to pick up her portmanteau.

'So sorry to be late,' Anthony Chapman burst out as he heaved his bulk from the trap to politely assist the young ladies on to it. 'A costermonger had turned his cart over and I had a devil of a job getting through the press of carriages. It all got very heated and I thought a fight might break out between two jarveys.' He wheezed in air. 'I hope the way is now clear or we will be delayed on the road back.'

Verity's papa seemed stricken to have missed the appointed hour to meet them on alighting from the mail coach to transport them to his home in Marylebone.

'It is no trouble to us to have waited a few minutes,' Elise replied soothingly. 'It is very kind of you to fetch us. We could have hailed a hackney, after all, and saved you the journey.'

'No…no…' Mr Chapman flapped a stout hand whilst

the other assisted in hoisting him back up on to the carriage seat. 'Wouldn't hear of it, m'dear. It's a pleasure to see you both and looking so very well.' Having sucked in a heavy breath, he turned his head and beamed at the young ladies seated beside him. 'And your papa is in good health, I trust?'

'Indeed he is, sir, and he sends you and Mrs Chapman his very best wishes.'

Anthony patted at Elise's closest hand. 'Verity will be so pleased to see you. As will Fiona, although she is in a tizz over Mr Whittiker.' His mouth drooped to blow a sigh. 'Her mama is pleased, of course, that she has a beau.'

Elise noticed his furrowed brow and had the impression that Mr Chapman was no more enamoured of the idea of Mr Whittiker joining his family than was Verity.

Chapter Three

'For country misses you have pretty manners.'

Elise rewarded the fellow's faint praise with a cool smile. 'Indeed, thank you, Mr Whittiker.' He'd come too close to her and, stepping away, she added, 'We like to think ourselves housetrained.' She dipped him a curtsy but he continued smirking and Elise realised he was too thick-skinned to comprehend the insolence in her answer.

'We were reared in London, sir,' Beatrice cheerfully explained, having overheard his crass remark yet seemingly unaffected by it. 'We moved to Hertfordshire many years ago, worse luck…' She fidgeted uneasily beneath Elise's swift cautionary look.

'Have some more tea, sir.' Verity had grabbed up the pot and hurried towards him to hinder him from pursuing the conversation, or Elise for that matter. He had seemed to dog her friend's footsteps as she moved from bookcase to bookcase, attempting to shake him off her shoulder. 'I tried to give a hint about him when I last wrote to you,' she murmured, refilling Elise's cup.

'I fear no hint could do justice to Mr Whittiker,' Elise

returned ruefully, stirring her tea and watching Fiona shyly conversing with her beau. Elise had always considered Fiona to be a bit too nice, but nobody's fool. She certainly still thought her over-obliging, but was beginning, sadly, to suspect perhaps she might be a fool to be encouraging an oafish fellow to court her.

'I'm baffled, too, by what Fiona thinks she is about.' Verity had correctly read Elise's concerns as they settled down together on a sofa. 'But I know what's drawn him in.' She glowered sideways at James. 'Our grandmother has recently passed on and left Fiona a little nest egg.' Despite their distance from the room's other occupants Verity continued concealing her lips with her teacup. 'She has left me the same amount, but in trust until I reach twenty-one. On reflection I'm quite glad of that as Mr Whittiker might have turned his attention to me instead.'

Verity was six months younger than her, thus Elise knew her friend must wait another year and a half to lay claim to her cash. 'You think Mr Whittiker has found out about the inheritance and is a fortune hunter?'

'I'm almost certain of it. It is three thousand pounds, not a fabulous sum, but I overheard Papa telling Mama that the fund is enough of a lure for a man like James Whittiker who has his pockets permanently to let. Papa seems very suspicious of his motives, but Mama is simply relieved that one of us might soon be sporting a ring.' Verity sighed. 'She has been chivvying Fiona to get herself off the shelf. Whittiker can claim good connections—and believe me, he does constantly boast about his uncle who is a baronet.'

'Perhaps there is a genuine fondness between them.'

Elise glanced at the couple, noticing they appeared to be chatting amiably.

'Hah!' Verity snorted quietly. 'He has a habit of ogling me that makes me think he is not as besotted with my sister as he'd like us all to believe.'

Elise knew the fellow had an unsettling habit of sidling up and standing far too close for comfort while ogling her bosom.

On their arrival earlier Verity had immediately whispered an apology to Elise because they were to be burdened with Mr Whittiker's presence. She'd explained that he'd called on Fiona yesterday and, discovering that young ladies were expected on the morrow, had prised an invitation from Mrs Chapman to join them at teatime to welcome the Dewey sisters to London.

'Mr Whittiker has offered to accompany us to Vauxhall on Friday. We'll have a nice time, won't we?' Having noticed her younger daughter and Elise were deep in private conversation, Maude Chapman had loudly addressed the pair in an attempt to draw them into discussing the week's social agenda.

Maude was always glad to offer hospitality to her daughters' friends. Her husband was not a tight-fist, but he was careful with his money. Yet Maude had noticed that when the Dewey sisters came to stay Anthony's generosity seemed to improve. She took no offence at her portly spouse's silly attempts to impress the pretty girls, for everybody benefited from it.

'But Elise and I have something else planned for Friday.' It was the only excuse Verity could dream up on the spur of the moment.

Elise didn't relish spending an evening with James

Whittiker either. But a trip to such a popular venue might turn up introductions to a suitable gentleman who might take a fancy to Beatrice. Her sister had also pounced on the opportunity and she gave Elise an energetic nod.

'It would be nice to go, Verity. I've heard Vauxhall is an enchanting place,' Elise enthused, appeasing her friend with a subtle wink that promised a private explanation would soon be forthcoming.

'Please do a recce for me, Alex. It won't take you more than a few minutes. I'll take care of Celia while you're gone.' Hugh's eyes darted from his friend's dark profile to settle apprehensively on the petite brunette dangling from one of his arms. He knew every fellow in the vicinity had her lush body under covert observation and would gladly swap places with him. But Hugh was under no illusions as to what he was taking on. Keeping such a fiery temptress entertained whilst his charismatic friend was running his errand was going to be no easy task. The prospect of fending off her gallants until Alex returned to claim her was alarming.

Celia Chase's full red lips were aslant, displaying her boredom, because her lover was dividing his time between her and Hugh. One of her slender white fingers began twirling an ebony ringlet, then her exaggerated sighing could be heard as she glanced about.

Viscount Blackthorne turned from his mistress to his friend, a low curse in his throat. Hugh had been hovering at his shoulder and muttering in his ear for some five minutes.

'There's no time to lose,' Hugh insisted, noticing he finally had Alex's full attention.

Suddenly Alex propelled him away from their group so they might speak privately.

'I'm due to meet Lady Lonesome at nine o'clock and it's almost that now.' Hugh plucked out his watch to check the time.

'For God's sake, you've got eyes in your head,' Alex ground out in irritation. 'If you're determined to carry on with this lunacy, you can see for yourself if she's a fright.'

'Well, yes, I can do that,' Hugh admitted readily. 'But I'm not a good judge of character where women are concerned…as you well know.' The corners of his mouth drooped in self-mockery. 'Lady Lonesome might be a bewitching beauty, up to no good. I'll get taken in as I did with Sophia and end up in a worse mess than I am in already. If she's got a sob story prepared, I'm done for. You know I have a soft heart.'

'Soft head, more like,' Alex snapped, jerking his eyes heavenward. But he couldn't argue with his friend's self-confessed incompetence with the fairer sex. A good few gentleman who'd had previous dealings with Sophia Sweetman had told Hugh that she was a mercenary madam out for all she could get. He'd not heeded warnings and had acceded to her demand to set her up in style, not casting her off until he'd been almost down to his last shilling.

'Whereas you…you are pretty clued up about the petticoat set and I'd trust you to spot a fraud a mile off.'

A sour smile acknowledged Hugh's compliment.

Alex pivoted on a heel to glance back towards his mistress and gauge her mood.

Celia was watching them, in between chatting to Sidney Roper. The young Hussar, resplendent in his brocaded uniform, was one of her admirers and had dared to approach her first before Alex had moved far from her side. Aware he was under observation, the young officer jerked him a nod. Alex leisurely returned the salute with a quirk of the lips intended to allay the boy's fears and stop his Adam's apple bobbing so violently. Alex's smile strengthened as he transferred his attention to Celia. He wanted her to know her flirting didn't bother him.

And it didn't. He just wished she would allow him similar licence. Their relationship was only six months' old, yet Alex was already thinking it had run its course. She'd irritated him several times by being too possessive and flouncing over to find out what he was up to if he left her side for too long.

'I'll take care of Celia for you,' Hugh again promised, having noted the direction of Alex's gaze. He imagined his friend to be, understandably, enthralled by the sultry lovely. Celia was known to be very selective about the gentlemen she allowed to woo her and liked rich influential lovers. She'd be hard pressed to improve on Alex Blackthorne on either count in Hugh's opinion. Added to which his friend had the broad physique and rugged dark looks that made females flutter and fawn as soon as he entered a room.

'I'll have a scout around and have a brief conversation with your blind date—if she's turned up.' Alex's eyes swerved to Hugh, gleaming with mordant humour.

'But that's all I'll do. If you decide to go ahead and meet her, you can charm her yourself.' He took a prowling pace away, then pivoted and walked backwards while muttering, 'If Celia cross-examines you…I've spotted my mother and have gone to speak to her.' It was a valid excuse; he'd caught sight of Susannah Blackthorne parading with Lord Mornington about twenty minutes ago. He wanted a word with his mother, although it needn't have been this evening that he brought up the subject of Miss Winters.

His widowed mother's long and happy marriage had made her convinced her only child must hanker after the same blissful state of union. But Alex had no intention of being paired off by his doting mama and he wished she'd stop matchmaking him with Rachel Winters or any of the other nubile young women she thought suitable to be his wife because they were her friends' daughters.

'Where have you agreed to meet her?' Alex retraced a few steps to get that vital information. He jammed his clenching fists into his pockets. If Hugh hadn't been such an old friend, he might have throttled him on the spot for making him feel obliged to get involved in this farce.

Having told Alex in which direction to head, Hugh grabbed his friend's elbow before he could stride away. 'I made up a name to catch her attention. I guessed she'd get a lot of replies to her advert and I wanted to stand out.' He smiled bashfully. 'She is to meet a *Mr Best*,' he whispered, significantly poking a thumb against his chest.

'Ingenious…' Alex muttered caustically, stalking off.

* * *

'You promised me you would not contact those gentlemen!' Elise's angry astonishment caused her to stop
dead on the path. A woman who'd been strolling behind
bumped into her and glared, prompting her to apologise.

Beatrice linked arms with her sister, urging her on.
But a guilty colour stole into her cheeks as she felt
Elise's stony stare on her profile. They had been walking beneath twinkling globe lights strung in the trees
in Vauxhall Gardens when she'd dropped her bombshell
and let Elise know she'd contacted one of her respondents and arranged to meet him that evening.

'I know I said I wouldn't and I'm sorry for the deceit,
but I have to be sensible and make the most of this time
in town. We only have a few days left before we return
home.' It was an earnestly made case. 'So far we've
been out and about every evening with the Chapmans,
yet no gentleman has shown much interest in me.'

Elise knew that wasn't quite true. Last night Bea
had collected several admirers when they'd attended
a soirée held by the Chapmans' neighbours. She, too,
had attracted a fresh-faced young fellow who had
loitered by her chair and courteously fetched her drinks
and titbits from the buffet. But when they had retrieved
their coats to leave, no gentleman had seemed keen to
further an acquaintance with them.

Seven years might have passed since their parents
separated and their father had left town in disgrace, taking his two teenage daughters with him, but Elise had
noticed a sharp glint in the eyes of some individuals on
discovering their identities. Mrs Porter and her friend
had last night distanced themselves quickly once the

name Dewey had been mentioned. Elise had watched them whispering behind their gloved hands while sliding sly peeks their way.

'Where are you to meet this fellow?'

'A pavilion by the lake.'

'And where on earth is that?' Elise curtly enquired.

'As I recall, it is somewhere over there…'

'You don't even know the location?' Elise sounded exasperated, snatching at her sister's wildly gesturing hand to prevent her attracting attention.

'I can't recall exactly; it's many years since I was last here,' Bea stated defensively. 'I only had one trip here before we got carted off to the countryside by Papa.'

'It doesn't matter, in any case, where it is as you shall not go and meet him.' Elise tightened her grip on Beatrice's fingers to physically restrain her. 'If you are spotted dawdling about on your own, or, worse still, with a stranger, it won't only be Mrs Porter and her friends who are shredding our reputations.' Elise nodded at two middle-aged ladies who were strolling just yards away. Mrs Porter raised a gloved hand, letting them know she'd got them in her sights.

Huge crowds were thronging the pleasure gardens that evening to enjoy the music. People were already milling about the stage, jostling for a prime position as the orchestra tuned up.

'I'm not daft, you know!' Beatrice protested. 'I have arranged to meet *him* when everybody else will be occupied listening to the concert.' She dimpled a smile, pleased with her strategy.

'You shall not go!' Elise vowed through gritted teeth. 'And that's final.'

'I want to go home and tell Papa a gentleman is soon to come and speak to him,' Bea announced defiantly. 'I know you think me brazen for using such tactics, but who is to say that we might not suit well enough to make a go of it.' She pressed back against the hedging, allowing people to pass them, obstinately refusing to move despite Elise's tugs on her arm. 'A marriage of convenience brokered by a couple's parents for property and pedigree is equally distasteful.'

'Not in the eyes of polite society,' Elise hissed in frustration. 'Anyway, you might yet meet a gentleman without resorting to sneaking about. Mr Whittiker claims his friends are here in abundance this evening.'

That comment elicited a grimace of mock horror and Elise sympathised with Bea's sentiment. If Mr Whittiker's friends were even a little like him then the stranger by the lake might indeed be a better bet.

'I hope I *do* meet a fellow in the customary way,' Bea said with asperity as they started to walk on. 'But—'

'Do you even know your blind date's name?' Elise interrupted crossly before her sister could again bombard her with reasons to act rashly.

'He calls himself Mr Best.' A little chuckle escaped Bea. 'I imagine that is not his real name.

'I imagine you are right!' Elise acidly concurred. 'Just as he knows full well you are not actually Lady Lonesome.'

'It is quite dramatic is it not?' Bea's eyes were alight with excitement.

Despite her grave misgivings, Elise felt a twinge of the thrill enlivening her sister. Her compressed lips softened slightly. 'Maybe…but you cannot go through with it because you will get us both hung.' She gazed sombrely at her sister. 'Promise me you will not go there and risk disgracing us all.' When Bea remained silent Elise demanded more forcefully, 'Promise me, Bea, or I will never forgive you for your selfishness.'

'I promise…' Bea sighed. 'I shall try and make another arrangement to meet Mr Best in the daytime. And you can come along, too.'

'Papa has found us a wonderful spot, very close to the stage.' Verity had been walking ahead of them, with her parents, but had skipped back towards her friends to impart that news. She linked arms with them, urging them to hurry.

Chapter Four

Battling against a flow of revellers was forcing Elise to dodge nimbly to and fro to avoid sharp shoulders and elbows. But she couldn't escape those people's sly looks and she understood what prompted them.

Generally only one class of female went about Vauxhall Gardens unaccompanied and they were usually touting for business. Mortified as Elise was to be mistaken for a doxy, she nevertheless knew that finding Beatrice before she disgraced herself was more important than fretting over strangers' hateful imaginings. Finally the throng thinned out and she settled into a fast walk along the shadowy path.

Elise felt her lungs burning with exertion, yet despite her discomfort she longed to hurtle on at an even faster pace. It was her first outing to Vauxhall and she hoped she had correctly remembered her sister's vague indication of where the lake was situated. If she were heading the wrong way, she and Beatrice would both be in grave trouble. She'd be too late to drag her sister away before dratted *Mr Best* arrived for their tryst. Elise knew she mustn't dash like a hoyden hither and thither and risk drawing further attention to herself. The entire matter had to be dealt with as discreetly as possible.

Inwardly she berated herself for letting Bea slip away from her side. At one moment they had been in a conversation with Mr Chapman, offering opinions on the talent of the musicians, at the next Elise had turned to find Beatrice had vanished. At first Elise had felt furious that her sister had gone back on her word; then she had striven to conceal her panic from the others in their party. Fortunately Mr and Mrs Chapman had seemed oblivious to any change in her. Fiona appeared quite serene, as she always did, waiting for Mr Whittiker's return with some refreshment. Only Verity had interpreted her frantic glances.

Rightly or wrongly Elise had, on the day they'd arrived in London, confessed to Verity that she'd angled for an invitation because her sister was yearning to escape the gloom of the countryside and find a husband. She'd gone on to admit that Bea had been foolish enough to advertise for a mate.

Verity was a true and trustworthy friend. Despite being quite scandalised a few moments ago when Elise had whispered her fears over Bea's sudden disappearance, Verity had promised she would try to concoct a plausible tale for their absence, if asked about it.

On the periphery of her vision Elise was again vaguely aware that someone else was striding away from the entertainment on a parallel path to the one she was taking. From beneath the brim of her bonnet she swung a discreet glance at him. He was tall and swarthy and imperious looking and from his sternly set profile she guessed he might be in a similar black mood to the one burdening her. Despite the vital nature of her mission she felt an odd compulsion to slacken her pace so she might study him more closely. He had an aura of such angry hauteur that, even at a distance, she felt a *frisson* of alarm ripple through her.

Suddenly he turned his head, glancing over before dismissing her. Just as abruptly his gaze snapped back and it narrowed on her as though an idea had struck him.

At the same time something struck Elise. The idea seemed so ludicrous that her eyes spontaneously widened on his handsome face and her steps faltered. He slowed down, too, calculatingly, so he was now behind her and able to watch her whilst she must twist her head awkwardly and obviously to see him. Before he'd slipped from her eye line Elise had noticed a subtle unpleasant change in his expression.

Despite her now sedate pace Elise felt her heartbeat increase tempo until the thud beneath her ribs seemed to quake her body. Her eyes darted along the prickly hedging to one side of her. But there was no gap, no escape route through which she might plunge to avoid that sardonic stare she sensed was boring into the back of her head. Yet, tense with anxiety as she was, an inner voice continued scoffing at her suspicion that such a gentleman might be Mr Best. From the glimpses she'd had of his distinguished bearing he certainly didn't look to be on his uppers and in need of a spinster's modest inheritance.

He was probably judging her, as had others she'd encountered whilst racing through the dusk, and had concluded she was hunting for customers. Her insides knotted as she realised he might be studying her from behind to assess whether he liked enough of what he saw to approach her. That notion inflamed Elise's indignation to such an extent that she came to an abrupt halt and turned towards him, chin up, eyes sparking anger and defiance.

He stopped, too, and Elise felt ice shiver her spine. There was no longer any doubt that she interested him and he seemed undeterred by her hostile glare. She'd hoped to embarrass him into moving on, but he turned fully towards her, plunging a hand in his pocket. The other was abruptly raised and he beckoned her with a crooked finger.

At first Elise felt too astonished by that curt summons to react, then her pride surged to the fore. How dare the arrogant man assume she'd go to him!

But she did; stumbling in her haste and with every intention of giving him a piece of her mind. Having marched diagonally across grass and cobbles she came to a halt with the breath hacking at her throat and stared up into a lean angular face. She read from his expression that he was still amused…unpleasantly so.

'Why are you following me?' she demanded in a shaky voice.

'I'm not. I suspect I'm just heading to the same place as you.'

'And…and where is that?' Elise demanded in a suffocated voice.

'The lake pavilion.' Having provoked the response he needed to satisfy himself he was talking to Lady Lonesome, Alex gave her a cynical smile. 'We needn't bother traipsing the whole distance, my dear. Here will do.'

His tone had sounded insultingly familiar and Elise guessed that was exactly his intention. But her shock at knowing this was Mr Best momentarily deprived her of speech. She had been correct in her assessment of him from a distance. Everything about his deportment, from the top of his stylishly cut dark hair to the tips of his expensive shoes proclaimed him to be a man of wealth and breeding. His bored drawl could not disguise the culture in his voice any more than the lengthy black lashes, low over his eyes, could conceal that he was looking her over very thoroughly. But his saturnine features remained impassive; there was no indication if he liked what he saw.

'Come…let's not draw out the charade longer than necessary,' he said curtly. 'There's a spot close by that's secluded enough for us to get to know each other a little better. It'll serve while I determine whether Lady Lonesome's to my liking.'

A firm grip on her arm was immediately propelling Elise towards another wall of hedging. Before she'd gathered wit enough to forcibly shake him off she was being steered through an arch and towards a bench set at the apex of converging dark paths. A single light above the seat was undulating in the breeze, casting eerie shadows over his features. At that moment Elise would sooner have been alone in twilight with the devil himself.

'Let go of me at once! There's been a dreadful mistake…' Elise shoved at him, attempting to slip past and speed back whence she'd come.

Alex easily barred her flight with his body. 'I'm afraid that won't quite do, my dear. You instigated this little tryst. Having lured me here, the least you can do is give me a few minutes of your time…if nothing else is on offer.'

Elise recognised the throaty lust in his voice and glanced about to spot someone who might come to her aid should the hateful brute make a lunge for her. But the only sight was a wall of shrubbery, the only sound the soughing of a million leaves and strains of a far-away melody. She slowly moistened her parched lips with her tongue tip.

Alex felt a stirring in his loins at her teasing little trick. She was good, he acknowledged sourly, the out-raged innocent act was convincing and erotic. She even looked the part. Now he'd got a closer look at her he could see she had an unusual, fresh-faced beauty and her abundant hair looked to be a shade of dark blonde. Her quietly stylish clothing betrayed a hint of a sweetly curvaceous figure beneath her cloak. But he'd sooner she stopped acting coy and owned up to the game im-mediately so they could get down to business. She'd be-trayed herself straight away by allowing guilt to show in her eyes when he'd mentioned a tryst by the lake. If she were a harlot—and no genteel young woman in pos-session of her sanity would be out alone—he guessed she was new to the profession to have made such a basic mistake.

'If you do not let me pass this instant, I shall scream and accuse you of behaviour most unbecoming to a gentleman.' Elise clung to her indignation in the hope it might subdue her rising panic.

'Indeed?' He sounded bored. 'And I shall accuse you

of behaviour most unbecoming to a lady. But I think we both know you are not.'

As she backed away from him, darting glances to and fro, Alex swept back his jacket to plunge his fists on his hips. He was tied between impatience and intrigue. Novice Jezebel maybe, but she had perfected the persona of a prim maiden and it was definitely not the reaction he was used to arousing when he was stranded with a woman in the dark. 'Are you saying you aren't Lady Lonesome?' he demanded.

'Do I look as though I might adopt such a ridiculous soubriquet?' Elise returned him a question of her own while struggling to compose herself. The last thing she wanted was for this man to think he could intimidate her despite her fearing it was well within his power to do so. But she understood why he felt entitled to be crudely familiar with her. He hadn't leered at her quite as nastily as some of the other men she'd hurried past earlier on her hunt for Bea, but still she knew he considered her some sort of vulgar trollop used to being mistreated.

Her chin jerked up and she made herself squarely meet his eyes. She'd had an amount of success in deterring him; from his thoughtful expression she gleaned he was renewing his assessment of the situation, wondering if he'd made a mistake and had accosted the wrong woman.

He had; but despite her anxiety for her own safety Elise was glad that Mr Best now prowled in her vicinity rather than Bea's.

She'd been correct from the outset as to where her sister's folly in advertising for a mate might lead. She'd warned Beatrice she risked attracting lechers who'd imagine her advert to be a doxy's ruse.

A degenerate, keen to enliven his jaded appetite, might enjoy playing such a game, but Elise had not expected the fellow would turn out to be as dangerously attractive as this man. Had Mr Best met Bea at the lake she feared her sister might have allowed herself to be seduced on the spot by such a handsome and compelling character. Elise couldn't deny *she*'d experienced a thrill from the moment her eyes met his; she'd yet to decide if she hated the odd sensation.

'Very well…my excuses and apologies to you if you are not Lady Lonesome.' Alex had been watching her inner turmoil transforming her delicate features. He guessed she was indeed Hugh's blind date, but for some reason had changed her mind about proceeding with the pantomime. He'd previously flattered himself on having a far more positive effect on women than startling the life out of them. 'If you'll excuse me, I'll continue to the lake.' He gave her an exaggerated bow. 'Would you allow me to escort you back to the main path?'

Elise blinked, beginning to fully grasp the peril that lay ahead, and not simply from having her life ruined should she be spotted emerging from the bushes with this man. Mr Best intended heading off to meet Beatrice and the consequences of that were unthinkable. Her sister was likely to swoon at his feet in delight at the sight of him.

'No…please don't go…' she gasped shrilly, grabbing at one of his arms. 'I admit I am Lady Lonesome. It is just…' Her fingers sprang away from the sensation of hard muscle beneath a sleeve. Frantically she sought a plausible excuse for rebuffing him having, as he'd rightly implied, wasted his time in arranging this meeting. 'You startled me, sir, by being too brusque. I was indeed coming to meet you by the lake, but simply to…to apologise to you. I have found a fiancé in a conventional manner, you see.'

Alex took a step back towards her, his narrowed eyes scanning her tense visage. She was courageously trying to hold his gaze, but couldn't and every move he made was increasing her nervousness. He continued to approach, forcing her to retreat until the backs of her knees bumped into the bench and she abruptly sat down. Immediately Elise shot up again and in doing so skimmed herself against his hard masculine body.

Alex could feel her softly curving hip pressed into his thigh, and her rapid breathing brought her warm firm breasts to chafe his chest.

Spellbound, Elise felt suddenly too weak to move although his hands remained by his side and she could have attempted to push past him.

'I think that's not quite fair, my dear…' Alex murmured.

His husky voice stirred the hair at her brow, making her eyelids feel weighty.

'How do you know you might not prefer me to this other fellow, once we've had an opportunity to become acquainted?' Alex knew he was behaving idiotically. He should go right now and head straight back to his dratted friend and tell Hugh that his blind date was a… rather wonderful surprise.

Alex had not been expecting to feel the way he did at that moment. When he'd started out earlier he'd been exasperated. Now he was burning with passion of a very different kind. In turn, his lust was being tempered by an inexplicable tenderness. He didn't know anything about Lady Lonesome, but was beginning to suspect the chit had immersed herself in a drama she now knew to be out of control.

This slender girl with huge doe eyes fascinated him and he wanted to know more about her and why she was lying. She hadn't suddenly got engaged to anybody, he'd put money on it.

He could tell she was teetering between ducking aside to flee and allowing him to touch her. Much as he was tempted to take advantage of her shy confusion, he knew he couldn't seduce her. He didn't consider himself a saint and, without doubt, most red-blooded men would have made her suffer for her recklessness, but he kept his hands clenched at his sides.

Without understanding her reason, Elise swayed closer, tilting up her face as she sensed he would move away. Her breathing slowed and her lashes lowered as she waited without knowing why she did so or what she was expecting from him.

It was too much for him to withstand. With a strangled oath Alex bent his head, sliding his mouth on her closed lips, tasting a honeyed sweetness on her skin that began dissolving his self-control and made him crave more of her. A hand cradled her nape, long fingers spearing into thick silken hair to keep her close as he sensed her flinch in uncertainty as his tongue touched her lower lip. His hand skilfully manoeuvred her chin to part her lips and his mouth moulded on hers with slick speed and increasing pressure.

Elise felt heat flowing through her veins, fizzing beneath her cheeks where their faces touched. She felt dizzy with sensation and her arms, ramrod straight at her sides, jerked up so she might clutch at the stranger's sleeves as though to keep him close.

It was a tiny encouragement, but all Alex needed as permission to deepen the kiss. The little moan in her throat mingled with his breath and he felt his control slipping. His hands drove beneath her cloak, tracing her silhouette before cupping her breasts. His palms rotated until he felt the warm little nubs hardening and her back bowing towards him. This time when his tongue plunged, hers met it with a tiny tormenting touch before darting away.

Novice doxy maybe, Alex inwardly mocked himself as his urgent fingers worked buttons from hooks to slip inside her bodice and enclose a small silky breast. But she knew exactly what she was doing. She'd aroused him in record time and put a hugely uncomfortable bulge at his groin that normally would have resulted from ten minutes of erotic attention lavished on him by a naked mistress. He sat abruptly on the seat, pulling Elise astride his lap, his hand immediately flowing up towards her thigh, dragging her skirt with it.

It was the brutal treatment Elise needed to shock sense into her.

'Please don't…' she whimpered even as she curved into him, courting more of his relentless touch. Her body felt rocked by a throb that had started in her bruised lips and now had streaked to a place low in her belly.

Alex's mouth stilled on hers, his hand curved over

her thigh, tightening towards the moist core of her and he waited, unable yet to release her.

'Please let me go…' Elise whispered, her cheek resting against the side of his head where their light and dark hair mingled.

Alex abruptly stood up with her in his arms and dumped her on the ground before walking away.

Inwardly squirming in shame, Elise watched, thinking he might just go and leave her without a word even after what they'd just done. But he turned, strolled back to stare at her in a way that renewed the heat in her cheeks. He thought her a harlot; worse, he thought her a dishonest harlot—one who would lead a man on, then back out of the deal. 'I'm sorry,' she whispered. 'I know what you think me and you've every right to suspect me a disreputable character. But I'm not,' she gasped, unable to quell a note of despair in her voice. She sniffed, cleared her throat. She straightened her clothes with brisk shaking fingers, remembering her sister and the reason for her being with him at all. 'I must go…' She approached, hoping he would stand aside and let her pass. Hoping, too, he wouldn't notice her smearing tears of mortification off her lashes. 'Please don't try to stop me; I swear I won't let you kiss me again,' she threatened, spearing him a combatant look.

'I've no intention of kissing you again. I'm no masochist.'

Elise blushed at his savage tone despite not wholly understanding what had caused it. She'd angered him, she knew that, and frustration was evident in the thin slant to his mouth…a mouth that moments ago had been welded to hers…

Quickly she dipped her head and hurried past.

'I have a confession to make,' Alex said.

Elise pivoted about, glancing up into his narrowed eyes.

'I'm not actually Mr Best.' His gaze roved her face, partly shadowed by her bonnet's brim. He undid the strings and pushed the bonnet back, unsure why he knew she wouldn't object. He wanted them to see one another clearly before parting.

Her eyes clung to his, a few of her small pearly teeth nipping at her lower lip, as he continued, 'A friend of mine replied to your advert. He nagged me to come here first in case you weren't genuinely interested in marriage, but were plotting some deceit.' He shrugged. 'I'll recommend he meets you if you want.'

'Why would you do that?' Elise gasped, outraged that he might want to pass her on to somebody else. 'Do you make a habit of stirring trouble for your friends? How do you know I'm *not* plotting some deceit?'

'You just said you weren't disreputable,' he reminded drily. 'Were you lying?'

'Of course not! But you can tell your friend I'd not consider a man too timid to come in person and make up his own mind about me.'

'He'd have very quickly made his mind up about you,' Alex said sourly. 'He's not lacking courage, just sense. And I dare say he'd have been so smitten he'd have forgotten to enquire about your two-thousand-pound dowry.'

Elise whipped aside her face before he could see her stricken look. 'We would not suit…you must make your friend clearly see that.'

'You'd sooner I told him you're a fright?'

'I'd sooner you told him…' Elise hesitated, trying to unscramble her wheeling thoughts. 'I have already explained myself to you, sir. Please convey that I have found a suitor in the usual manner and I apologise to you both for every inconvenience suffered.' She fumbled with tying her bonnet strings and made to hurry towards the main path.

In a couple of strides Alex was blocking her exit.

'I don't think there is anything more to say,' Elise said coolly, attempting to dodge about the obstacle of his broad figure. 'I have already apologised to you and it is all you will get.'

'I think you owe me more than just an apology,' Alex returned firmly. 'I've had the decency to be honest with you, my dear, I think you owe me the same courtesy.'

A blush flooded warmly up Elise's throat; he'd flatly let her know he'd not been taken in by her tale. 'I've given you my explanation.'

'Indeed…but now I'd like to hear the truth from you,' Alex drawled.

Chapter Five

'Are you accusing me of lying?' Elise was unable to summon the audacity to continue with the deceit and avoided his eyes.

He'd explained his involvement moments ago and she'd believed him because his reasons for becoming embroiled in this ridiculous game were strikingly similar to her own. They'd both hoped to protect someone else and now were suffering the consequences of their concern. Yet, regrets aside, she knew she would remember for ever being kissed and caressed by a stranger who'd made her ache in an exquisitely pleasurable way.

'I am not Lady Lonesome…' Elise spontaneously volunteered, forcing her mind away from memories that had rushed blood to her cheeks. 'I am very fond of… the person I am helping and was on my way to intercept her and bring her back to the safety of our group before she disgraces herself. If she is spotted dawdling about on her own or, worse, is accosted by a gentleman, she will ruin her future and that of her family.'

'Your family?' Alex suggested in a way that was sympathetic yet demanding.

A single nod from Elise answered him. 'I must somehow slip back unseen to my friends or personally risk the shame I was dreading might befall my sister.'

'Is your sister likely to still be waiting by the lake for Mr Best?'

'I certainly hope not,' Elise choked. 'As you have not turned up I'm praying she has returned to our friends with no more harm done than a fit of the sulks got from imagining she was stood up.'

'If your sister is as alluring as you, she has a right to feel miffed over it.'

'Beatrice is a real beauty...' Elise's praise for her lovely sister tailed away. She didn't want him to think she was fishing for more compliments. Charming this gentleman might now appear, his reputation would suffer no lasting damage from their meeting, should it be discovered. For her, however, it would be a catastrophe. It was imperative that she got back to the others. Verity would be unable to smooth over their absence for long and if Bea had returned while she had not, everybody would imagine harm had befallen her.

'Might I ask you to stay here a while longer and give me a chance to head back first?' It was a muted plea. 'It will not do for us to be seen together.'

'Why is your beauty of a sister forced to advertise for a husband?'

Elise made a hopeless little gesture. 'It is a private matter, sir; I beg you will ask no more. I'm sure after this evening's fruitless escapade she will understand how foolish she has been.' She glanced at his angular features, half in shadow. Moments ago his face had abraded hers, his hands had stroked intimately against flesh no man had ever touched. Now they were as remote as strangers. 'If you would deter your friend from any further communication with my sister, that would be appreciated.'

'And your name?'

His imperious demand hastened Elise in darting out of the walkway, having first taken a look to and fro to make sure the coast was clear. She sped with a hammering heart in the direction of the soothing music, only once taking a glance over a shoulder to reassure herself that he had allowed her to put a good distance between them. A woman in a feathered bonnet hove into view, but there was no gentleman to be seen. Hugging her cloak about her in relief, Elise quickened her step.

Lily Watson was in a bad mood as she loitered in the shadows. She'd been sauntering to and fro in the dusk on the lookout for a client for an hour or more with no luck. She knew that if she returned home with nothing to show for the fancy hat Johnny had bought her he'd give her a bruise for what he'd call her laziness. But she hadn't been idle; she'd been pipped to the post, she reckoned, and her lips twisted resentfully because of it.

If she'd been in the right spot a few minutes sooner, she'd have nabbed the fine gent that another girl had led off into the bushes. Or rather, he'd been taking her, and Lily knew that a cove as eager as he'd seemed to be would have paid up handsomely for his pleasure. She was dawdling now, pressed into the hedge, hoping a gentleman on the loose, looking for a bit of fun, might happen by. But the concert seemed to have drawn all to it so Lily was waiting for the only randy fellow

who seemed to be about this evening to emerge from
the dark path.

A few moments ago Lily had seen her rival speed off
and she'd wondered whether the lucky thing had another
client lined up and was heading there now.

Lily tilted her hat to a jaunty angle as she noticed the
fellow strolling into view. With a final pat at her curls
she moved forwards.

She knew it was a vain hope that he might be interested in another session so soon after the last; but
Johnny was able to perform more times than she liked
so she reckoned it was worth a try because this fellow
looked big and virile.

'Oh…sir…I'm lost and looking for my friend.' Lily
had slipped up from behind to clutch at Alex's arm before he could move too far. 'I don't like to wander alone
in search of him—would you accompany me to find
him?' She tugged his sleeve, urging him back the way
he'd just come, while peeking up from beneath many
ostrich feathers. Her coy gaze floundered beneath cynical dark eyes. She knew at once she was wasting her
time. And what a shame that was! Now she was closer
she could see that he was the sort of gent a girl might
only be fortunate enough to have once in her working
life. A tumble on the ground with him would be no
hardship at all.

Her fingers were disengaged from his arm and, defeated, Lily watched his broad back as he strode off in
the direction his previous fancy had taken.

'Where on earth have you been?'

'Where have *I* been?' Elise hissed furiously at her

sister. 'You know where I have been. I have been searching for you.'

'That's what Verity said,' Bea whispered back,
frowning. 'But I've been here all the time. Or rather a
little way away in order to escape *him*.' Her eyes narrowed on James Whittiker standing with Fiona. 'He sidled up to me while you were engrossed in discussing
the violins with Mr Chapman, and hinted he would take
me to meet his acquaintances whether I would go or not.
Naturally, I made myself scarce in case he carried out
the threat.' Bea grimaced in mock alarm. 'I have been
just over there with Aunt Dolly.' She flicked a finger,
squinting into the distance.

'Aunt Dolly?' Elise echoed faintly, striving to cope
with the awful realisation that she'd dreadfully mis-
read the situation.

'Aunt Dolly is here with one of her neighbours. She
was most surprised to see me, I can tell you.' Beatrice
craned her neck again before raising a gloved hand,
waving to a woman stationed close to the stage. 'I told
her I would bring you over to her to say hello.' Bea
frowned. 'So where did you go?' Suddenly her eyes
widened. 'Did you think I'd gone to meet Mr Best, after
all?'

'Of course I did!' Elise suddenly felt very silly and
close to tears.

'But I promised I wouldn't, Elise!' There was hurt
in Bea's eyes and tone as she realised her sister had believed she'd easily broken her word.

'When has that ever made any difference?' Elise
muttered, but she flushed guiltily, pressing quivering

fingers to her throbbing brow. 'I panicked when I could not locate you.'

'But you might have been in dreadful trouble had you been spotted!' Bea's eyes were alight with scandalised amusement. 'I wish now I'd shared the adventure with you. I have been thinking about Mr Best and whether he might have been a fellow for whom it was worth taking a risk. Did you see him? What is he like? Did you speak to him?'

'I…I didn't get as far as the lake. I soon regretted what I'd done and returned here as soon as I could.' Elise was glad that she'd been able to give her sister an honest, if very abbreviated, account.

She had slipped back beside Verity a few minutes ago. Her friend had been watching for her return and had immediately given her a most relieved look, discreetly indicating that Bea was close by. A slight shrug and an elevation of her eyebrows had been Verity's method of requesting an explanation. But Elise had no time to give it and had grimaced an apology before drawing Beatrice aside to give her a piece of her mind. Uneasily she knew now that she deserved a scolding, not her sister.

'Let's forget about it and enjoy the entertainment.' Elise took a deep, calming breath as she linked arms with Bea. 'I should like to talk to Aunt Dolly. Let's go and see her.'

'What delightful nieces you have, Dolly.'

Dolly Pearson beamed proudly at Elise and Bea. 'They are very pretty girls aren't, they, Edith?'

'Indeed they are pretty! Are either of you young ladies spoken for?'

Edith Vickers glanced from one to the other of the young women, awaiting a reply, unabashed at her blunt question having elicited three startled expressions. In fact, she'd already taken a discreet peek at gloved hands and had spotted no bumps beneath kid that might have hinted at the presence of rings on fingers.

Edith had thought the elder of the two a charming beauty when she'd come alone for a brief conversation with her aunt earlier that evening. Now the younger girl had been brought over by her sister and in Mrs Vickers's opinion didn't quite have the same appeal, being a shade too tall and willowy for what was considered attractive to gentlemen.

'We are both unattached,' Elise quickly informed her before changing the subject. 'Are you close neighbours, living in the same street?' She swung an enquiring glance between the older women.

'Mrs Vickers has the large villa at the end of the terrace,' Dolly informed her. 'You have not long been in Hammersmith, have you, Edith? About a year and a half I suppose it must be now.'

'Twenty months, I'm afraid.' Edith sighed. 'But it is nice to have found a good friend in you, Dolly, despite the miserable circumstances that brought me to the area in the first place.' The mourning pearl pinned to her grey silk cloak received a pat. 'My husband died two years ago, you see, and circumstances were such that I must move out of Chelsea, although I was happy there. My girls had flown the nest to marry some years previously so it wasn't the disaster it might have been. I should have hated it if my darlings had had their home snatched from under them—' She broke off to dab at an eye with a scrap of linen.

'Oh…I'm sorry to hear of your loss,' Elise murmured and Bea echoed a similar condolence.

'Well, let us cheer up and hear what you two young ladies have been up to,' Dolly said brightly. 'It is a long while since I saw either of you for a nice chat.'

Dolly had lost her husband Percy some fifteen years ago so time had smoothed the rough edges of her sorrow. She hadn't been reduced in circumstances as had her friend, and thus didn't have that additional regret burdening her. Dolly had always lived in comfort rather than luxury, whereas Edith Vickers had been used to a grand lifestyle until her husband suddenly expired, leaving his collateral at the mercy of his creditors.

'How long will you be staying in London with your friends, the Chapmans? I think them delightful people.' Dolly inclined forwards to murmur, 'I must say the rumour that the elder daughter is receiving Mr Whittiker greatly surprised me.' She diplomatically said no more, but her expression betrayed her opinion of the fellow.

'He has accompanied us here and Fiona seems to like him,' Bea confirmed.

'I've heard that gentleman has his pockets constantly to let,' Mrs Vickers chipped in with a knowing nod.

'The music is very fine this evening, don't you think?' Elise had no liking for Fiona's suitor either, but she felt uneasy talking about any of the Chapmans behind their backs. 'I'm sure Mr and Mrs Chapman would like to say hello—would you come over with us a little later?'

'That would be nice, Dolly, wouldn't it?' Edith enthused. She drew her cloak tidily about her in readiness to make a move.

Aunt Dolly appeared not to have heard her friend's comment. 'Why is that fellow staring at us, I wonder?' Dolly had been having an innocent glance about when she'd noticed a gentleman taking an interest in them.

'Oh, it is Hugh!' Edith clapped her hands in delight. 'Hugh Kendrick is my nephew and a capital young man.' She waved her hand at him, before beckoning excitedly. 'I have not bumped into him in town for an age. He was probably hanging back, unsure whether he'd correctly identified me. He appears a little stockier, but just as handsome,' she chattered on, while urging her nephew to hurry over with an impatiently flapping hand. 'He is my sister's youngest, you know, and a very popular chap. One of his good friends has a country estate and Hugh spends a lot of the year in Berkshire.' Edith shook one of Dolly's arms to emphasise the information she was about to impart. 'Viscount Blackthorne has a vast acreage. And with Hugh being the youngest son he has not much in the way of prospects or property to look forward to, so gratefully accepts such favours.' She sniffed. 'It is a shame because he is so much nicer than his older brother who will get the lot. Toby Kendrick is a stuffed shirt and mean with it—' She broke off that hissed aside to welcome her nephew.

'How have you been, Hugh? And your mama?' Edith clasped her nephew's hands. 'I'm afraid I must scold my sister soon; I have been waiting for a letter from her for the past six months. I was just saying to my companions, you and I have been strangers for too long.'

'Had I known you had the acquaintance of such pretty young ladies, Aunt Edith, I would have been a far more regular visitor to Hammersmith.'

Edith's nephew had spoken teasingly and the compliment made Elise chuckle rather than cringe.

'And *we* are pleased to make *your* acquaintance, sir,' Bea responded with a smile that brought a dimple to her cheek. Her eyes darted to her sister before her lashes lowered.

Elise remembered that look very well. A mix of anticipation and excitement had gleamed in Beatrice's eyes the first time Mr Vaughan had paid her attention on a previous occasion when they'd been in town visiting the Chapmans.

And Hugh Kendrick *was* paying attention to Beatrice, Elise realised. Although he was politely conversing with their aunt Dolly, his warm gaze was returning again and again to her sister.

Elise could understand why he had quickly impressed Bea; in the short while since he'd joined them Hugh Kendrick had displayed an amiable manner, lively conversation and he was good-looking to boot.

But he had no prospects. His aunt had disclosed that he was the youngest son with little to look forward to, hence his grateful acceptance of favours from his rich and generous friend. Inwardly Elise sighed for she feared her sister might again pin her hopes where there was little chance of success.

'We are going over to talk to the Chapmans—will you come and say hello too?' Now Hugh had joined them, Edith wanted to keep his company for a while; he had a way of fitting in and enlivening the atmosphere.

Having spotted the group Hugh's smile faded. 'I believe Mr Whittiker might not appreciate my presence. We are not the best of friends.'

'Then indeed you must come with us, sir,' Elise insisted in a dry undertone. 'And we will all approach him in like mind.'

Hugh chuckled, swinging a glance between the sisters. 'I knew straight away you were sensible as well as pretty girls.'

'He is courting Fiona Chapman,' Bea chipped in with a grimace that gave enough of her opinion to render words unnecessary.

Hugh politely offered Bea an arm to clasp and she immediately took it with a shy smile. He would have extended the same courtesy to Elise, but she'd skipped a little ahead and joined their matronly aunts who were already squeezing a path through the crowd.

Chapter Six

'Must we stay longer, Alex?'

'You're ready to leave? I thought you were enjoying yourself.'

'Of course, if you'd sooner stay…' Celia Chase gave her lover an arch smile. 'But I know of better ways of enjoying myself than listening to tedious melodies.' Her sultry eyes flashed a promise at him. 'I thought we could return to Vale Court. I have told Paulette to prepare us a little supper for later. Are you hungry?'

A gruff chuckle escaped Alex, but he continued scanning the crowd as he murmured, 'I'm always ravenous, you know that.'

'Good…for I am, too,' Celia purred, subtly rubbing her hip against his thigh. 'It is wonderful we share a similar appetite.'

Despite Celia's sensual nudging against his sensitive groin Alex continued glancing about.

When he'd returned from his rendezvous with Lady Lonesome's sister he'd been surprised and not a little irritated to find that Hugh was nowhere to be found. His mood had not been improved by the realisation that he couldn't put the young woman he'd met from his mind, and not just because his body was throbbing with unrelieved sexual tension because of her. He'd been searching for her slight figure in the throng, but had not had a glimpse of her. From the way she'd bolted off into the night he guessed she might have decided to drag her sister off home before the chit brought shame on them both. Alex hoped they hadn't yet quit the gardens because he wanted to see her again and find out more about her.

Once he caught up with Hugh he'd tear him off a strip. His friend ought to have realised that an *ingénue*, eager for excitement, might imagine it great fun to invent such a harebrained scheme.

But it wasn't fun at all, as Hugh's own sister could testify. She had been ostracised for a similar folly, causing heartache and financial crisis to her family, when she'd allowed herself to be compromised by a fellow with seduction on his mind.

Alex knew that he had no right to a moral high ground on that score. If Lady Lonesome's luscious sister hadn't fled when she had, he might have been tempted to kiss her again and finish what he'd started. He could still sense her soft flesh filling his palm, the lissom length of her leg flowing beneath his fingertips and the fresh lavender scent of her skin seemed to again be teasing his nostrils…

'Are we to go, then?'

Celia's petulance cut into Alex's pleasurable reflection, making him frown at her. But his eyes were soon swooping back to a group of people close to the stage

and he stared in disbelief before cursing softly in a mingling of surprise and satisfaction.

'I won't be going yet—I have some business to attend to.' A ferocious determination had entered Alex's
voice and he swiftly turned his head, searching for a
temporary companion for his mistress. He noticed the
gallant young Hussar still watching them, so gave the
fellow a nod causing him to look rather confused. A
moment later Alex was propelling Celia towards her
admirer. Ignoring both his mistress's furious, suffocated indignation and Sidney Roper's startled smile,
he strode away.

'Oh…I say! It looks as though Hugh's great friend is
heading our way. Indeed, what an honour it would be
if he were to join us, Dolly,' Edith squeaked excitedly.
She started to waft a hand in front of her pink cheeks
before digging in her reticule to find a small fan. Having snapped open ivory sticks, she hissed from behind
them, 'Have you spotted him, Dolly…the tall Conti-
nental-looking gentleman who appears rather severe?
He is a viscount, you know…and I swear we are about
to have his company.'

It seemed Edith had been more vigilant than her
nephew in noticing Alex Blackthorne approaching,
stony-faced. Hugh continued chatting to the group of
ladies that now included Maude Chapman. Mr Chapman and his eldest daughter had James Whittiker as
company and only Fiona was looking comfortable about
that arrangement.

When Alex clapped a heavy hand on Hugh's shoulder a few moments later, his arrival went unnoticed by

Elise as she was slightly apart from the others, turned sideways, talking privately to Verity. The two friends had finally managed to start a whispered dialogue about what had occurred during Elise's mission to rescue Bea. But before Elise had got very far into her doctored account, an abrupt quiet had descended close by and the change in the atmosphere penetrated her consciousness, making her turn her head.

'Ah…Alex…how nice of you to join us.' Hugh quickly overcame his surprise at having been rather roughly handled by his noble friend. 'Sorry to disappear like that, but I spotted my mother's sister in the crowd and came over to say hello to her. Let me introduce you to my Aunt Edith.'

'Oh, but we have been introduced, Hugh.' Edith gave the newcomer a breathless beam, hoping for a smile in return. But the viscount's expression softened only a mite and she wondered why he had joined them if he'd sooner be elsewhere. 'Perhaps you do not remember me, Viscount Blackthorne, but I recall we met at my sister's—Lady Kendrick's—when she lived in Eaton Square with her husband—Hugh's father—because at that time he was still among us—'

'I do remember you, ma'am, and trust you are well,' Alex smoothly interrupted her rambling discourse before his eyes drifted, in a deceptively casual manner, to Elise.

But Elise, frozen in shock as she was, knew there was nothing innocent in his regard. His dark eyes might have seemed coolly enquiring to others, but she understood the glitter of dangerous amusement in their depths.

'Are you not going to introduce me to your new ac-quaintances, Hugh?' Alex prompted mildly.

Elise started to her senses, instinctively darting an alarmed glance at her sister…and then wished she had not, for she had betrayed to him the identity of Lady Lonesome without having uttered one word. She made a small movement as though to forbid Hugh Kendrick to disclose to his friend a solitary thing about them.

'I imagine the two fair-haired young ladies are sis-ters,' Alex said silkily, the smile in his eyes deepening as Elise shot him a baleful look.

'Oh, how clever of you, my lord, to know that.' Aunt Edith clapped her hands. 'Is that not clever, Dolly? Your nieces, I would say, are not that alike. Indeed, I think Miss Verity Chapman, being tall and slender, could be mistaken for Miss Elise's sister…'

'Oh…let me introduce my nieces to you properly, sir…my lord…' Dolly burbled, having recovered from her amazement at being in the presence of one of polite society's most distinguished—and rakish—bachelors. Dolly had heard the exhilarating rumours about Vis-count Blackthorne's conquests among the petticoat set and, having just gawped at length at his fine physique and handsome visage, she could understand why the ladies found him irresistible.

And now he was asking to be introduced to her rel-atives, and seemed particularly interested in Elise, al-though the silly girl seemed incapable of giving him a welcoming smile. Dolly sent her wan-faced younger niece a glance of fierce encouragement while hoping Elise wasn't feeling too overawed by the fellow as to appear soppy or the viscount would soon be looking elsewhere. He didn't seem the sort to suffer fools gladly.

Maude Chapman was very much hoping he *would* look elsewhere. The woman was feeling giddy with excitement, but she knew such an opportunity was unlikely to ever again present itself so took heart and a deep breath. While introductions to Dolly's nieces were underway, she tugged Fiona and Verity forwards, one either side of her, to ensure the viscount was aware there were four spinsters present.

Abruptly depriving Mr Whittiker of Fiona's company had put the fellow's nose out of joint—Maude noted he was looking exceptionally sulky, but gave it little heed. There had been no talk yet of an engagement and Maude was glad about that as she watched the viscount paying courteous attention to her girls. Although Maude wanted her eldest wed before she got any older, in truth she knew the idea of having James as a son-in-law would be hugely disappointing. The niceties over, she dejectedly noticed the viscount's eyes straying again to Elise Dewey and inwardly sighed. Mr Whittiker might have to do if Fiona were not to sit for ever on the shelf...

'You look as though you've seen a ghost.'

The whispered words made Elise snap her unblinking gaze back to Verity. She forced a smile. 'Do I?'

'He is rather gorgeous,' Verity said with a light chuckle, 'But please don't swoon even if he does stare at you.'

'I won't swoon over him, I assure you,' Elise announced hoarsely, having brought some of her shock under control. But still she sensed her heart racing and moisture was dampening her clenched palms.

She wished he'd not made his attention to her quite so obvious. But he wouldn't betray her antics earlier that evening, she reasoned. He'd hardly behaved well and wouldn't want his part in the risible drama disclosed any more than would she. He and his friend Mr Best— suddenly Elise shot an enlightened glance at Hugh Kendrick and inwardly groaned. Of course! A fellow with no prospects to look forward to might be grateful for a spinster's few thousand pounds. Elise let her eyes travel on to her sister, noticing, with no satisfaction, that Bea seemed on sparkling form as she chattered away to Hugh.

'Will you come with me to join the other ladies and get closer to his lordship?'

Verity's teasing words penetrated Elise's troubled thoughts.

'It might be the only chance I get to bask in such exalted company and be the envy of every lady here this evening,' Verity continued on a theatrical sigh. 'Miss Clemence's mama has been sending us daggers for ten minutes or more.' Verity inclined her head at a sweet-faced brunette, chaperoned by her mother. Caro Clemence had recently made her come out and was expected to do very well in this Season's marriage mart.

'Go ahead and join them all,' Elise urged ruefully. 'I intend to go and keep your papa company. I have hardly exchanged a word with him all evening.' Elise had noticed that Mr Chapman was on his own now James Whittiker had sidled off to eavesdrop on conversations.

Anthony Chapman was feeling happier now he was

free of Fiona's beau's tedious company. He could tell the fellow was irked at having been thoroughly cast into the shade by the arrival of two handsome young bucks. Anthony remained unruffled at the sight of his wife and the other middle-aged ladies fluttering more feverishly about the charming fellows than were the youngsters. He was aware Maude was anxious to find husbands for their girls. But Anthony knew that if his wife's aspirations now included Alex Blackthorne she was clutching at straws. He was utterly out of their league in that respect and, in Anthony's opinion, was merely being polite in coming over to renew his acquaintance with Hugh's aunt. Anthony expected both gentlemen would take themselves off quite soon, although young Kendrick did seem partial to the older Dewey sister, and, in turn, Beatrice seemed to have taken to him.

As for the viscount, Anthony had spotted him earlier with the pretty little lady he was rumoured to have recently set up in style. No sane fellow would leave Celia Chase at a loose end for too long. She was reputed to have a circle of gallants drawn from the finest Mayfair addresses. Anthony had not heard that Blackthorne was on the lookout for a wife and, when he did decide to get an heir, the fellow's connections and bank balance would make a duke delighted to have him come calling on his daughter.

'We have turned into a lively gathering,' Mr Chapman greeted Elise's arrival at his side with that cheery comment.

'Indeed we are lucky,' Elise said, attempting to sound sincere as her eyes glided over the saturnine features of a man who held the power to destroy her life. 'But…it is a shame that the entertainment is drawing to a close.' She glanced at the podium where the musicians were starting to pack away their instruments.

'Perhaps we may have entertainment of a different sort,' Anthony remarked with mild humour. He nodded to where a gaggle of ladies were stealthily approaching their party. 'I could have sworn my wife told me Mrs Porter cut her dead in Baldwin's fabric emporium the other day.' His head vibrated in feigned surprise. 'Yet it looks as though the woman and her friends are now desirous of catching Maude's eye. I wonder why that might be?'

Elise chuckled—she found Mr Chapman's amusing manner relaxing. Several young women had joined Mrs Porter and her cronies, hovering on the perimeter of their circle hoping for an opportunity to butt in and draw the viscount's notice. Mrs Porter's patience expired and she tapped Maude on the shoulder, then squeezed a place beside her. Her friends began delicately elbowing some space, too.

'I imagine the hour is getting quite late,' Elise remarked. She glanced up at a crescent moon shimmering in a starlit sky of navy blue. Despite the danger in which she had foolishly placed herself earlier she had to admit it had been an exciting evening. Viscount Blackthorne, as she now knew him to be, might forget her before he reached home that night, but she would never be able to put him from her mind, or what he'd done to her. Heat stole into her cheeks at the memory of a sensual mouth moving on hers, of cool night air on her skin as he bared her body to his hands. And tomorrow, she inwardly scolded, when you are sane once more, you will realise just how much you risked for that sordid thrill.

'It is almost a half past ten, my dear,' Anthony supplied, returning his watch to a pocket. 'I'm afraid it will soon be time to hail our transport home, if I can drag the other ladies away.'

'We have not had an opportunity to talk properly this evening. How do you do, sir? And you, Miss Dewey?'

Unnoticed by Anthony and Elise, Alex had detached himself from the press of female admirers to stroll to join them, unaffected by the disappointed sighs drifting in his wake.

Mr Chapman allowed his hand to be taken in a firm grip. Although he rarely socialised in the same circles as the aristocracy he'd seen this fellow in his club and had approved of the fact the viscount never felt the need to impress his status on lesser mortals.

'Glad you and Mr Kendrick have come over to liven things up, sir,' Anthony said cordially. 'Was feeling rather outnumbered by the ladies—just Mr Whittiker and myself, you see…' He cast on his daughter's suitor a mournful look.

'And how are you, Miss Dewey?'

'Very well, sir, thank you,' Elise replied in an admirably level tone despite the fact her heart had a moment ago leapt to block her dry throat.

'Are you staying long in town?'

Elise's tawny eyes clashed on a deep-brown gaze, but he wasn't deterred by her hostile stare.

'Your sister mentioned a moment ago that you reside in Hertfordshire with your father.'

'We do, sir, and will be in town a very short while as guests of Mr and Mrs Chapman.'

'Always welcome…you know that…' Mr Chapman chipped in.

Anthony had always thought Elise very pretty in a quiet way. Her sister had a popular beauty with her petite figure and pale hair and skin, but in his opinion Elise's warm character made her the more attractive of the two. 'You must stay as long as you like, my dear,' he offered magnanimously.

'Thank you, you are very kind, but we cannot accept…' Elise began evenly.

'I shall speak to Mrs Chapman about a few more days with us.' Anthony patted one of Elise's hands comfortingly. 'There's…no need to feel it will put us out. I assure you it won't. Besides, now your aunt Dolly knows you are in the capital, I expect she'll like you to go about with her to a few places, won't she.' He gave her a beam. 'Now I really must tell the ladies it is time to go or we will not find a ride home till goodness only knows what hour.' He ambled off, leaving a very tense atmosphere in his wake.

Chapter Seven

'Am I forgiven yet?' Alex asked quietly as soon as Mr Chapman was out of earshot.

'Forgiven?' Elise echoed, eyeing him warily. 'Why… what have you done, sir?' She pounced on the possibility that he was about to admit to having betrayed her.

'I confused you with a woman of ill repute for a while,' Alex murmured, amusement far back in his eyes. 'Too reckless and loyal to a fault…I'll accuse you of that, but a hussy? No…I couldn't have been more wrong, and I apologise for that and what followed.'

A fizz of heat prickled Elise's cheeks at what he was alluding to. But she realised there was still hope their meeting remained a secret. 'I trust you have not mentioned to anybody…?' she murmured, attempting to suffocate a note of panic in her tone.

'Did you imagine I would?'

Elise gave a small shake of the head and even managed to bestow a shaky smile. 'I guessed you would not want to be plunged into a scandal any more than I.'

'And the irony is…' Alex let his eyes drift sideways to where his friend and Elise's sister were merrily laughing within a group of friends and relatives '…they seem to have taken to one another without our help.'

'Hugh Kendrick is Mr Best, isn't he?'

Alex gave a sardonic smile that was answer enough for her.

'He has no prospects and I imagine no proper interest in a woman without a dowry.' She sighed. 'I can assure you he would be disappointed in my sister. It would be best to deter him in a subtle manner, if indeed he needs to be dissuaded from pursuing her. Perhaps he likes to flirt as well as fortune hunt.'

'Who told you Hugh has no prospects?'

'His aunt…but she meant no harm in it, I assure you,' Elise quickly added. 'Mrs Vickers made it clear she is very fond of Hugh and prefers him to his brother, who has inherited everything.'

'Sensible woman,' Alex muttered drily. 'So, your sister has lied about having a little fortune.'

Elise bristled at the implied criticism, warranted though it was.

'Your friend has not behaved impeccably either, sir, by encouraging a gentlewoman to arrange a clandestine tryst, and neither have you,' she added sharply.

'How were we to know she was a gentlewoman?'

'How were you to know she was not?' Elise returned immediately.

'Only you have behaved decently, Miss Dewey, is that it?'

'I have done my utmost to prevent Beatrice from getting embroiled in this lunacy from the very start—' Elise broke off to nibble her lower lip; he didn't know her efforts had worked and her sister had been more sensible than she in staying put with Aunt Dolly earlier. 'When you waylaid me—no…abducted me,' she spluttered in an angry undertone, 'my intention was to find my sister and return her to safety.' Elise shot him an accusing glower from beneath dusky lashes. '*You* were going to report back to your friend, thus prolonging the madness, whereas *I* was determined to bring it to an end.'

'I've not yet found an opportunity to tell Hugh my opinion on the woman he despatched me to meet.' Alex slid a sideways glance at Hugh before his eyes captured Elise's anxious gaze.

She inched up her chin, aware of the mordant humour in his attitude. 'And now you've met Lady Lonesome, is she to your liking, sir?' She discreetly tilted her head in her sister's direction. 'Do you approve of Beatrice and will you be advising Mr Kendrick to carry on? Or will you do the honourable thing and say the woman you met was a fraud and advise him to forget all about her?'

'I'm not a convincing liar; the woman I met wasn't a fraud, far from it. But I'll advise him to forget about her, although I doubt I will,' he finished self-mockingly.

'I think you will, sir, quite quickly,' Elise rebuffed coolly although his words had enhanced the pink in her complexion. The memory of what they'd done was for her not easily pushed aside and she was sure he knew it. He, however, might have forgotten the colour of her hair by tomorrow. 'Now I must join the others. Mr Chapman is keen for us to leave soon before all the hackneys are taken.' A light touch of his fingers on her arm made her start and momentarily she halted close by.

'Will you own up to your sister about what happened and that you know Mr Best's identity?'

Elise hesitated, then shook her head. She didn't want to lie or tell half-truths but she knew she had no option but to do so. Beatrice was a lively gossip and might unwittingly betray her confidence, thus bringing disaster upon them both. She glanced up at the viscount about to say goodbye, but suddenly became aware that their conversation had been under scrutiny by many people. With a curt bob for him she ignored the whispering behind gloved hands and, head high, joined her family and friends with a smile pinned to her lips.

'Well, I must say, the trip to Vauxhall turned into a thorough success.' Maude Chapman bit into her toast and beamed at the four young ladies seated at the breakfast table with her. She seemed oblivious to the fact that her daughters and their guests seemed unusually quiet as each of them pondered on the previous evening's excitement.

Beatrice was looking dreamy-eyed while pushing kedgeree to and fro and thinking of Hugh Kendrick's warm hazel eyes. She was also congratulating herself on having sensibly refrained from going to meet Mr Best and vowed henceforth to chase all such nonsense from her mind. She determined to tell Elise of her decision as soon as possible and apologise for worrying her over it all.

Verity was smiling privately while attacking her poached eggs. In her opinion the Dewey sisters—and by association, she and Fiona also—were undoubtedly under animated discussion at many a breakfast table right now. She had observed several ladies yesterday who appeared ready to surrender their eye teeth for a chance to swap places with Elise and keep moody Viscount Blackthorne company.

Fiona was forcefully banging a spoon on a boiled egg while wistfully hoping that Mr Whittiker would stay away today and give her an opportunity to finish the still life she'd started some weeks ago. She knew she had a duty to her parents, and her mama in particular wanted to see her married, but she'd sooner keep the status quo if they could afford to and send James to look elsewhere for a wife.

Elise darted glances at reflective expressions and took a sip of tea, but felt little inclined to eat anything other than a slice of toast. A new day had brought no lessening of the turbulent emotions she felt over her behaviour last night with Viscount Blackthorne. Added to which Beatrice was no closer to realising her wish to have a husband and a move to town. During the journey home yesterday evening her sister had chattered on about charming Mr Kendrick and how she hoped their paths would cross again before they returned to Hertfordshire. Elise knew dispiritedly that she must nag Beatrice to pay attention to the fact that Hugh Kendrick had no prospects.

Maude Chapman patted her lips with a napkin. She'd been happily mulling over the events at Vauxhall while she ate and could find nothing wrong in what had occurred despite the fact that the Dewey girls had obviously netted the attention of two handsome bachelors and it had drawn spiteful comments from green-eyed people. Were the girls' success with the gentlemen to give rise to gossip…so much the better in Maude's opinion. She knew that she and her daughters had long remained on the fringes of the *ton,* but she had a feeling all that was about to change thanks to Elise and Beatrice.

The post was soon due to arrive and Maude was confident it would bear exciting news. She anticipated receiving cards from families who a week ago would have overlooked her and her daughters when drawing up their guest lists. Before the day was out Maude was expecting her mantelshelf to be littered with invitations for them all to go to balls and parties. She knew the workings of the minds of mothers keen to pair off their spinster daughters: women such as she herself wanted present at their soirées people sure to lure the rich and influential to their doors. Maude had an inkling—as she was certain did many other ambitious hostesses— that if Elise Dewey were to attend a party Viscount Blackthorne might turn up, too. And, of course, he had many eligible bachelor friends and one thing might lead to another…

Maude saw exciting opportunities opening up for her two daughters. Of course, gowns would be needed; she couldn't allow her girls to be made a laughing stock by appearing plainly dressed while mingling with the cream of society. But Mr Chapman would understand that the expense of a few new frocks and fripperies would be an investment in their daughters' futures. She frowned, wondering whether to ask her husband to pen a note to Mr Dewey and hint that his girls might require a few additional clothes as they were doing well socially and were welcome to stay longer in town. It was a delicate matter to broach; Maude knew Walter Dewey was under siege financially with no likelihood of a change in circumstances, but Anthony would have to find a way of raising it with the fellow. It would be unfair to expect the Dewey girls to go about clad in the same dresses every evening. If Beatrice and Elise chose to return home rather than feel humiliated all plans would go awry... Maude rose abruptly from her chair.

'I have to speak to Mr Chapman before he goes off out,' she told the girls, hurrying away.

'She didn't turn up?' Hugh sounded indignant. 'In that case I'm glad I didn't bother traipsing off to the lake pavilion to meet her.'

'As I recall, you gave me the task so I might waste my time instead,' Alex returned sardonically as he expertly negotiated a zigzagging path between a brewer's dray and a coal cart. The phaeton returned to an even keel as Alex eased the spirited thoroughbreds to a more sedate pace.

Hugh was unperturbed by the precariousness of the journey they were undertaking to Cheapside. He had complete confidence in his friend's skill with the ribbons and knew they would arrive for appointments with their respective attorneys, in good time and good health. The frown furrowing Hugh's brow was caused by guilt, not fear they might be pitched off the high-flyer and into the road.

When Alex had called at his lodgings earlier to give him a ride the first question Hugh had ready was concerning Lady Lonesome. A few days had passed since they'd seen one another because estate matters had taken Alex to Berkshire. But now his friend was back and, in Hugh's opinion, looking decidedly moody…and that was making him uneasy.

'Sorry about sending you off on a fool's errand,' Hugh mumbled, glancing at his friend's lean profile. 'Had I believed Lady Lonesome was a fraud I'd not have nagged you to get involved.'

'If she were a fraud, I imagine she'd have turned up and attempted to part you from your money,' Alex pointed out.

'True…' Hugh admitted on a rueful grimace. 'Mayhap she was a harlot who found rich pickings elsewhere that night. If she writes again, I'll let her know that I'm no longer able to continue our correspondence. If I hadn't remained in the thick of things I might not have spotted Aunt Edith by the stage and that would have been a great shame.'

'Particularly as she had with her Beatrice Dewey,' Alex remarked drily.

Hugh suppressed a slightly self-conscious smile. 'She is a delightful young woman, don't you think?'

'I think you should concentrate on putting your finances in order before you contemplate romance. You replied to that damned advertisement hoping to marry a stranger for her fortune because of the mess you're in.'

'You're right on that score, too.' Hugh sighed dolefully. 'It's pointless getting keen on a young woman who is as hard up for cash as I am myself.'

'How do you know Miss Dewey is hard up?' Alex asked sharply. He didn't imagine that Beatrice would have divulged anything personal to Hugh so quickly, especially not in such company as was tightly congregated about them a few nights ago. It might easily have been overheard and the tabbies would delight in putting such rumours about to give their own favourites a head start in the marriage stakes.

'Aunt Edith told me a bit about the family after I'd escorted her and Dolly Pearson home to Hammersmith.' Hugh plunged a leg out in front of him, easing his position on the carriage seat. 'I went in and took a nightcap with my aunt before I set off home. She told me the Dewey girls had moved to the countryside with their papa because of some difficulties the family had years ago.' Hugh grimaced disappointment. 'I expect Edith realised I rather took to Beatrice and she was gently putting me straight. My aunt knows I have no option but to fortune hunt for a wife. Apparently her neighbour Dolly only related bare bones about her brother's fall from grace. But whatever happened resulted in a scandal and Walter Dewey's financial ruin.'

Alex steered the phaeton towards the kerb outside his lawyer's offices. He scoured his mind for some memory of the Dewey family and details of the calamity that had befallen them. A few years ago his father had still been alive and Alex had been serving on the Continent as a colonel in Wellington's army. A great deal of the London tattle had passed him by. But he doubted his mother would have forgotten it if it had been noteworthy at the time. The Dowager Lady Blackthorne was noted for her fine memory. She was not a gossipmonger, but neither did anything interesting elude her. Alex realised it might be time to pay his mother an overdue visit…

'If you would sign these documents, my lord, the transfer of Grantham Place will be finalised in the next day or two.' Mr Tremaine gave his august client a dry smile, wondering why the fellow seemed rather apathetic about acquiring the land that abutted Blackthorne Hall and would increase his acreage considerably. Previously the viscount had seemed impatient to have it. Now the deal was done the victory seemed to be of little note.

Alex took up the pen and swept his name over the parchment that had been pushed towards him on Tremaine's leather-topped desk. He had honoured the price he had first offered James Whittiker, although he knew he could have negotiated a discount once it became common knowledge the fellow had again lost heavily at Almack's faro table. Alex was aware, but for that setback, James would never have grudgingly taken up his offer.

'Oh…and just one more item for you to have, sir.' Mr Tremaine had noticed his client getting immediately to his feet as though impatient to be gone. 'You will recall, my lord, that your uncle Thomas Venner bequeathed you something. It was to be handed over once you had attained the age of thirty and only if you had taken your birthright.'

Alex nodded. At the back of his mind it struck a chord that he'd been mentioned in his uncle's will. Alex didn't expect it to be anything of value; his mother's brother had been known as a gambler and a spendthrift who, despite being a prolific womaniser, had died a cash-strapped bachelor. But Alex had liked him and Thomas had returned the sentiment.

'And if I had turned thirty while my father was still alive?'

'The document was to be destroyed, unopened. I

calculate you turned thirty last month so the letter can be released to you.' Tremaine pulled open a drawer and drew forth a folded parchment sealed with scarlet wax.

Alex turned it in his hands. 'Did he confide in you as to what this might be?'

'He did not, my lord.' Tremaine sniffed disapprovingly. 'I rather fear it is a catalogue of his debts. That would be reason enough for your uncle to want the document withheld in your father's lifetime. I'm aware that the old viscount did not approve of his brother-in-law,' Mr Tremaine said with some understatement. He knew the men had hated one another. 'Of course, if it is such a list, you are not legally obliged to pay any of it.' He snapped his head at the letter.

'Why wait till I turned thirty to present me with a roll-call of his creditors?' Alex asked. 'My father has been gone two years.'

'It is not unknown for some people to defer in that way.' Mr Tremaine's sunken features lifted in a rare smile. 'They think to salve their consciences by leaving a list for a rich relative to settle…but not too soon, you see, just in case some of the fellows demanding payment have had the good manners to also shuffle off this mortal coil.'

With a dry chuckle Alex dropped the document into a pocket and departed.

Mr Tremaine shook his head in disbelief. Not many fellows would have taken that news so lightly, but then Viscount Blackthorne had inherited from his father an estate with significant yields, and since then had greatly added to the family wealth with shrewd and successful land deals. Nevertheless, Tremaine knew the late Thomas Venner's debts were swingeing enough to make even a young millionaire wince at the idea of settling them.

He was aware the viscount was reputed to be a rogue with the ladies. Tremaine's opinion was that his lordship was ridiculously benevolent when he tired of a mistress. He knew this because it invariably fell to him to arrange pensions for those paramours.

In business matters Alex Blackthorne was nobody's fool, but a fair opponent, hence his refusal to snap up Whittiker's estate at a knock-down price despite all parties being conscious he could have done so. In matters relating to kith and kin Alex was magnanimous to a fault, as his friend Hugh Kendrick could testify. No doubt his late uncle had also noticed and schemed to make use of that trait, post mortem.

So…being as the viscount was basically moral and generous, Tremaine was glad the fellow had taken himself off with the letter unopened. He didn't envy any person who happened to be in that gentleman's vicinity when he broke the seal, did some sums and had his virtues tested…

Chapter Eight

Mr Tremaine was correct on two counts: the bequest did contain details of Thomas Venner's debts and the deceased's nephew did spit out an oath on reading it. But it wasn't the lengthy list of figures that had caused Alex Blackthorne to grit his teeth; it was the sight of a surname that had been haunting him since the night he'd visited Vauxhall.

The whisky tumbler held in a fist was thumped down and his booted feet, propped on the corner of his desktop, were swung to the floor.

Unable to believe what he'd seen in the shady room, he strode to the window, yanked at the blind and allowed sunlight on to his uncle's scrawl in case his eyes had deceived him.

The paper was divided into two columns: the first held the creditor's name and the second what the fellow was owed. What had stunned Alex had been reading that, according to his late uncle, Walter Dewey was due an unspecified amount of cash and also…a wife.

Alex knew his uncle had been deemed an eccentric by some, a reprobate by others. His own opinion now was that lunatic should be added to those character assessments. Alex had seen his uncle just a month before he died of consumption, and although Thomas had appeared gravely ill, he had conducted himself as though of sound mind.

There was only one person of Alex's acquaintance who, beside himself, had liked Thomas Venner and that was the man's sister. He knew his mother had adored her brother despite his failings. His father, on the other hand, had loathed his brother-in-law and had made no effort to disguise his feelings.

Having only recently returned home to Upper Brook Street, Alex strode out into the hallway of his town house, shrugging on his tailcoat. He gave his stoic butler, Robinson, an order for his choice of transport and in less than five minutes was down the graceful sweeping steps of his mansion and waiting impatiently by the kerb for his curricle to be brought round.

'I sent a note to your papa earlier in the week and today received his reply.' Anthony Chapman had entered the parlour, pulling a letter from a pocket.

'He is very pleased to know you are having a nice time with us and wishes you will stay for as long as you like.' Anthony gave the Dewey sisters a beam while tapping paper on a palm. 'Now it is a pleasure to have you stay and you must not think that you are putting us to any trouble—'

'Indeed you must not,' Maude interrupted, rising from her chair by the fireside. 'You are very welcome to remain for a month or more.' She noticed that Elise was about to say something. She knew of the two sisters it would be Elise who would elect to go home rather than feel indebted for her keep. But Walter Dewey had sent a bank draft to meet costs and, if it were not quite as generous a sum as Maude had hoped for, it would suffice. Besides, the girl's aunt Dolly had made it clear she would like to have her nieces as house guests before they returned to Hertfordshire. Maude had guessed the woman wouldn't want to miss out on her youthful relatives' sudden popularity. So between them Maude was confident they would be able to afford Beatrice and Elise a fine time in town.

Already this week they had been for tea with some ladies who had unmarried daughters, and Maude had accepted invitations for two balls for next week and numerous afternoon salons. She had felt torn between elation and frustration to have so many cards arrive that she must pick and choose and disappoint some people by turning them down.

'Now, listen to me, girls, the dressmaker is due to arrive and your papa is keen for you both to have some pretty clothes to go out in. You must not fret that he will mind.'

'But the cost is sure to be great and...' Elise paused. She felt awkward discussing her father's financial situation even with good friends such as the Chapmans who knew about, and accepted, their reduced circumstances.

'Your papa has sent the means to meet it,' Maude soothed quickly. 'He understands it is a great opportunity for you to socialise with new people and secure your futures.' To avoid further argument she turned to her own daughters who had been quietly attending to proceedings, hoping the sisters would be able to extend their stay in London.

'Mr Whittiker is to take you for a drive at four o'clock, Fiona, so you will have your fitting with the dressmaker first.' Maude started tidying away the pencils and charcoal with which her eldest had been sketching.

Anthony Chapman gave a frown on hearing Whittiker's name mentioned. Lately, he'd been getting caught up in his wife's enthusiastic ambitions for the girls and hoped that James might soon be elbowed aside by a candidate worthy of Fiona's hand. Maude was keen to keep the fellow in reserve in case no other man showed an interest in their eldest child; Anthony would sooner have the girl at home with him than see her saddled with such a weasel. Voicing that opinion was sure to result in a flare-up with his wife, so rather than sour things too soon while there was still hope of a positive outcome, he withdrew from the room with a nod for the ladies.

As Anthony strolled the corridors in the direction of his den, he pondered on the fact that now Whittiker had sold property to Blackthorne he would again have money in his pocket, if no freehold to call his own home. James had only a short lease on his London property. A proportion of the funds from the sale of his country seat would no doubt pay off urgent creditors to keep the duns at bay, but Anthony had heard on the grapevine that Whittiker had again been spending heavily.

He'd also heard that he'd been cosying up to Mrs Porter's granddaughter now he was feeling flush. Anthony had believed the rumour as he'd seen the popinjay posturing close to the girl in Hyde Park. Whittiker obviously felt that now he had some ready cash he'd lure a plumper dowry than Fiona's small inheritance. Mrs Porter had boasted that she intended to leave ten thousand to the girl. Most people believed she wasn't embellishing the amount by much. Mr Porter had been a canny fellow and had amassed quite a fortune as a tea importer prior to his early demise.

Anthony smiled; it would suit him very well—and he guessed Fiona, too—if Whittiker started making his excuses so he could go and bother the Porters.

In the parlour a lively discussion was taking place regarding the imminent arrival of the dressmaker.

'I will choose a cheap fabric, I promise,' Bea whispered to Elise. 'There are some very nice cottons.'

Elise's rueful expression strengthened on hearing that. She knew that the modiste would carry very few samples of cottons and a great many of expensive silks and satins.

'Please don't be offended…but I have several pairs of gloves, and other bits and pieces that I rarely wear.' Verity had come over to Elise and Beatrice to quietly make the offer. 'You have no need to purchase new accessories if you'd rather not. You can borrow some of mine and very welcome.'

Having escaped her mother's droning instructions on preparations for James Whittiker's arrival, Fiona also approached. 'I have a few shawls I don't need. Mama insisted I had several when I had my début. They are still in the tissue paper, although some years old.'

Elise clasped a hand of each of her friends, gratitude in her smile, words unnecessary. She was not too proud to accept such well-meant generosity. She knew the offers had been made out of consideration rather than charity to ease the load on her father.

'We are lucky to have such kind friends as you,' Bea said emphatically.

'We *will* stay in London a little while longer and are very happy to be invited, but two new gowns only?' Elise's fiercely enquiring look demanded an agreement from Bea. 'If we must go about in the same frocks some evenings, then we must.'

Bea nodded excitedly. 'I will choose blue for one and perhaps lemon for the second.'

Caught up in the excitement Elise blurted, 'I think I might want lemon. We *could* have the same…or perhaps I'd sooner a darker shade.'

Maude had been hovering by the door, aware her daughters would have more success than would she in persuading their friends to stay. On hearing the girls' excited chatter about fabrics she smiled in relief and slipped from the room to await Madame Joubet's arrival.

'To what do I owe this great honour?'

'To the fact that I am a dutiful son,' Alex drawled incling to give his mother a kiss on an olive-skinned cheek as she stabbed at her embroidery.

He would have straightened from his stooped position, but Susannah Blackthorne clasped him about the neck, hugging his abrasive jaw against her soft complexion. 'You should come to see me more often, you know I miss you when you stay away too long.' Her light Scottish accent always strengthened when she was annoyed with him.

'I saw you at Vauxhall earlier in the week,' Alex protested, removing her clasped fingers.

'You saw me and gave me a wave, that's all,' Susannah complained, pushing away her tambour so she could get to her feet. 'I was hoping you would talk to me, Alex. But perhaps your new friend doesn't allow you out of her sight for too long, is that it?'

Susannah had noticed Alex escorting Celia Chase. She knew that the liaison was unlikely to last till the end of the year. Her son's mistresses tended to see him as a challenge because he was notoriously changeable. Each successive young beauty seemed to believe she'd be the one to enslave and shackle him to her side, thus her behaviour became too possessive and hastened her departure from his life.

But that night Susannah had also glimpsed her son encircled by a gaggle of genteel ladies, some of whom appeared to be débutantes. It had been so unusual and noteworthy a sight that she had been impatient for an opportunity to bring it up. 'Are you looking for a wife, Alex?'

Alex spluttered a laugh and placed down the teacup he'd just filled from the silver pot on the table. He slanted his mother a quizzical look. 'You may rest assured that I have no plans to propose to my new friend.'

'I don't mean *her.*' The fêted beauty was dismissed with a flick of an elegant finger. Susannah approached the table against which her son was resting and gazed up into his handsome features. 'I noticed you with some sweet-looking young ladies at Vauxhall; there seemed to be quite a crowd of them. Were you interested in one in particular?'

Alex shot her a look. 'I'm interested in one of the families…but not in the way you mean, ma'am,' he answered with mild amusement on noticing a glimmer of optimism sharpening his mother's dark eyes. 'There were two sisters with their aunt, Dolly Pearson, and Hugh's aunt, Edith Vickers.'

'The Dewey girls?' Susannah asked abruptly, with a frown.

'Yes…you know of the family?'

'Mmm…' Susannah strolled to look out of the window on to a rose garden. It was late May and some beautiful blooms had unfurled to perfume the air. She drank in the scent wafting in through a half-open sash.

'And? What do you know of them?' Alex got the impression his mother wasn't keen on elaborating and that was making him determined to have more information.

'There was rather a scandal some years ago when the girls' parents went their separate ways.' Susannah turned to face her son. 'Mr Dewey took his daughters with him and moved out of town. I know Dolly Pearson is Walter Dewey's sister.'

Alex continued to gaze at his mother in an attempt to extract further news, but she seemed to have sunk into her own thoughts.

'I'm guessing there was more than that to the calamity. Are you going to tell me what it is?'

'Why do you want to know?' Susannah asked.

'Because your late brother has bequeathed me a list of his debts to clear.'

A tut of mingled anger and astonishment was Susannah's initial response. 'Thomas is a devil to do that! You must throw it on the fire, Alex. It is a dreadful thing to expect you to clear up after him.' She paused to consider. 'Does this list have anything to do with your interest in the Dewey girls?'

'In a way…my late uncle has noted that he owes their father a wife and an amount of cash.'

A spontaneous giggle escaped Susannah before she frowned and shook her head. 'Obviously you could pay back the cash if you'd a mind to, but a wife? What in the Lord's name does he expect you can do about that now?'

'I wish I were able to ask him,' Alex said. 'For I haven't the vaguest notion.' His mother's surprise on being told of her brother's odd bequest hadn't been as pronounced as he'd expected.

'Did Uncle Thomas steal Mrs Dewey from her husband? Is that why the couple went their separate ways?' Alex sensed his mother was veering between fibbing and telling all. He'd considered the possibility that his uncle's roving eye had landed on Mrs Dewey and an *affaire de coeur* had ensued. If the woman had been as attractive as her daughters, Alex could understand his uncle's temptation. According to Hugh a scandal had blighted the lives of more than the adults involved; the girls had been affected, too, by having their family name sullied.

'Thomas did have an affair with Arabella Dewey,' Susannah said slowly, 'but it was not a lengthy liaison. She went on to become Lord Reeves's mistress, then passed away. Officially, she expired of influenza in Norfolk, having gone there for bracing briny air to aid her recovery.'

'And unofficially?'

'It was rumoured she died in labour, being too frail for another pregnancy. She had turned forty some years previously. If I had to choose between my brother and Lord Reeves, I know which of them *I* would say owed Walter Dewey a wife.' Susannah snapped a nod, her loyalty to Thomas obvious.

'Your brother obviously felt guilty enough to want to repay Walter Dewey in some way.'

'Thomas must have got addled in the attic towards the end, I can think of no other reason why he would act so peculiar.' Susannah frowned, her mind travelling back through the years. She'd heard other gossip about the liaison between her brother and Arabella Dewey. When questioned by her, her brother had never owned up to there being truth in it and, by all accounts, Walter Dewey had kept his lips tightly sealed on the whole matter.

'You know more about it?' Alex prompted on seeing his mother's concentration.

'Just rumours…'

'Nevertheless I'd like to hear them,' Alex gently insisted.

'I've never known you show this much interest in any *decent* young ladies before.' Susannah gave him a penetrative look.

'I've never been required—by one of your kin—to do so before.' Alex had emphasised his mother's vexing relative in the hope she'd feel obliged to offer up a full explanation.

'Oh…very well…if you want me to feel guilty on Thomas's behalf I'll tell you what I've heard in reparation for his sins.' Susannah approached the table to shake the teapot. On finding it only half-full and lukewarm, she rang the bell for fresh to be brought. Reseating herself, she began, 'There was more of a scandal than simply Arabella defecting to begin an affair with Thomas. Mr Dewey didn't take being cuckolded lightly. Oh, he must have been furious, and mortified, but he wanted his wife back and attempted to buy your uncle off. He settled Thomas's gambling debts—which were huge—on the understanding that my brother would end the affair. Thomas reluctantly agreed. He was by then in a financial mess that might have ended with him in the Fleet. I believe it wasn't just a mercenary decision— he thought sacrificing Arabella was the right thing to do. She was a clingy woman and obsessed with him. I've no doubt she would have willingly followed him to gaol and the scandal would have hit new heights.' Susannah shook her head. 'Those poor girls would have suffered dreadfully. They were still in the schoolroom, but in their teens, so old enough to understand a good deal.' She glanced at her silent son. 'I know what you're thinking—why wouldn't your papa help Thomas settle his debts?'

'I know my father had scant patience with him and it's becoming clearer why that was.'

'Scant patience?' Susannah echoed ruefully. 'It was a sadness to me that the two of them loathed one another. Thomas would never have asked for a penny piece from George and neither would he have got it if he had.'

'Perhaps my uncle has got the last laugh. If I settle his debts, it could be argued the money will have come from my father's estate.'

'None of this tale has been corroborated. Thomas would never speak about it,' Susannah said truthfully. Quickly she carried on her account. 'That's not the worst of it: the money with which Mr Dewey paid off Thomas's debts was not his to use. It belonged to clients; he was a lawyer, you see, and held money in trust. I don't think Walter intended to defraud anybody; he was a desperate man and borrowed the funds until an investment he'd made in the East India Company turned up trumps. Unfortunately, the whole enterprise turned as sour as a barrel of vinegar. And Arabella refused to go home into the bargain. She turned to Lord Reeves instead of her husband when Thomas put her off.'

'So Walter Dewey lost his wife, his good reputation and I imagine his business because of your brother,' Alex stated in an emotionless voice.

Susannah bristled. 'Some people might say his hussy of a wife brought about his downfall. I believe Thomas managed to repay some of what he owed before the end of his life and he did so voluntarily.'

'Have these *rumours* come via Lord Mornington?' Alex asked drily. He knew his mother was the Earl of Mornington's mistress. 'I imagine if Uncle Thomas didn't confide in you another fellow has supplied the details.' Alex was aware that Lord Mornington had relatives in the judiciary.

'I'd sooner have left it all well alone.' Susannah evaded answering. 'The two people who caused the misery have passed away so it is pointless raking it over now.' She looked crossly at her son. 'Why have you only just mentioned this, Alex?'

'Because I've only just found out. I was given the letter yesterday. Thomas stipulated I have it after I turned thirty and only if my father had passed on.'

Susannah gasped in surprise. 'You see, he was a complete henwit at the end.'

Behind his casual façade Susannah could see that her son was disgusted by what he'd heard about his uncle and that saddened her because they'd been close. 'Thomas tried to act honourably,' she insisted, championing her dead sibling. 'He ended the affair and urged Arabella to go home. When she knew Thomas wouldn't take her back she hooked herself a lord instead.'

Alex paced to and fro, thinking deeply on what he'd heard. 'So I take it that the official version of events is that Mr Dewey stole money through selfishness and avarice and was caught red-handed when his ship failed to come in?'

'More or less…' Susannah agreed. 'Despite what Arabella had done he wanted her name kept out of it as much as possible. I imagine again that was to protect his daughters. The eldest made her come out at sixteen under her aunt Dolly's wing. But it was a quiet affair. I think by then Mr Dewey knew that his girls would be the butt of malice and sought to protect them in the countryside. I was surprised to hear you say they are again out and about. But some years have passed and fresh gossip always overshadows ancient scandals.'

The tea arrived and Susannah immediately offered her son a fresh cup. But Alex seemed keen to get going.

'What will you do about Thomas's bequest?' Susannah asked.

'At present I've no idea,' Alex said.

Once Alex had gone Susannah drank her fresh tea

and helped herself to a cinnamon biscuit from the plate. She sighed. She had loved her brother dearly, but her darling late husband would easily have won a contest for her affection. George had never made her choose between them, but he had begrudged the fact that his son and heir seemed fond of his dissolute brother-in-law. Alex had visited his uncle frequently when he was of an age to do as he pleased. With hindsight Susannah knew George had been right to want to keep them apart. No bad character traits seemed to have rubbed off on Alex—although Susannah realised Alex's success with the ladies could rival her brother's conquests. Nevertheless, if the two men hadn't been quite so close her brother might not have felt entitled to draw his nephew into a tragedy revived from beyond the grave.

Chapter Nine

Maude Chapman was pleased to be proved right in her theory that the Dewey sisters would attract well-connected followers—as she proceeded into Mr and Mrs Clemence's sparkling ballroom the first person she saw was Hugh Kendrick. His delighted smile acknowledged their arrival and Maude noticed that Beatrice was shyly mirroring his pleasure. Her eyes darted to and fro to discover if his good friend Viscount Blackthorne had also turned up to pursue Elise, but couldn't spot him. She cheered herself up; the illustrious viscount might not be in evidence, but many other eligible bachelors were and some, stationed close to the entrance, were giving her pretty charges appreciative glances. The Clemences' son Jago seemed particularly interested in the girls. Yesterday James Whittiker had sulkily imparted that he'd not been invited to this ball. With soaring spirits Maude had recognised a perfect opportunity for Fiona to improve her prospects without Whittiker dogging her footsteps.

'Come…let us mind our manners and say hello to our hostess,' Maude whispered, ushering her daughters and the Dewey sisters towards Mrs Clemence and her daughter Caro.

As the ladies took care of niceties Mr Chapman and Hugh Kendrick strolled towards one another.

Anthony fanned his face with a hand. 'It's a warm evening, sir; I think I'm in need of some cold refreshment.'

'Champagne is on its way, Mr Chapman.' Hugh tipped his head at the waiters circulating with silver salvers filled with fizzing drinks. 'And very good it is, too.' He elevated his empty glass, then deposited it on a tray as a waiter halted in front of them. The two gentlemen helped themselves to filled crystal flutes. Anthony immediately savoured a refreshing mist of bubbles on his skin before tasting his drink.

'Is your chum Alex on his way?' Anthony asked, smacking his lips.

'He's here,' Hugh replied and nodded at the doorway just as a footman's booming voice heralded the presence of Viscount Blackthorne.

Elise wasn't alone in swivelling about on hearing that announcement. Their hostess and her daughter had started to attention; so had Maude, and Dolly Pearson who had arrived some time earlier with her friend and neighbour Edith Vickers. Elise's expression was apprehensive whereas the other ladies simply seemed overjoyed at the sight of him.

'I had a feeling he might turn up,' Verity whispered with an arch look for her friend.

Elise smiled wryly. 'I had a feeling Hugh Kendrick might turn up.'

'He has been giving Bea some fond looks,' Verity interpreted the hint.

'She likes him, too.' Elise sighed. 'She has barely let a waking hour pass without mention of him since they met at Vauxhall.'

'You don't approve?'

'Oh…I like him very well; he seems charming and sincere…' Elise's praise withered away. How could she think him sincere when he had proved himself a fortune hunter too craven to meet Lady Lonesome in person? But, on reflection, Elise adhered to her first assessment of his character. Hugh Kendrick was not a bad person, she was sure of it, just as her sister was not dishonest in scheming to get a husband and family to love and cherish. Unfortunate circumstances and soulful yearnings could make good people act foolishly.

'But you don't think anything will come of it?' Verity asked.

'How can it when neither of them has a bean?' Elise gave a hopeless gesture.

'Perhaps this evening Bea might catch the eye of a fellow in a position to propose.' Verity gave her friend's arm an encouraging pat.

'And if such a gentleman comes up to scratch, will she accept him now she is smitten?' Elise was frowning at the sight of her sister gazing dreamily in Hugh Kendrick's direction.

'My mama wasn't very optimistic about such a notable turning up.' Caro Clemence had nudged Elise, then drawn her aside to murmur that in her ear. 'But I said if we received an acceptance from the Chapmans then there was a very good chance Viscount Blackthorne might come along. He is very attractive, isn't he?'

'Mmm,' Elise replied neutrally. She was aware eyes had turned on her as soon as he passed over the threshold. He'd devoted time to her at the pleasure gardens and started chins wagging. Had the reasons for his attention circulated…none of her party would have been invited here this evening. Of course, the viscount would have been welcomed in with open arms. Little disgrace would have attached to him following the exposure of their night-time tryst in the bushes.

'He seemed to take a fancy to you at Vauxhall.' Caro went on to prove Elise's concerns valid. 'I know my mama would be ecstatic if he were to come calling on me.'

There was no hint of envy or malice in the belle of the ball's limpid gaze. 'And you?' Elise asked. 'How would you feel?'

'Disappointed.' Caro wrinkled her nose. 'Oh…I know he is such a wonderful catch, but—' She glanced at a group of young army officers resplendent in their scarlet uniforms. One of the fellows, who looked little more than nineteen, appeared to be blushing and peering their way. 'I have a sweetheart, but my parents know nothing about it, nor would they approve if they did.' She pulled an unhappy little face. 'They like Wilfred well enough as my brother's friend, but as a son-in-law they would find him sadly lacking—no money, you see.'

'It seems to be the way of things.' Elise gave Caro a sympathetic smile. On turning about, she found the Chapmans and her aunt's party had moved some yards away to talk to new arrivals.

'How are you this evening, Miss Dewey?'

'Very well, sir, thank you.' Elise darted a glance up into a startlingly handsome face, her heart racing.

She hadn't realised that Alex had strolled closer, then casually cut off her path to her group of friends. When last they'd met, in twilight broken only by palely flickering lamps, Elise had not noticed what he wore other than to recall he'd had an aura of wealth and distinction. Now, under the sharp crystal light of the chandeliers she realised he was magnificently attired in snug-fitting evening clothes cut from smooth charcoal-coloured cloth. A grey-silk cravat sat atop an ice-white shirt, its intricate folds pinned in place by an oval diamond the size of a button.

Alex's lips tilted in wry humour as he noticed her innocent admiration. 'And you look very nice, too,' he murmured, his eyes slipping over her slender, satin-clad figure.

Elise had chosen to have a dress made up in an amber hue. It matched her eyes, Mrs Chapman had said. The woman had been glad, too, that it was not a colour that any of the other girls had wanted or there might have been a delay in getting the gowns finished while good-natured bickering over fabrics continued. The modiste had done sterling work to deliver the clothes earlier that day after such a short time.

'Thank you, it is new,' Elise burbled, smoothing her shimmering skirt as a quiet settled between them.

'The colour is unusual, yet it suits you very well.'

Again Elise murmured her thanks for the compliment and nervously flicked a honey-coloured curl from a fragile shoulder. 'I see that Mr Kendrick is here. I have not yet had an opportunity to speak to him,' she rattled off.

'He seems quite content to devote himself to your sister,' Alex replied drily, tilting his head to indicate that Hugh Kendrick and Mr Chapman had joined the ladies. Hugh and Bea did appear to already have drawn away from the group to chat, eyes locked.

'I wish I could say I'm glad to see my sister looking happy, but it will not do,' Elise murmured. 'There is no future in the relationship and I would beg you to steer him elsewhere. I must ask Beatrice to keep her distance, too.'

'Why interfere? Hugh won't heed what I say if he is besotted with her. And your sister is old enough to decide her own fate…older than you, I recall your aunt said.'

'Why interfere?' she echoed in a stifled tone. 'My sister has no dowry, but is determined to find a husband to provide her with a new life in London. Your friend is after a wife with money because he has none. You know all of this following the fiasco that occurred at Vauxhall.' Elise tore her eyes from his subtle amusement, heating as she remembered what he'd done to her that night…and her response to his lust. She lowered her face to hiss, 'Pray, tell me how they will suit?'

'It is not my place…or yours…to act the controlling guardian. As far as I know they are both aware of the other's financial situation and must make up their own minds about one another.'

Elise felt a bubbling anger. Mrs Chapman had told them at breakfast that very morning that Viscount Blackthorne was renowned as one of the wealthiest gentlemen in the country. What did he know of being restricted and humiliated for want of money? This trip to town to socialise was possibly Beatrice's last chance to realise her dream of having a husband and family. If the rich viscount had a sister, no doubt the lucky young lady would be afforded numerous new gowns and new opportunities to meet her mate. Beatrice had one week and two dresses before her time and her credibility ran out.

'My sister has been disappointed before and I would not like to see her hurt again,' Elise uttered coolly. 'Neither would I like to see her waste precious time on a fellow who cannot come up to scratch however nice he might be.' Elise bobbed her head and made to pass him.

'Don't run away, I have more to say.'

Elise pivoted about. A casually encompassing glance confirmed her fears that they were under observation. She pinned a smile to her lips and again stepped closer to him so they might not be overheard. 'Please do not order me about as though I were one of your lackeys. And please do not think I am running away. I am not frightened of you just because we met under…odd circumstances.'

Alex laughed, chillingly in Elise's opinion, but she continued holding his eyes squarely, her full rosy lips pleasantly curved. She prayed that their audience believed they were enjoying some light banter, nothing more to it.

'We met under highly improper circumstances, Miss Dewey, and I imagine you would not want further scandal attaching to your family name.'

Elise blenched, moistened her lips. So he knew about

her parents' *mésalliance*, and her father's disgrace, and was vile enough to raise the subject with her in a society ballroom. 'Are you threatening me, sir?' she whispered.

'I'm stating the obvious,' he drawled, nodding curtly to an acquaintance to deter the fellow's approach.

'Nothing is *obvious* about that most regrettable incident at Vauxhall unless you make it so, sir,' Elise replied tightly. 'As far as I am concerned it is already forgotten, never again to be mentioned, and a gentleman would concur with that.'

'I don't take kindly to being ordered about either,' he echoed her reprimand. 'So don't tell me how to behave.'

'If you conduct yourself in a way appropriate to your breeding and position, I will not need to do so.'

Elise knew she would be defeated in this verbal duel and her confidence and composure were also withering beneath his dark sardonic stare. Etiquette could not be ignored and before their antagonism became clear to those keenly watching them she must withdraw. Had they been alone…in the dark in bushes as had been the case at Vauxhall…she would have told him exactly what she thought of him. But here, under the unforgiving glare of a thousand candles and sharp eyes, she was constrained to respond in a ladylike manner. With gritted teeth and lowered lashes she curtsied, more deeply this time, hoping he understood the insolence in it.

Her defiance drew a mirthless chuckle from Alex. 'I'll call on the Chapmans later in the week and we can finish our conversation,' he murmured silkily. 'I promise it is to your advantage to receive me. Perhaps you and your sister would come for a drive in the park with Hugh and me.'

Elise said nothing and moved past, her heart pounding as though she were running rather than walking away from him, her moist palms clenched into fists at her sides.

'It is very bad of the viscount to disappear so soon after arriving.'

'At least he did arrive, my dear. I've heard he rarely attends these débutante balls.' Anthony Chapman handed his spouse a glass of lemonade and set about another flute of champagne with gusto, as though it were the first of the evening instead of the tenth.

Maude sipped the cool brew and continued looking around. She had hoped that Elise might tempt the *ton*'s most eligible bachelor to partner her in a dance. But there had been no sign of Alex for some while. 'Perhaps he has gone into an ante-room to play cards. You know how gentlemen occupy their time if they've no wish to jig about.'

Mr Chapman did indeed know about that as he'd only recently thrown in his hand in Mr Clemence's library, having lost a guinea to their host in less than fifteen minutes. But there had been no sign of the viscount around the faro table. Anthony knew that the fellow had gone as he'd seen him on his way down the stairs.

'I suppose he might have escorted a lucky lady to the balcony to take the air,' Maude mused, not to be dissuaded from her belief Alex Blackthorne would reappear. She'd had high hopes of that distinguished fellow pursuing Elise and stirring up a frenzy of interest, which in turn would guarantee the girls were showered tomorrow in more social invitations. But if the viscount were promenading outside, it wasn't with Elise. Maude could see all four of her charges dancing the quadrille partnered by young officers in red coats. Hugh had ceased charming Beatrice for long enough to allow her to accept an invitation to dance from another fellow. Maude was glad he had, for propriety's sake.

'Oh…I had hoped the viscount would dance with one of our girls!' Maude came close to stamping a foot in annoyance.

'I expect the fellow has gone off to female company more to his taste,' her husband soothed with an accompanying dirty chuckle. Anthony cleared his throat and stuck a finger between his hot neck and his cravat. He was still sober enough to realise he'd had rather too much alcohol to have spoken in such a vulgar manner to his wife.

'More to his taste?' Maude sounded affronted rather than outraged. 'He won't find prettier… Oh…you mean that sulky-looking brunette might have the viscount wound about her crooked finger.' Maude knew, as did most people, about the viscount's popularity with *demi-reps*. It made no difference to her—or any sensible mother with daughters to settle—how many mistresses prospective beaux kept prior to their marriages. 'Perhaps you're right,' Maude grudgingly agreed. 'Celia Chase is quite comely, I suppose, in a common fashion, and might have lured the viscount away. How tiresome that he's more interested in his mistress than a roomful of débutantes.'

'Would either of you young ladies like a drink of lemonade? I'm happy to fetch it,' Anthony babbled, having just noticed that the Dewey sisters had rejoined them. He hoped that the young ladies had not overheard the unseemly exchange between him and his wife. The older girl seemed more interested in locating somebody in the throng, but Elise's forced smile dismayed Anthony as she declined his offer of refreshment.

'Jago Clemence seems a nice young fellow.' Elise nodded in the direction of their hosts' son. 'I'm sure he would have asked you to partner him again if you'd not immediately disappeared into the supper room with Verity.'

Beatrice bit her lip, looking anxious. 'I hope Hugh won't think I encouraged him for I did no such thing. I only accepted him to be polite.'

Elise sighed. 'Why *not* encourage him? Jago is a charming fellow and his family seem nice. I thought you wanted to meet eligible bachelors and get one to propose.'

'I've met one I like very well,' Beatrice breathed, eyes glowing.

'He is in no position to propose,' Elise muttered wearily. 'As you well know.'

'How do you know that Jago is in a better position?' Beatrice mumbled moodily.

'Look around you.' Elise darted admiring glances at their sumptuous environment. 'If that is not enough to persuade you he has a wealthy family and sufficient prospects, his sister told me that he has bought a country manor with his grandfather's bequest. Caro hinted he's buying his own property because he is on the lookout for a wife.'

Bea shrugged, turning her head to and fro as though

she'd given little heed to her sister's homily. The ball
was coming to an end and the crowd had thinned out
considerably. The orchestra were packing away their
instruments. 'Oh…where is he? Do you think he's gone
without even saying goodbye, as the viscount did?'

'For goodness' sake, Bea!' Elise snapped. 'Don't
make your pining quite so obvious. You'll have every
tabby in town knowing you're besotted with a certain
gentleman. Do you want to end up a laughing stock
when nothing comes of it?'

'Miss Elise, Beatrice…' Hugh had materialised
beside them, bowing gallantly. 'Would you like to
promenade on the balcony and take some air before
departing?'

Elise feared her sister might swoon with relief at the
sight of him. It was obvious Bea wanted to have Hugh
to herself, so with a sigh Elise let her have her way. 'I'll
go and say goodbye to Aunt Dolly and Mrs Vickers. I
expect Mr Chapman will want to leave very shortly,
Bea, in case all the hackneys are taken.'

'Well, what a wonderful evening.' Mrs Chapman
sighed, settling back in the squabs of the cab conveying
them home from the Clemences' ball. Mr Chapman had
gone on ahead with Fiona and Bea. Maude had elected
to accompany Elise and Verity to Marylebone in the
hope of discovering what had occurred between the viscount and Elise when he had singled her out for a chat.

'It was a shame Alex Blackthorne left so early.'
Maude squinted through the dusk to read Elise's expression. She was disappointed when the young woman
gave her usual amiable smile. She tried again. 'The

viscount is not usually persuaded to attend such functions. I think he came along to see you, my dear. He certainly didn't seem interested in talking to any other young lady.' She sniffed. 'I couldn't engage him in a conversation although he did talk to Mr Chapman for some minutes.'

'He was no great loss to the party in that case,' Elise said lightly. 'We all had a fine time without him, didn't we?'

'Oh…a fine time indeed.' Maude frowned. It wasn't quite the reaction she'd hoped for. Most spinsters with a modest country début some years behind them would have been elated to have the undivided attention of such a rich and influential man. 'So…did Viscount Blackthorne ask after your family…your papa?'

Elise gazed into the night, wondering if Maude was worried the noble fellow might lose interest on discovering her family's name was sullied. In fact, it had seemed to her the opposite were true. From what Alex Blackthorne had said, Elise suspected he desired seeing her again *because* of the scandal in her background.

Their prickly exchange had been playing over and over in her mind during the evening although she'd refused to allow it to spoil her enjoyment. He'd demanded she didn't run off because he'd more to say to her and the thought wouldn't quit tormenting her that he'd been on the point of probing into things she'd no wish to discuss. Yet she must be nice to him because she knew he had the power to ruin not just her future, but Bea's, too. What she didn't know was whether he'd be mean enough to use her folly against her. He hadn't liked her lecturing him on how to behave and…she inwardly sighed…it had been impertinent of her. She wished she hadn't provoked him. The last thing she wanted was a tiger by the tail, for this particular one could quite easily turn and maul her.

'Did the viscount speak of his relatives?' Maude tried a different tack.

'No…but we did briefly mention my family,' Elise informed, aware that Mrs Chapman was peering at her, awaiting an answer. 'Oh…and the viscount also said he would call on us in the week. He might have been jesting, though.'

Elise received a nudge from Verity sitting beside her; it was her friend's way of congratulating her remarkable achievement. Mrs Chapman was momentarily stunned into speechlessness, but her wide beaming smile was replete with gratitude.

Elise stared again through the window, wishing she could shake off a prickle of foreboding that the Chapmans might eventually view the viscount's patronage as a curse, not a boon.

Chapter Ten

'Lily…you are a good girl.'

'Am I, sir? I try to be.'

'Sometimes I think I should marry you.'

Lily Watson ceased fluffing up her fiery curls in front of the spotted glass. She turned on the rickety stool to look askance at the fellow reclining naked on the bed, his fleshy top lip hiked in a libidinous smile. She'd sooner marry her pimp Johnny and he was no good. But at least Mr Whittiker seemed to have money to flash around at last. He'd been one of her clients for many months and had always haggled with Johnny over her price. The sight of him huffing up the stairs to her dingy room had previously dispirited her.

But he seemed to be more generous lately and thus her service was less grudging. This evening he'd presented her with a little brooch. Lily knew it was trumpery, worth only pennies, but she was cute enough to coo over it and hint at how much she'd like another gift. In the mirror's reflection she saw that James had scooped up the brandy bottle from the dirty floorboards and, in between watching her lacing the ribbons on her

chemise, was swigging from it. Her eyes flitted over
his stumpy torso. Although he'd only rolled off her fifteen minutes ago he appeared nearly ready to try again.
He was a fellow who liked his money's worth and Lily
wasn't expecting Johnny to come back with another
punter for about half an hour.

She swivelled her posterior on the stool and made
a show of fixing her garters, peeking provocatively at
James from beneath her lashes. When he'd hurriedly
pulled off his clothes earlier she'd seen his plump purse
discarded on the chair atop his breeches. She wouldn't
mind a dip in it before he got bundled out. If she could
distract him, she was sure she could slip some coins
out of sight. All she must do was help him sink further
into his cups so when he noticed the loss tomorrow he
wouldn't remember where he'd been this evening. As
Johnny wouldn't know she'd been light-fingered, he
couldn't help himself to a cut of the takings. She got
to her feet and gave James's flagging erection a saucy
smile.

James elbowed himself off the bed and staggered
to give Lily's rump a playful slap. 'You're a minx to
make me fall for you,' he slurred, breathing hot alco-
holic fumes against her cheek. 'I swear if you were just
a tiny bit decent I'd forget the vinegar-faced misses and
take you down the aisle instead.' Despite his inebriation
James realised he'd spoken truthfully. He felt piqued at
not getting an invitation to the Clemences' ball and was
sick of all the people who thought they were better than
him. He and Jago Clemence had been friends…until
he'd taken a loan from the fellow and failed to deliver
on a repayment. But he'd sooner be here with a good-

natured whore, he told himself, than prancing about with some silly chit who'd have a fit of the vapours if he so much as tried to kiss her.

Maude listened intently to her housemaid's whisperings, then, as a wondrous smile spread across her face, she pivoted about to quietly clap her hands, drawing the attention of the four young ladies seated in the drawing room. Fiona had been sketching with charcoal; Verity, Elise and Bea had been taking it in turns to rifle through a journal and give and seek opinions on the fashion plates. They had been cooped up inside all day, watching grey clouds scudding over ivory sky, hoping the drizzle might blow over so they could take a walk and stretch their legs.

'Viscount Blackthorne and Mr Kendrick have come to pay a call just as Elise said they might,' Maude excitedly squeaked to her audience.

Having been shooed away, Winnie, the young servant, hurtled back out into the hallway to tell the gentlemen they were to be received. Maude's bosom swelled high under her chin in pride as she gazed reverentially at the embossed parchment in her grip bearing the name and crest of the Blackthorne dynasty. She had impressed on the girls they should dress with care every morning for just this eventuality. As the days had passed with no sign of the illustrious fellow's calling card, Maude's hopes had flagged. She glanced about, pleased Winnie had remembered her instruction. The best china and silverware were set out for tea and she was determined to ensure that their guests stayed long enough to take refreshment. She would be the envy of every hostess in town…

On hearing the exhilarating news, Beatrice had jumped to her feet, but had been pulled back to sit on the sofa by her sister.

Elise's countenance was grave. Once Beatrice had found out they might receive a call from Hugh and Alex following the Clemences' ball, her sister's expectation had rivalled Mrs Chapman's, her pleasure transforming to moroseness as days wore on with no sign of them. They had socialised with their friends every evening, but neither gentleman had appeared at those *soirées*.

'What will you do if Hugh asks you to marry him?' Elise whispered, frowning and trying to quell her own butterflies at the realisation that Alex Blackthorne was close by and they had parted on bad terms only days ago.

'I shall tell him yes, then say he must speak to Papa,' Bea burbled joyfully.

'But you know he has no means to make you his wife.'

'Well…he won't propose then, will he?' Beatrice was again on her feet.

Elise's small teeth nipped at her lower lip; she desperately hoped that Hugh Kendrick would also take that logical view, but people falling in love could act irrationally and cause great hurt to those they professed to care about. She only had to recall her own mother's behaviour to know that. Arabella Dewey had promised her daughters they were the most precious people in the world to her…yet it had not prevented her abandoning them to go off with her lover.

Elise's unhappy memories were curtailed as Winnie shyly reappeared, eyes saucer-like, to show the viscount and Hugh Kendrick into the drawing room.

'Oh, how very nice to see you. We are honoured.' Maude's welcoming beam drooped a little as she noted the viscount looked as sinfully handsome as ever, but rather too stern. She didn't want this to be a fleeting visit, so breathlessly rattled off, 'You must take tea with us.'

'That would be very nice.' Hugh gave an encompassing smile despite seeming rather subdued. His eyes had soon drifted Bea's way, but instead of stationing there moved on.

'Please do sit down.' Maude indicated a vacant sofa.

Hugh immediately went to it, but before the viscount could follow Beatrice had whipped to sit beside him.

Elise winced at her sister's excruciating lack of modesty, momentarily closing her eyes in despair. They opened to clash on a deep-brown gaze that she was sure mocked her. He'd told her the couple would not be nagged apart and must sort things out themselves and reluctantly Elise recognised the truth in it. She could sensibly advise her sister till she was blue in the face but Bea wouldn't heed one word of it if she didn't want to. If her sister had listened to her fears over the dratted Lady Lonesome business their family would not have come to the viscount's notice. Elise sensed that might have been best.

'Do take a seat, my lord,' Maude urged as the viscount braced a dark hand negligently on the mantelshelf as though he would stay where he was. 'There's a place by Miss Elise.' She opened the door to hiss at Winnie—who'd been instructed to hover outside—that it was time to put the kettle on.

Alex sat down on the edge of a blue-velvet cushion, clasping his linked fingers on his knees. 'And how are you, Miss Dewey?' he asked evenly, gazing at a spot on the ceiling.

'I'm well, sir. And you?' Elise replied in an equally placid tone that belied the fact she was overwhelmed by his proximity. The warmth from his body was seeping through the thin dimity of her day dress and a scent of sandalwood was in her nostrils. A sliding glance took in his impressive appearance: highly polished Hessians and tight buff breeches were in her line of vision. She averted her eyes from a muscled thigh's hard contours that mere days ago she'd straddled with her skirts awry.

'I'm glad to be back in London,' Alex answered, sitting back and turning his dark head towards her.

Maude had been eavesdropping. 'You've been out of town, my lord?' It was unusual for people to be drawn away from the metropolis during the height of the Season, but she had heard from her husband that the viscount had recently bought Whittiker's country acreage that abutted his own. She prayed that particular fellow wouldn't put in an appearance this afternoon and ruin everything. He hadn't visited this week and Maude sensed her eldest daughter was relieved rather than sorry about that.

'I've had estate matters to deal with in Berkshire. Some newly acquired land needed fencing.'

Alex caught a muffled sound to one side of him. 'You find fencing amusing, Miss Dewey?' he asked without removing his gaze from his long, loosely entwined fingers. They freed themselves so a few could brush a speck from a conker-brown sleeve from which protruded a pristine shirt cuff.

'I find the idea of you personally doing it quite funny. But then I'm sure you did not.' Elise cast her eyes down to her lap, wishing she'd managed to control her spontaneous giggle.

'I personally did a good deal of it.' He slowly turned to face her.

Elise stared at him, moistened her lips, then stilled her tongue when she noticed she'd drawn his eyes to her mouth.

'You believe me incapable of swinging a hammer?' he asked quietly with a half-smile.

'No…' Elise could remember very well the strength in the arms that had held her captive in the bushes at Vauxhall. 'I believed you incapable of lowering yourself to do so,' Elise blurted truthfully, feeling uncomfortably hot with embarrassment.

'Ah. An easy mistake to make if you're used to jumping to conclusions about other people. Before my father died and I took my birthright I was in the army and learned many practical skills.'

'Oh…well done,' Elise praised icily, fuming at his set down. Every time they met he either ordered her about or reprimanded her. But what irked her most was her own behaviour; she'd been wrong to speak too openly. In future she'd guard her tongue and give him no opportunity to air his sarcasm. Then she'd have no need to retaliate in kind.

'Surely you have estate workers, my lord, to carry out such work?' Verity, although a distance away, had heard snippets of the conversation and gamely came to her friend's assistance as she saw Elise's blush heighten.

'I have many staff at the Hall, but we have a measles epidemic in the surrounding villages. It has laid low men in their prime and hit some families particularly hard.' Alex paused. 'Cattle have been escaping fields and causing a nuisance, roaming free in the lanes. It's no real hardship to get my hands dirty once in a while if an urgent job requires it.'

'Ah…refreshment,' Maude cried in relief. She sensed a tricky atmosphere was fomenting, yet oddly was quite sure that his lordship would not yet take himself off. Under cover of pouring tea and distributing cups she gave the sofa to her left thoughtful glances. In her opinion Elise was very sweet in looks and character, but not a raving beauty. Yet something about the girl interested him; and something about him made Elise nervous.

Maude suppressed a smirk. She had high hopes of where it all might lead.

'We were going to take a constitutional as soon as it stops raining.' Bea turned to Hugh and inspected his jacket for signs of drizzle. 'Have the clouds gone at last?'

'It's fine enough for an outing.' Hugh glanced at his friend, hoping he would remember what they'd discussed on the way over.

Alex spoke on cue, including the Chapman sisters in his invitation. 'Perhaps all the young ladies would like to take a short drive in the park. If it does come on to rain, the landau has a hood.'

'That is most kind, sir!' Maude abruptly rattled her cup on to its saucer. 'Verity, Fiona, fetch your outdoor things…quickly now.' Maude's beam commended the viscount for his gentlemanly conduct. She knew he'd sooner have taken just the Dewey girls and Hugh Kendrick, for it was bound to be a squash seating everybody. 'By the time you return I shall have some spiced biscuits hot from the oven,' she promised.

Hugh gave his friend a rueful glance. Alex had a celebrated pastry chef in his kitchen in Upper Brook Street and could have fancy delicacies brought to him freshly baked at midnight if that was his whim.

'I'll look forward to that, ma'am,' Alex said graciously on standing up.

'I'm sorry I—'

'There's a matter I—'

'Please…you speak first, sir.' Elise made a small apologetic gesture.

'No, I insist you do so. You began fractionally before me.' Alex sounded quietly amused. 'Besides, it would be churlish to interrupt your apology when one is quite overdue.'

Elise bristled, spearing him a darkling glance. She turned her head and carried on walking, pondering on her response now he had interrupted her train of thought.

They had only recently alighted from the landau; Beatrice and Hugh had quite naturally drawn together like magnets and set off at quite a pace along the path as though wishing to put distance between themselves and their friends. Verity had spotted the Clemences in their carriage and had given them a wave. Caro and her mother had openly goggled at the sight of them all seated in the viscount's crested landau. The Clemences' barouche had pulled up sharply just yards in front of Alex's vehicle. Verity and her sister had got down and dutifully gone off to have a gossip with their friends, leaving—quite deliberately, in Elise's opinion—just her and the viscount to stroll on alone towards the water. She glanced over a shoulder to see that the Chapman sisters now trailed a long way behind and Jago Clemence was at their side riding a large black horse. Caro and her mother had their heads together with more people and Elise could guess what held their interest.

'Do I need to prompt you again?' Alex asked softly.

'No, you do not, sir,' Elise answered with admirable aplomb and level tone. She turned back to him, putting from her mind that talk about them would be circulating in every society drawing room before the day was out. 'I am thinking on how to phrase my conversation so that you do not immediately take me to task over it.'

'Is that what I do?' Alex wryly enquired. 'I apologise in that case.'

'And not before time,' Elise returned, but her tone held a hint of levity. 'Pax?' she ventured appealingly.

'Pax,' Alex agreed. 'Now that's over with, what else were you about to say to me?'

'I'm sorry if you thought me rude earlier. I meant no offence; it is just unusual to hear of a gentleman acting as a labourer.'

'Has your father never used tools or mended things?'

'Oh yes…' Elise chuckled. 'A few years ago when he had better health he would from necessity make economies and do odd jobs around the house. He loved his gardening, too. I would scold him often for coming to the table with soil beneath his fingernails…' Elise frowned, suddenly wishing that the conversation hadn't turned in that direction. 'It must be a worry to you that the measles is infecting people close to your home.' She fluidly changed the subject. 'It is a nasty disease. Both Bea and I had it when quite young.'

'I also had a dose as a child,' Alex said. 'Perhaps I was lucky, but I don't recall being much put out by it.' He frowned. 'Yet one family has lost two children out of six and the parents are both afflicted.'

'How dreadful!' Elise gasped. 'Is the doctor of no help? Can such country folk not afford to pay for his care?'

'He has been regularly in attendance and done what he can for everybody…I made sure of it. A woman from the village is going in to help out with the everyday needs of people worst affected.'

Elise guessed he might have paid for the woman's generosity and the physician's visits, too. 'You are a good landlord and employer?' she asked simply, wanting to know he was a benevolent man.

'I hope so…I try to be.' Alex plunged his hands into his pockets. 'The matter I wished to discuss with you concerns your family.'

Dejectedly, Elise realised he hadn't been put off for long in pursuing the subject that really interested him and her admiration for his philanthropy withered a little. She was conscious of deep-brown eyes warming the top of her head and knew he was gauging her reaction to his blunt announcement.

'I imagine you have heard that my parents had their problems before my mother died,' Elise began coolly.

'You might also have heard gossip about a scandal concerning my father's business. I've no wish to revisit any of it, so please do not press me to do so.'

'I've no desire to hurt you by talking about distressing topics,' Alex returned quietly. 'I have brought up the matter because I would like your advice on something.'

Elise frowned, her interest quickening. 'Something that concerns my family?'

'Yes…' Alex indicated a bench set beneath a canopy of branches. 'Shall we sit down while we talk?'

Elise allowed him to lead her to the seat.

After a quiet moment Alex leaned forwards to plant his elbows on his knees and gaze into the distance. 'Some days ago I had a meeting with my attorney. He gave me a letter bequeathed to me by my late uncle. In it he made mention of members of your family.' Alex turned to look at her. 'Tell me…did you know my uncle, Thomas Venner?'

Elise repeated the name in a murmur, looking reflective. 'I don't think so. Was he a friend of my father's?'

'No…more a friend of your mother's, I gather.'

Elise's puzzlement transformed to an expression of wariness. She glanced at his face, noticing there was a softening to his mouth as though pity moulded it. 'Are you about to tell me they were romantically involved?' Elise whispered.

Alex pressed his spine back against the wooden bench, let an arm unfold along its top rail. 'It seems they were. I was abroad serving in the army at the time, so have no personal knowledge of any of it.' He paused, pursing his lips thoughtfully. 'I have spoken to my mother. She recalls what went on between our kin many years ago. Her brother seems to have had the affair still on his conscience when he died.' Alex glanced sideways at Elise to find her watching him intently. 'He has written out a list of his creditors and included in it that he owes your father a wife and a sum of money. For reasons only known to him he expects me to make reparation for that sin.'

Chapter Eleven

'My mother ran off to Lord Reeves, not Mr Venner,' Elise blurted, too shocked for a moment to properly form a questioning response.

'I understand she accepted that gentleman's protection afterwards. My mother informs me her brother had only a brief affair with Arabella Dewey.'

Elise snapped down her face, frowning at her agitated fingers. It seemed incredible that she was discussing such personal family details with a man who a short while ago had been a stranger. Yet she believed all of what he'd said. She might not quite trust him in some ways, yet knew he would not lie to her over this. It seemed a bizarre coincidence that the scandalous drama that had altered the course of her and Bea's lives had encompassed his family, too. But what disturbed her, and brought a surge of blood to stain her cheekbones, was the revelation that her mother had moved quickly from one lover to another. She hoped very much that Alex Blackthorne wouldn't consider Arabella wanton and neither should she. Elise was determined to stay loyal to her mama's memory no matter the extent of her peccadilloes.

'I'm in a dilemma over whether to act on my late uncle's wishes or to leave well alone,' Alex explained.

'What on earth does he expect you can do about it now?' Elise cried in a stifled tone. 'How can you make amends for all the hurt and humiliation your uncle heaped on my father's head?' She bit her lip, swinging away her tense countenance. There was no point in apportioning blame. She knew her mother must bear her share of the guilt.

'Did your uncle's family suffer as we have because of the liaison? Did his children feel ashamed?'

'Thomas Venner was unwed.'

Elise felt unaccountably angry to know it. So the fellow had not committed adultery like her mother. But still he was guilty in her eyes. Thomas Venner might have been unattached, but he knew her mother wasn't.

At the ball Elise recalled overhearing Maude and Anthony Chapman discussing Alex Blackthorne's paramour. Perhaps Celia Chase was a married woman, cuckolding her husband, and the viscount was a hypocrite to affect an attitude of regret over his uncle's bad habits. He would have betrayed his mistress with her at Vauxhall had she not come to her senses and put a stop to his seduction.

'Even had your uncle been married, the disgrace would not have ruined him, would it? Gentlemen can often act the cheat with impunity.'

Alex raised his eyes heavenwards, impatient fingers massaging his shady jaw. 'I've no wish to stir antagonism between us. I'm not defending Thomas in any way, although I liked him.'

Elise twisted to look at him, feline eyes springing to his face. 'So…what advice do you seek on this tawdry topic, sir?'

A quiet descended, broken only by the whispering of the sycamore leaves overhead as they danced in a strengthening breeze.

'I've no idea how your father might react to a visit from me to discuss this matter,' Alex finally said.

'You would rub my father's nose in his wife's adultery?' Elise accused, whitening in fury and disbelief. 'My advice to you and to all your relatives is to leave him be!' She shot to her feet but her elbow was gripped and she was unceremoniously tugged back to sit at his side.

'The last thing I want is to fire the embers of his bitterness.' Alex had turned towards her, his body positioned to thwart any further escape she might attempt. 'I've sought to consult you for that very reason and would have done so sooner if you'd been a bit more amenable on the night of the ball.'

'Had you stayed more than half an hour perhaps we might have talked,' Elise snapped. 'But I believe you were in a rush to get away to other company.'

'Explain what you mean by that.' Alex's lazy drawl was at odds with the way he shifted threateningly closer as she made a tentative move to bolt.

To an observer they might have looked like a couple having a delightfully animated chat, he sitting forwards, facing her. Only she understood his looming torso was pinning her in place. Elise felt her chest tighten in a mingling of thrill and trepidation.

But she wouldn't again try to flee. She'd no intention of drawing more eyes to them or of giving him the satisfaction of forcing her to submit. She had told him she wasn't frightened of him…and she wasn't!

Elise lifted clear golden eyes to clash on his impassive regard, reading his challenge. He knew very well what she'd heard about him. No doubt his womanising was common knowledge in polite circles and people enjoyed gossiping about it. Elise sensed he didn't give a damn what they said.

'I heard that you stayed just a short while at the Clemences as you were more interested in your mistress than a roomful of débutantes.'

'I doubt you would have been included in that conversation so I take it you were eavesdropping.'

'I was not!' Guilty colour crept up to the roots of Elise's silky fair hair.

'So who were you talking to?'

'Nobody…' Elise ejected through gritting teeth.

'You didn't enquire about me?' Alex's mouth slanted sardonically.

'I did not! And I'm sorry your conceit has led you to imagine I ever would.' She twisted aside her head.

'And did you believe that?'

'What?'

'That I had left to seek other diversion because I had no interest in the assembled company?'

'I gave it no heed,' Elise returned icily. 'And would sooner you didn't hint at your sordid habits.'

'You started it,' Alex reminded, drily amused. But he

shifted back from her, lounging into the wooden slats with his long legs stretched out, crossed at the ankles.

Elise moved pointedly sideways and turned her head away from him.

'If you hadn't annoyed me, I would have stayed longer. I might even have asked you to dance.'

'In that case thank goodness you did not tarry. A refusal is not always well received.' Elise continued squinting away into the distance.

He threw back his head to shout a laugh at whispering leaves. 'You've obviously heard I'm out of practice on the dance floor.'

Elise knew he was offering an olive branch, but she felt too piqued to take it.

'Our truce didn't last long,' he idly observed, studying his nails.

'I should like it to,' Elise answered after a short quiet in which she brought her temper under control. There were things she very much wanted to know and she regretted having jumped at the bait he'd dangled and acted hot-headed. She hoped he didn't think her jealous.

That worrying thought spurred her to quickly face him, although she avoided looking into his sultry brown eyes. 'I…I have been shocked by what you have said about our kin's involvement, but will tell you what my conscience will allow.'

'There's no need to discuss it further,' Alex said gently. 'You've made it clear you believe your father will be distressed by unearthing the past. I shall let sleeping dogs lie so there's nothing else to say at present.' Alex pushed to his feet.

'I have more to say, if you please, sir,' Elise insisted,

spontaneously and rather rudely pulling on his sleeve to make him again sit beside her.

Alex covered her quivering fingers with his, stilling them with very little pressure while he looked deep into her eyes. Mockery was still present in his long-lashed regard, but so was another emotion that tightened a coil of sensation in Elise's stomach. He'd looked at her in that way when their bodies had been pressed together on the dark path at Vauxhall.

When he again took his place beside her his thigh nudged hers but she made no immediate effort to slide away from his proximity. To her consternation she sensed she wanted to cleave to his warmth and strength. She forced herself to put a seemly distance between them.

'I don't want to hurt you…any of you…' Alex said, his face turned from her as he watched the approach of her friends. 'But if you want to pursue the subject, let me say I'm aware your father's financial position is such that he'd welcome repayment of a debt owed to him.'

'Is it a good deal of money?' Even if it was not Elise knew it might make a huge difference to her father's household accounts. He moaned often about the cost of feeding them all and had made economies lately. The butcher's visits had dwindled to once a week and she and Bea had accepted a small reduction in their already meagre allowances.

'I've no idea of the amount; Thomas didn't let on. That is why I wanted to speak to your father. I've no wish to insult him by transferring to him a woefully inadequate figure.'

'So it might be a lot?' Elise ventured.

'It might…'

Elise digested that information. 'Your uncle was indeed a wretched individual to take a man's wife and his cash, too.'

'I made a similar remark when I discovered what had gone on.' Alex tipped up his face to frown at a canopy of leaves. 'I know you consider me a reprobate and perhaps I am, but I have my own codes of conduct and would ask you to remember that no matter what tales you hear about me. They are almost upon us…' He indicated the Chapman sisters by tilting his dark head. Jago was still at their side, keeping his mount to a sedate pace. Of Beatrice and Hugh there was no sign.

'Do you want me to speak to your father?'

Elise sighed, made a small gesture of uncertainty. 'Old wounds are best left alone…but if repayment of your uncle's debts resulted in a dowry for my sister, then good would come out of it.' She spoke her thoughts aloud. 'It is daft to speak of weddings after such a short acquaintanceship, but Beatrice would accept a proposal from your friend if one were forthcoming, she has told me so.' Elise gazed earnestly at him. 'But then if the sum owed is very little there can be no wedding—' She broke off immediately and stood up as Verity skipped over the grass towards her. Elise sent a fleeting glance over a shoulder and as their eyes locked felt satisfied Alex had understood her caution. No more mention would be made of the matter today.

James Whittiker brought his elderly mare to a halt in Hyde Park, narrowing spiteful eyes on the happy party congregated under the sycamore tree. He sourly noticed that Fiona Chapman was looking gay despite the fact he hadn't paid a call on her for some time. He saw, too, that Jago Clemence seemed interested in the younger Chapman girl. But it was Alex Blackthorne who drew James's full attention. He still harboured resentment over the sale of his estate to the man while conveniently overlooking the fact that if he'd exercised some self-control he would have been able to keep a hold on it. In James's opinion Blackthorne had taken unfair advantage of his execrable pecuniary position. He was brooding so deeply on what he regarded as a great injustice that he failed to hear a familiar giggle the first couple of times that it was let rip.

James's eyes suddenly veered sideways and landed on Lily Watson's tumble of red tresses. She was promenading with a dark-haired friend, the two of them boldly eyeing up passing gentlemen. James suddenly forgot all about Alex Blackthorne's triumph over him and concentrated on a very recent treachery. He knew where his missing golden guinea had disappeared to: it had been slipped down the bodice of that thieving little whore the last time he'd visited her. And he'd have it back. He'd lost again at cards last night and was quickly running through the proceeds of selling Grantham Place. No doubt Lily had thought him too stupid or too drunk to miss one coin from the many he'd carried in his purse. But James knew to the last penny how much he was worth, even on those mornings when he counted out his money with a very sore head.

Since discovering the theft he had several times secreted himself outside her lodgings, hoping to catch her alone. But she'd always emerged from the hovel where she lived with Johnny and he knew better than to get on the wrong side of such a felon. James feared getting skewered if he accused her pimp of theft. Besides, he had a feeling that minx Lily would have kept to herself that she'd been light-fingered. Johnny might know nothing about it and believe him lying.

At present, Johnny was nowhere in sight and James saw an opportunity to recover his money. After that he'd make sure he went elsewhere for his pleasure.

Kicking his mount into action, James trotted over the grass towards the sauntering women, but reined back when he saw they'd had some success in finding a client. With a satisfied smirk James observed the elderly fellow thread the brunette's arm through his, then stroll away while his own prey sulkily watched them.

'Oh…I wasn't expecting to bump into you, sir.' Lily tried to dodge past James, but he'd wedged her against a hedge with his horse's flanks.

'And I don't suppose you're too pleased about it, are you, my girl? But I'm glad to see you, Lily. I'll be happier to see my money.' Jumping down, he held her arm in a pinching grip, preventing her from bolting. 'Give back that guinea you stole or it'll be the worse for you.'

Lily squirmed, but James tightened his hold until she threw back her head and gave him a defiant glare from beneath a wagging feather. 'Too late—it's gone and serve you right for bringing me a brooch worth a farthing.' She pulled at her lapel to show him a gaudy set of coloured stones. 'See…bought a nicer one and told Johnny it came from you.'

James's mouth disappeared into a hard line and his cheeks whitened in rage. 'I'll take payment in some form, you little trollop!' James began leading his horse and dragging her along with him towards dense shrubbery. He was so fired up he knew he'd forgo decency and tumble her right now in the bushes—with the cream of society close by—rather than let her escape punishment.

'Let me go or I'll scream blue murder,' Lily squeaked.

'Do so and I'll broadcast that you're a thieving harlot who needs a spell in Newgate to cure her sticky fingers.'

Lily knew that the magistrate *would* send her to prison, too. She'd been up before the beak just last month on a charge of soliciting and he'd said if he saw her again he'd have her in gaol.

James abruptly hissed at Lily to keep quiet and be still as he noticed Alex Blackthorne frowning his way. He didn't want anybody—especially not that fellow—poking his nose into what he might be doing arm in arm with a notorious doxy in Hyde Park. Although many gentlemen might be acquainted with some of the rougher women sashaying about, they ignored them until after dark.

Lily followed the direction of James's eyes and gave a sour chuckle. 'Bet that fine fellow won't be taking *her* into the bushes this afternoon,' she muttered. 'He'll wait for another go at it when they're alone in the dark at Vauxhall.'

James whipped his attention to Lily. He found it hard to believe the viscount would dally with such as Lily when he could take his pleasure with the beautiful fêted brunette rumoured to be besotted with him. 'You know Alex Blackthorne?' he demanded, shaking her arm to hurry her response.

'No…more's the pity.' Lily sighed, giving the viscount a lascivious peek. If such a handsome gentleman showed an interest in her, she'd go very willingly wherever he suggested. 'But *she* does,' Lily added grudgingly. She nodded at Elise.

'Who do you mean? The taller blonde young lady?' James demanded, puzzled.

'Looks like butter wouldn't melt, doesn't she?' Lily sniped. 'But I saw the two of them coming out of the bushes together at Vauxhall. Wished it had been me in there with him, I did.'

James's jaw sagged. 'Are you sure?'

''Course I'm sure,' Lily insisted. 'I went up to him… but no use…he wasn't interested.' She narrowed her eyes on Elise. 'And I took a good gander at her, too, before she ran off. She'd been poaching on my patch and I promised myself I'd have her guts for garters if she tried it again.' Lily sensed she had in some way pleased James and she gave him a faltering smile. 'Was that worth a guinea to you, Mr Whittiker?'

James smiled maliciously. 'Oh…I think so…' He let go of Lily's arm, then gave her a small disdainful shove. 'Be on your way.'

Lily needed no second telling. She trotted over the grass towards the path, pulling her feathered hat to a jaunty angle.

Chapter Twelve

'Please stop crying!' Elise sighed as she stared into the busy street from the bedroom window. Across the road a young housemaid was half-heartedly rebuffing a delivery boy's raucous advances and vehicles and horses were clattering over cobbles. The cacophony was quite audible through the glass, but Elise was only conscious of the hiccupping sobs coming from the bed behind. She felt sorry for her sister's dreadful disappointment, but was exasperated with Bea because it had been plain from the start how it all must end.

A few days ago when the gentlemen had brought the young ladies back from their drive in the park Alex and Hugh had departed almost immediately without entering the house.

Mrs Chapman had been dismayed that her offer of tea and biscuits hadn't been taken up, but it hadn't been a surprise to Elise when the landau swiftly set off along the road. Hugh and Bea had reappeared for the journey home looking tense and solemn, making the other female passengers quieten in sympathy. Only the viscount had seemed unaffected by the leaden atmosphere.

Straight away Elise had guessed that Hugh had done the decent thing and apologised to Bea for encouraging her to think he might court her when he was actually in no position to do so. Beatrice had confirmed that to be the truth as soon as they had set foot in the Chapmans' hallway. In a tearful whisper she had imparted that Hugh had honestly admitted he would need to improve his prospects before being able to support a wife.

Beatrice sat up with a sniff and dabbed at her red eyes. 'Are the others back yet?'

Elise shook her head, turning from the bustling vista below to come and sit down beside Bea on the coverlet. Mrs Chapman had accompanied Verity and Fiona to an afternoon salon at the Clemences' house. Elise would have liked to go, too, allowing Beatrice to wallow in her miseries, but knew she and her sister must have a serious conversation. It was pointless for them to remain in London as the Chapmans' guests if Bea were to continue moping about creating a bad atmosphere. It had been several days since their outing to the park, yet yesterday evening Beatrice had again chosen to remain upstairs pining for what might have been rather than join them all at dinner. Their host had noticed her absence and asked if something was amiss despite his wife's attempts to deflect his concern with mutters and meaningful frowns.

'Do you want to go home, Bea?'

Beatrice pulled a face, looking undecided. Eventually she nodded. 'But I don't want to spoil things for you if you'd sooner stay in London. Aunt Dolly has said we may lodge with her if you think we are outstaying our welcome with the Chapmans.'

'I'll forgo Aunt Dolly's company if you've done enough husband-hunting.' Elise gave a rueful chuckle. 'But I shall miss the opportunity to observe how Jago and Verity fare.' Elise was certain that Mrs Clemence's invitation had been issued at her son's behest. Elise wouldn't be surprised to learn that Jago had attended the ladies' tea party simply to devote more time to her friend. Elise had hoped to take her sister's mind off her own troubles, but when Bea dipped her head to dab at her eyes she realised she'd been tactless mentioning that blossoming relationship.

The matter of the money owed to her papa by Thomas Venner was constantly on Elise's mind and once or twice she had almost confided in Bea that there might be a way. But she knew if she raised her sister's hopes and it all came to nought because the sum was small, Bea would be even further in the doldrums than she was now. So Elise had stayed silent on the matter of the possibility of a dowry, hoping soon to hear further from Alex. She was sure there must be a way for him to discover—perhaps from a solicitor who knew of the transaction between their kin—how much the debt was and whether it might make a difference to Bea's future.

'Come…let's not stay cooped up, but go out and get some air,' Elise urged, as golden warmth filtered through the lightweight curtains. 'The sun has come out and we can take a walk and do some window shopping.' She gave her sister's forearm an encouraging shake. 'It might be the last opportunity we get to enjoy Regent Street if we are to return home soon.'

Robinson phlegmatically regarded the portly indi-vidual standing on the top flag of a gracious flight of

York stone that descended to Upper Brook Street's cobbles. The fellow looked as though the climb had exerted him: his fat cheeks were florid and his vibrating chest was straining buttons on his garish waistcoat. But it was the visitor's pompous expression that grated on the servant. He had overheard conversations between his master and Hugh Kendrick in which it was apparent they found this fellow's company repugnant. Robinson could understand why that was.

Nevertheless the butler knew his master had had recent business dealings with Mr Whittiker so tonelessly invited him into the opulent hallway of the viscount's mansion. He led the way past soaring marble pillars and a twin sweep of graceful walnut banisters to indicate one of a pair of intricately carved ebony chairs, set against a pastel wall. Once the man had seated himself—with a bitter look at his sumptuous surroundings—Robinson announced he would ascertain whether Viscount Blackthorne was able to receive a caller despite suspecting it would be a wasted journey.

Alex had been absently tapping a pen on a blotter, his thoughts with Elise, when his butler arrived to tell him James Whittiker wanted an audience. In front of Alex on his desk was his late uncle's bequest. He had reread it several times in the last hour, hoping to spot something he'd missed previously. But still the damnable document failed to reveal an amount owed to Mr Dewey. Alex knew he would return to Elise's father every penny he was due so he must try to shed some light on the matter. His need to settle with Walter Dewey wasn't solely in the hope the funds might assist the ill-starred lovers by providing Beatrice with a dowry. Hugh and he had been good friends since schooldays, but gaining Elise's trust and approval was Alex's prime motivation. For a reason he'd yet to fathom a girl with golden eyes and overwhelming filial duty had intrigued and obsessed him in a way no ambitious débutante or seasoned courtesan could. He thought her beautiful, although he realised some people would consider her too thin and passably pretty. Those same people might think her character lacking vivacity, whereas he found her quiet wit and caring nature far more endearing than the shallow gaiety displayed by a good number of *beau monde* débutantes.

Mostly he desired her. He'd come close to losing control and seducing her at Vauxhall and even now just the memory of her silky mouth and warm pliant curves could cause an inferno to ignite within. Since then, whenever they were close, her slender figure captivated him causing his fingers to itch to touch her, making him forget his mistress's voluptuous body was readily available to him when the urge for a woman was undeniable.

Suddenly conscious that his loins were throbbing uncomfortably and his butler was stoically awaiting a response, Alex folded the parchment he'd been sightlessly staring at and thrust it away over leather.

'Did Whittiker state his business?' Alex asked in a voice roughened by frustration.

'He did not, my lord.'

An inaudible irritated sigh pursed Alex's lips. He could guess what had brought the fellow here. It was common knowledge that Whittiker was still brooding on the loss of his estate and would moan about it to anybody who cared to listen. But the deal was done and

Alex wasn't about to renegotiate any of it. He realised it was probably as well to give him an audience and spell that out one final time, then Whittiker need never again find the impertinence to bother him at home. A nod gave his butler permission to show his visitor in.

'You're aware I can be found at my club most days, I take it?'

An acid greeting met James as he bowled into the viscount's study while Robinson closed the door behind him.

'I don't think you'd want this matter aired in public, Blackthorne.' Whittiker's smug response came as he sat down, uninvited, in a hide wing chair. Deliberately he lounged back, eyeing the Viscount's brandy decanter on the corner of the desk.

Alex's expression remained impassive, but he was immediately on his guard. Despite the fact that they loathed one another, Whittiker customarily treated him with an amount of reluctant deference. At present the weasel seemed overconfident, prompting Alex to search for a reason for it. A memory of the last time he'd seen James surfaced in his mind. It had been on the day he'd been with Elise and her friends in Hyde Park and had heard James's raised voice. Alex remembered thinking he vaguely recognised the gaudy female with whom the fellow had appeared to be arguing.

It had niggled at Alex that he hadn't been able to place the woman, but with startling clarity he suddenly could bring to mind where and when they'd met. The curse was kept behind his teeth and the only change in his demeanour was a tightening in his jaw, causing a muscle to leap beneath a cheek. Despite the dusk that evening, and her luxuriously plumed hat, he had glimpsed the doxy's face and red hair when she'd accosted him at Vauxhall. He recalled at the time thinking it was of little importance if she had spotted Elise emerging from that dark walkway just minutes earlier for their paths would never again cross. He had a feeling Whittiker was about to shatter that foolish assumption.

'State your business, Whittiker, I've appointments to keep.'

James bristled beneath Alex's unconcealed contempt. He tapped together his fingertips, staring slyly over them from beneath his brows. 'I think you owe me some more money for Grantham Place. Let me tell you why...'

'Please do,' Alex sardonically invited.

'Its worth wasn't reflected in the price you paid.'

'Its worth was the highest bid. I believe that was what I paid. You had the choice to withdraw from the sale rather than sign the deeds over.'

'I had no choice! I was desperate for funds and you knew it,' Whittiker furiously hissed, sliding forwards on his seat. 'I know where you get your hard-nosed ways. Like father, like son. The old viscount tried to lay his hands on what was rightfully mine before I even took my birthright.'

Alex pushed back his chair and stood up with an air of tedium. 'I think you need to have a talk with your attorney, before I have a talk with mine,' he suggested dulcetly. 'Ask the fellow to explain the rudiments of business to you.' Alex strolled to his mantelpiece and negligently propped an elbow on marble. 'I—and my father before me—have done nothing wrong in offering to purchase land that abuts Blackthorne Hall. Your father refused to sell to mine, as was his right. But you agreed to sell to me. Now, if there's nothing else to discuss…'

Whittiker sprang upright, his veneer of composure crumbling away. Just being in the presence of this powerful man could intimidate him, making him lose the nerve to immediately threaten to expose Elise Dewey as a disgraceful wanton. But he was determined not to leave empty-handed. 'Oh…there's something else to discuss,' he uttered in a poisonous whisper.

'And will you ever tell me what it is?' Alex prompted drily.

Whittiker licked his lips. He didn't relish what he was about to do because he knew there was a risk it might backfire. Lily was an inconsequential witness to the tryst. But James didn't think Lily was being fanciful—he had seen the way this man looked at Elise and singled her out. He believed the seduction had taken place at Vauxhall. Whittiker was banking on the viscount not wanting the young lady's reputation sullied and thus paying him an additional sum to seal his lips. James would enjoy seeing Blackthorne squirm and dance to his tune. If the young lady were compromised, her future was ruined beyond repair…unless the viscount did the decent thing and proposed. Inwardly James guffawed at the idea. Blackthorne's sense of honour would never extend to taking a country miss to wife when aristocrats' daughters were vying to receive him to add a vast dowry to his bank balance.

'What is it you wanted to discuss, Whittiker?' Alex demanded exceedingly quietly.

James sensed a dangerous atmosphere fomenting and it occurred to him that the viscount had guessed

what he was about to say. Perhaps Alex had recognised
Lily in the park and had been expecting a visit from
him. He stroked his chin, adopting an air of regret as he
said, 'It is a very sensitive matter that you won't want
aired in public.'

Alex leaned back against the fireplace, his impatience intentionally apparent as he crossed his arms
over a white linen shirt that displayed the muscular
breadth of his shoulders.

'Miss Elise Dewey will not like it to become common knowledge that a friend of mine spotted her alone
with you in the bushes at Vauxhall.'

'Are you threatening to make such an accusation?'
Alex's expression and stance hadn't altered an iota.

'I will if I need to,' Whittiker returned in a rush.
'And I'll name my witness. On the other hand, if you
pay me…' He shot back a step and blinked nervously
as the viscount suddenly moved from the mantelpiece
to pick up the decanter.

Alex refilled his empty tumbler and sipped, remaining silent and inhospitable as he stoppered the bottle
without offering his guest a drink.

'You might deny it ever happened to protect her, but
Miss Dewey seems an honest chit and I imagine will tell
the truth under questioning.' Whittiker wished that the
viscount would look at him or answer him. The length-
ening silence was more unnerving than a bawled denial
or counter-threat.

Suddenly Alex lifted his head and James could feel
hard despising eyes boring into him.

'I imagine you've prepared well for the consequences
of trying to blackmail me. Have you?' Alex asked quite
mildly.

'The consequences need only be a banker's draft for three thousand pounds. And I'm willing to give you a week to consider.' James edged towards the door, feeling it wise to retreat before the simmering rage he could sense heating the atmosphere became explosive. 'It's not as though you can't afford it,' he added sourly before slipping out into the corridor and hurrying towards the vestibule. He was smiling—but not as firmly as he'd expected to when he'd passed in the opposite direction a short while ago.

Chapter Thirteen

'Isn't that Alex Blackthorne's phaeton?'

'I believe it is,' Dolly Pearson replied. 'And look who is sitting beside him.'

Raising her lorgnette, Edith Vickers studied the splendid carriage's passengers more closely. 'It's not surprising he's smitten. Celia Chase is a lovely lady, isn't she?'

Dolly disdainfully eyed the flimsy muslin garment clothing the young woman. 'Pretty?' she sniffed. 'Maybe… Lady? I doubt it…' Her muttering tailed off and she smiled brightly on noticing one of her nieces had turned away from the display of fabrics cramming a shop window.

'We have noticed that the viscount is out and about today.' Edith Vickers helpfully pointed out the sleek vehicle, oblivious to Dolly's frown.

'So he is,' Elise breathed. She stared at the high-flyer drawn by two elegant greys. Even had she not overheard her aunt name the viscount's companion she would have guessed that he was taking his mistress for a drive. The woman looked to be about her own age and devoted to him. Celia had a possessive hand on his sleeve while gazing up at him with an intimate smile.

He, on the other hand, was watching her, Elise realised as she glanced at his face to see if he was mirroring his mistress's ardour. She pivoted away, hating the fact that he'd caught her gawping at the two of them.

'Shall we move along and investigate other shops?' Elise beckoned to Bea, indicating that they were ready to walk on.

The sisters had barely set foot on Regent Street before bumping into their aunt and Mrs Vickers, who'd also been of a mind to get outdoors for a constitutional before the weather again turned to showers. The two older women had seemed eager to join them and Elise had welcomed their company. Bea had barely surfaced from her fit of the glums during the cab journey to the centre of town. As they'd all slowly promenaded among the crowds, stopping to peruse the shop displays, her sister's spirits had seemed to improve.

Elise took a surreptitious peek from beneath the brim of her bonnet, noticing that the phaeton was on its way again having escaped the knot of vehicles that had brought the traffic to a temporary standstill. An odd tension curdled her stomach as she watched the couple disappear into the distance and a lump formed in her throat. She gulped in a breath, inwardly scolding herself. Just because he'd once kissed and caressed her, making her, idiotically, feel overwhelmed didn't mean he was special to her any more than she was to him. He was just a man who happened to be a practised philanderer and was friendly with the gentleman her sister wanted to marry. The sight of him with his mis-

tress should not have affected her at all for it was none
of her business what he did. She realised the sooner
places were booked on the mail coach for her and her
sister to travel home, the better it would be for everyone.

'You two young ladies are very welcome to stay with
me in Hammersmith, you know,' Aunt Dolly said, as
though she'd read her younger niece's thoughts. 'It is
good of the Chapmans to put you up, but if you'd like
a change for a little while…'

Elise guessed Dolly was hinting she was aware how
costly visitors could be if they outstayed their welcome.

'We have decided it is time to go home,' Elise informed her lightly.

'Go home?' Dolly and Edith parroted in unison,
peering at the two young ladies. They both knew how
well the Dewey sisters were doing socially. Since their
arrival they had propelled the Chapman family from
the fringes of society close to its core.

'But you are having such a wonderful time and are
very popular, too,' Dolly burbled. She'd enjoyed basking
in reflected glory while her brother's girls had Viscount
Blackthorne's attention. Had that infernal brunette not
been with him, making things awkward, she was certain his lordship would have stopped to speak to them
moments ago.

Elise gave a neutral smile. The time to return home
had been reached not just because they risked becoming a burden on the Chapmans and were reluctant to
decamp to their aunt's frugal hospitality; their lack of
appropriate attire had been noticed. Only yesterday
when at an afternoon *musicale* in a neighbour's house
Elise had heard some young ladies commenting on their

oft worn dresses when she'd been entering the with-drawing room. Bea had not been with her and Elise had been thankful for it. Had her sister heard the spite-ful comment she might have burst into tears given her current mood. Elise had simply given a warning cough before coming fully into view of the room's occupants, examining their reflections in the pier glass. Thank-fully the gossip had quietened, but she'd noticed some very pink cheeks before the three young ladies hur-riedly dispersed.

'I have enough money left to buy some ribbon be-fore we leave.' Bea was gazing longingly at a reel of sea-green velvet.

'It will probably cost less if you buy some in the market when we arrive home,' Elise remarked, ever practical.

'I shall never find such a wonderful colour as that out in the sticks,' Bea moaned, but she turned away from the drapery's entrance, prepared to walk on.

'Oh…why not buy it then?' Elise encouraged with a smile, drawing Beatrice back to the window by linking their arms. Her sister needed something to cheer her up and spending a few extra pennies on a final luxury might do the trick.

'I like those gloves,' Edith said, pointing at grey elbow-length satin reposing next to the shimmering spools of ribbon.

The matrons proceeded inside, Elise and Beatrice following behind.

'Please come outside and talk.'

Elise spun around at that clipped order to find Alex quite close, his angular features severely set making him look startlingly cruel. Her face drained of colour; she had almost forgotten about him while trying to decide which buttons to purchase for a winter coat in need of repair. Her sister and their two older companions were still fingering lace and ribbon at a different counter and had not yet seen him.

'I'm afraid I cannot,' Elise replied coolly. 'I am with my sister and aunt.' She tipped her head to where the ladies were congregated. Her aunt was the first to become aware of Viscount Blackthorne's presence. Dolly gave him a beam, her chest expanding in pride as she glanced about to ensure his interest in her younger niece had been noted. She need not have worried on that score. Many gloved hands had been raised to shield whispered conversations.

'It is important. I wouldn't have entered this confounded shop else.' Alex knew he'd sounded overbearing and raised his eyes heavenwards in mute apology. But he was exasperated at the way the whole day was turning out.

Following Whittiker's unexpected visit he had been in a black mood, but had set off to keep his promise to Celia. Yesterday she'd pleaded with him to drive her to an afternoon tea with friends. He rarely met her during daytime, but had agreed to the chore because the carriage he'd provided for her use had snapped an axle. He'd quickly dropped her off and had returned to Regent Street as soon as he could to locate Elise. It had been his intention to call on the Chapmans that day to speak to her privately. He knew that Whittiker was malicious enough to spread gossip whether he agreed to pay him off or not. Plans needed to quickly be put in place to avert a disaster because Alex wasn't prepared to bow to blackmail.

'Are you alone?' Elise's thoughts had spontaneously leapt to Celia Chase in case she was somewhere close by, watching them.

A grunt of mirthless laughter was his response. Alex dragged her nearest hand to his arm and held it there. Furiously Elise allowed herself to be escorted towards the exit. She had no intention of drawing more eyes to them by engaging in an unseemly tussle. She went quietly, until late afternoon sun touched her face, then immediately jerked her hand from beneath his fingers.

'How dare you act so high and mighty!' she hissed.

'When you hear what I have to say I'll warrant you'll be glad I did,' he returned through his teeth. 'The sooner this is dealt with the better.' Taking her elbow, he propelled her towards his empty phaeton parked some distance away.

'I'm not going anywhere with you,' Elise declared, thinking he might force her into it.

'I'm not expecting you to,' Alex replied with the weary patience one might reserve for an annoying child. 'The crowd is thinner close to the road. If you simply make it appear we're having a pleasant chat while I say what I must, that should suffice.'

'There is no need for you to explain a solitary thing. My aunt and Mrs Vickers hinted at your companion's identity when you passed by.' She turned from him. 'So there is no need to feel under any obligation to elaborate.'

Alex neatly caught her wrist, tugging her back towards him. 'Why would I feel obliged to mention my mistress or anything else which is none of your concern?'

Beneath his dulcet sarcasm Elise felt her face suffuse with heat. She had acted like a jealous rival for his affections rather than a casual acquaintance.

Discreetly Alex brought her closer, his fingers moving soothingly before reluctantly dropping away. 'Our meeting at Vauxhall didn't go unobserved as we'd hoped.' It was a bald statement, devoid of any attempt to soften the blow.

Elise stared at him, frowning, and it was a moment or two before the full significance of what he'd said sunk in. Her complexion turned chalky and she steadied herself against the bottle-green coachwork of his carriage. 'Somebody saw us together in that dark walkway?' she whispered.

'A friend of James Whittiker's witnessed us departing the scene.' An acerbic smile tilted a corner of his mouth. 'Whittiker was good enough to come and tell me that earlier today.'

Elise's face lowered and a hand spanned her brow as she strove to bring order to her spinning thoughts. 'He has known all this time? Why did he not warn you sooner?' Elise raised wide eyes to his.

'Whittiker's motives aren't philanthropic, Elise,' Alex explained gently. 'Quite the reverse. He has only just found out about it and came to see me to crow.'

Her wide tawny eyes searched his face, but there was nothing to reassure her that the situation wasn't as dreadful as she feared it to be. 'You believe he would relish a scandal? But why would he be so mean?' Elise had allowed her voice to rise and swept a look about to ensure she hadn't drawn attention. Thankfully the noise and bustle of Regent Street had buffered her hysteria. Most people were happily going about their own business.

'Whittiker and I have no liking for one another—actually, that's understating the matter. I despise him and I imagine he returns the sentiment,' Alex ruefully admitted. 'He thinks to blackmail me into paying for his silence.'

Elise's soft lips parted in a soundless denial of such villainy. 'How much does he want?' she asked in a squeak of indignation.

'It's the cost to your reputation that bothers me.'

'Tell me how much he wants to keep quiet!' Elise insisted on knowing, her voice and delicate features turning fierce.

'Three thousand pounds.'

'That is *outrageous*!' Elise's initial anguish was being overcome by anger. 'Will you set the authorities on to him for such criminal behaviour? The odious swine should end in court! No…better he go straight to prison!'

'Do you want the sorry tale reported in the papers, Elise? Do you want your family name smeared and salacious gossip to spread in such a way that it will affect the Chapmans and your aunt, too?' Alex pointed out the likely outcome of such public scrutiny.

'No…of course not!' Elise murmured, slowly shaking her head. She knew all he had warned of might come to pass. She had heard of genteel young women who had had their lives ruined by a single slip that sent their kith and kin with them into exile. 'But it is unfair!' she raged beneath her breath. 'We did nothing wrong…' She felt his smouldering eyes roving her face and the memory of his mouth moving magically on hers, his hands stroking her body, made her again seek his phaeton as support.

'That's not how polite society sees it,' he murmured. 'I kissed you and—'

'And that was not *my* fault!' she spluttered, interrupting him before he could elaborate and make her blush deepen. But, embarrassment apart, she'd detected a light teasing in his voice and it infuriated her that he could jest at such a time.

'My memory serves me differently,' he responded throatily. 'You were lucky you stumbled across me and not some lecherous rogue or you'd not have escaped so lightly.'

Despite his self-mockery Elise knew he spoke the truth. She had wanted him to kiss and touch her and had, at first, felt heady with delight when he did, but thank goodness he'd been gentleman enough to stop when she told him to. She'd seriously misjudged the situation and might have been ravished or murdered by a miscreant posing as Mr Best. She *had* got off lightly…or so she'd thought. But now all manner of calamity could ensue not just for her, but for people she cared about. As much as she was grateful for Alex's concern, she could understand why he felt able to banter about it. If the story broke, he would face tuts and reproofs for a while, but still be welcomed socially by top hostesses and his adoring mistress. Opprobrium for her would last a lifetime.

'I didn't mean to be facetious.' Discreetly he touched

together their fingers in apology. 'I'm aware it is a serious matter and we must find a solution.'

'If you manage to deal with Mr Whittiker…what of his friend? Will he then come forwards to blackmail you, too?' Elise's mind was attempting to grapple with the extent of the awful possibilities lying in wait.

'It was a woman who saw us together. She approached and spoke to me that night, so I'm afraid it is not a bluff. We *were* under observation.'

Elise knew he was hinting that a soliciting harlot had accosted him. On casting her mind back to that fateful evening, Elise did recall glimpsing a woman in a flashy hat moments before she'd sped back to join her party. A large number of the people she'd hurried past on her way to meet Mr Best had glanced at her with contempt, believing her to be a trollop. No doubt the genuine article thought she'd been a rival. Elise felt like wailing her innocence. But it was pointless brooding on injustices. She'd taken a stupid risk and now the damage was done she must take the consequences.

'Do you trust me to put things right?'

'What can you do?' Elise answered in a despairing voice. 'If you were to pay him, he would surely come back to swindle more money.'

'There's not much a man can do when he compromises a young woman and a fellow threatens to expose the matter. He can call for seconds or call on her father.'

'But it might yet come right! I beg you will not tell my papa about it, even to apologise,' Elise whispered.

'Apologising wasn't my intention…'

Elise bristled. 'I accept it is more my fault than yours, but you are not free of blame. I only made you stay with me when you would have gone on your way that night because I believed Bea was loitering by the lake and in danger of ruin… Oh…we're going home!' Elise remembered the vital news and immediately blurted it out with a protracted sigh of relief.

Once James Whittiker realised his quarry was miles away he might reconsider his actions. She raised her head, meeting Alex's earthy dark eyes. 'We had already decided to go earlier today. Beatrice understands that there is no hope of receiving Hugh's proposal and is adamant nobody else will do. If Mr Whittiker has no victim to torment, surely he will leave you alone.'

'Your disappearance won't put Whittiker off the scent, Elise,' Alex softly disabused her. 'In fact, such a tactic might fuel the fire. Once rumours have spread people will believe you've bolted out of town to escape the scandal.'

'What else can I do?' Elise demanded tightly.

'Marry me,' Alex said.

Chapter Fourteen

'You have just apologised for being facetious…don't you dare repeat the offence.'

'I'm not joking.' Alex's steady gaze captured her anxious amber eyes. 'I know such a proposal is not ideal or romantic, but there is no necessity for either in such a situation.' He cursed below his breath as he glimpsed Beatrice and the older ladies emerge from the shop and immediately approach them. 'Our time has just run out,' he muttered. 'When are you to leave for Hertfordshire?'

Elise simply stared at him, stunned into speechlessness on realising he'd meant his proposal. She sensed the tension in her limbs melting away, warmth and calmness coming over her.

'Tell me when you intend quitting town! Your sister and aunt are almost upon us!' Alex insisted.

Elise jerked to attention beneath his rasping authority, sure his frustration meant he was already reconsidering his spur-of-the-moment solution to their dreadful predicament. A welcome pride swelled in her chest, overcoming the warring emotions clogging her throat. If he were worried she would tie him to his word, he

need have no fear on that score! A moment ago a spark
of blissful optimism had put a glow in her eyes, but it
had only briefly flickered before dying.

'I have asked you before not to order me about,' Elise
quickly croaked, very aware of her kith and kin coming
within earshot. 'I appreciate the great sacrifice you've
indicated you're willing to make to protect my reputation, but you may rest assured it will not be necessary,'
she continued rattling off. 'As for quitting town—if we
can get our places booked on the coach we will leave
the day after tomorrow.'

Alex's mouth thrust in sardonic acknowledgement
of her icy rebuff, but there was no time left to continue
the battle. 'We'll speak further about this another time.
For now...I've no doubt you will be required to account
for my urgent interest in you.' His mouth pursed in
consideration. 'I might have felt compelled to apologise to you about my friend's poor behaviour towards
your sister. But I'm in no way ordering you to use that
excuse—' Alex broke off his ironic speech to politely
nod to the ladies.

'It is a fine day, is it not, Lord Blackthorne?'

'Indeed it is, Mrs Pearson. Unfortunately I have to
forego enjoying the rest of the afternoon outdoors. I'm
on my way to visit my attorney in a stuffy office.' His
manner was suave and encompassed them all. Then in
an agile spring he was on the phaeton and soon steering the greys away from the kerb.

'Oh...he is so wonderfully distinguished,' Edith
Vickers breathed. 'Hugh is lucky indeed to have such
a friend.'

Elise became aware of three sets of eyes on her.

'Well?' Dolly Pearson prompted, keen to know what was making her younger niece look shell-shocked. 'What made him take you out of the shop like that? What has he said?' She tapped Elise's forearm to hurry an answer.

'Such a masterful gentleman…' Edith sighed, recalling the incident.

Elise was unable to formulate a better excuse than the one Alex had supplied, so reluctantly used it. 'The viscount wanted to say sorry for Mr Kendrick's unwise attention to Beatrice.' Her voice sounded high and unnatural, but she retained sense enough not to want to upset her sister.

Beatrice pulled a forlorn little face, then peeked inside her paper bag containing her purchase of ribbon.

'I'm not sure the viscount should have blamed *all* of that on Hugh.' Edith's loyalty to her nephew caused her to review his good fortune in having a turncoat for a best friend.

'It certainly *isn't* an innocent young lady's fault if a gentleman singles her out for particular attention.' Dolly took up the cudgels on behalf of her niece. The two older women exchanged combatant stares. Edith sallied forth first, leaving Dolly to trail in her wake.

Elise linked arms with Beatrice and urged her on. Her heart was still racing from the vital news received from the viscount. Putting aside his marriage proposal, she knew there were other momentous facts that she must set her mind to. But not yet. She took a deep breath to steady her nerves. 'Let me see what you've bought.' She took Bea's paper bag and discovered inside a coil of thin turquoise velvet. 'It would look very fine stitched around the hem of your new lemon dress,' Elise said, handing back her sister's purchase.

'Oh…what is the point? There will be nobody to see it.' Beatrice sighed dolefully. 'Not that I care about going out now…'

'Oh, do cheer up, Bea!' Elise said with an impatience born of anxiety. 'I have had enough of your sulks and will be glad to be home!'

'It is good to be back, Papa.'

Walter Dewey patted at the slender white fingers resting on his shoulder. 'And it is good to have the two of you home again. I have missed your company, my dear.' Walter put down his pen on the ledger and turned stiffly. He had been logging household accounts when Elise softly approached to stand behind his chair.

The sisters had alighted from the mail coach at noon and been brought back on the pony and trap by their manservant, Mr Francis. Shortly after they had trooped tiredly up the steps to their home, their father, leaning heavily on his cane, had come into the hallway to fondly welcome them. Following a refreshing drink of lemonade and some newly baked buns, eaten in the sunny parlour, the young ladies had immediately retired to their chambers to remove their dusty travelling clothes and bathe in cool scented water provided by Mrs Francis, their housekeeper.

Beatrice had then rolled herself in her eiderdown and fallen into a deep sleep. Elise, also attired in just her linen underclothes, had snuggled into the comfort of her own bed. The window had been wide open and she'd luxuriated in the feel of balmy air sweeping her clean skin. She'd drowsed until the roiling thoughts ever present in her mind stole away the comfort and even the somnolent rustle of a million leaves couldn't give it back. Drawing up her knees beneath her chin, she'd stared out at green pasture and fields turning gold beyond their boundary wall.

Now it was early evening and in an hour's time they would dine. Having prepared their supper, Betty and Norman Francis had set off for their tiny cottage close by. In the kitchen a mutton stew bubbled on the stove, wafting mouthwatering aroma into the atmosphere. But Elise had no appetite. For the duration of the journey home she had been torn over whether to prime her father that dreadful rumours might even now be circulating in London because she'd disgraced herself. Beatrice was also unaware their world might come crashing down about their ears. Elise was determined to shield the two people who meant most to her from unnecessary alarm, so still held her tongue on it. Subconsciously she clung to her belief that Alex Blackthorne was worthy of the trust she'd put in him and would somehow bring everything right.

She hadn't seen him again after their meeting in Regent Street. She'd been convinced he'd find a pretext to call on the Chapmans the following day so they might discuss what to do. But he had not.

'Now…have you had a good rest and a bite to eat?'

Elise nodded as her father's concern broke into her troubled introspection. 'Mrs Francis gave us some buns before we went to freshen up and have a snooze. Bea is still fast asleep. The journey was very warm and tiring.'

'Indeed, it is too close.' Walter took a hanky from a

pocket and mopped his perspiring brow. 'So…did you have a nice time in London with your friends and has your sister returned in a better mood?' He took off his spectacles and placed them on his desk, his features crinkling in a smile.

'We had a fine time, Papa,' Elise confirmed rather huskily. 'And must thank you for your generosity in providing us with new clothes and for allowing us to stay with the Chapmans longer than was planned.'

Walter waved aside his daughter's gratitude with a mottled hand. 'It is no great sacrifice if good might come out of it.' He cocked his sparsely thatched head, watching Elise. 'Has Beatrice found herself a beau? Have you?' His tone was as poignantly optimistic as the look in his pale eyes.

Elise walked to the window and looked out over a small garden filled with lupins and foxgloves and trellises tangled with roses and honeysuckle. She hated having to disappoint her father with the truth. 'Bea met a gentleman she liked very well. But…he is unfortunately not in a position to court her.'

'Is he spoken for as was the other fellow?' Walter had learned from his sister Dolly that Beatrice had settled her heart on a newly betrothed gentleman last time the girls had gone to town. Walter had written to the scoundrel to give him a piece of his mind when he discovered from Dolly that Mr Vaughan had cruelly encouraged Beatrice, laying her open to ridicule.

'It is Hugh Kendrick's financial position that is the stumbling block,' Elise explained.

'The Kendricks, eh? I do recall the family. I thought

the younger son, Hugh, nice enough…better than that brother of his with his tight fists and airs and graces.'

Walter sighed, picked up his spectacles and fitted the wires over his ears. He knew the drawbacks of being a younger son with few prospects. He'd been the second of three boys and of necessity had gone into the City to earn his way in the world rather than enter the clergy. It had taken him much time and toil to get to a position where he could afford a wife. He had been in his late thirties, Arabella barely twenty, when they married. Inwardly he sighed. Had he only acquired a loyal spouse and better business acumen things might have been very different…

He felt guilty for not securing dowries for his daughters, then putting the cash out of reach of grasping creditors. They were both good girls and deserved to be happy, but with only their pretty looks and personalities to recommend them they would need to find wealthy suitors, unfazed by the Deweys' lack of money and standing. Walter knew that he and Arabella must share equal blame for having disadvantaged their daughters by besmirching the family's reputation at great financial cost.

Arabella had followed her heart rather than her duty to her family and thus had caused dreadful gossip. Walter knew he, in vainly trying to buy her back, had been equally guilty of neglecting his children in favour of his own needs; he had never stopped loving his errant spouse. Now his wife was dead and buried and his girls were the most important things in his world, but it was too late to be lavish for he had nothing left to give them but his love.

'No gentlemen will be coming to visit.' It was a melancholy mumble beneath Walter's breath as, done with reflection, he picked up his pen and recommenced inking a column of spidery figures.

Elise gazed quietly into the distance, aware of a floral scent wafting through the open casement. Adding to the rhythmic tick of the wall clock was the sound of summer as bees gathered nectar from lavender swaying beneath the sill.

But her mind was far away, back in London, with Alex Blackthorne. She wished it were not because she realised she missed him and yearned to see him for more reason than he had the power to protect her and her family from a miserable future. Now she was out of sight, was she out of mind, too? Would he simply tell Whittiker to do his worst when the evil swine returned to harass him for payment?

Instinctively Elise was sure the viscount was a courageous and an honourable man. Thus, he would not pay Whittiker his ransom; neither would she want him to. Bullies had to be faced down or never would they leave their victims alone.

So what course of action was left? Only the one Alex had mentioned: a forced marriage.

'I know such a proposal is not ideal or romantic, but there is no necessity for either in such a situation—'

The damning words would not quit her head, even if he might have forgotten them. If he were to come here to see her father and repeat his reluctant proposal because he had divined no other solution to their quandary, Elise knew she must decide whether she could endure a marriage to a man who didn't love her...and might eventually grow to despise her as an unwanted encumbrance.

Walter Dewey's sudden dry cough brought his daughter pivoting to face him. 'You sound unwell, Papa.'

'Oh…it is nothing much. You know how the summer months affect my lungs…all the seeds blowing about… that's what it is…nothing to worry about.' He took out his handkerchief and blew his nose. 'The doctor might be by later. He comes sometimes to see me if he is travelling in this direction.'

Elise frowned. To her knowledge old Dr Perkins was reluctant to visit the sick unless they were on their deathbeds. Even the children in the village had to be wrapped in blankets and taken to his house when ailing. But then Dr Perkins looked to be a lot older, and in far worse shape, than was her papa. The physician was quite stooped and rickety in the knees and simply getting on to his trap to travel to patients would be an ordeal.

'Doctor Perkins has been to see you?' Elise echoed in surprise.

'No…that fellow has gone to Brighton to live with his sister now he has retired. And not before time. He must have been close to his three-score years and ten and had dreadful arthritis.' Walter removed his glasses again and, crossing his hands on his chest in readiness for a chat, began, 'Colin Burnett has arrived from Harrogate to take up where Cedric Perkins left off and a good chap he is, too. He brought me a linctus he'd made up himself and it did stop the tickle in my throat for a while.'

As her father smothered another cough with a fist

Elise went to him to put a cool palm on his forehead. 'You don't feel feverish.' She smiled. 'Your dinner will do you good. I'll see if Bea is up and about and ready to dine.'

'I thought I'd made it clear that I didn't want you bothering me again at home.'

'And I thought I'd made it clear that I'm not bluffing in this.' The viscount hadn't done him the courtesy of facing him while speaking, but James Whittiker was aware of hard black eyes watching him in the glass.

'Am I losing track of time?' Alex pivoted away from the huge gilt-framed mirror in front of which he'd been adjusting his neckcloth in readiness to exit the house. 'If my memory serves, I recall you generously allowing me a week to consider matters. I don't believe seven days have passed since your last intrusion.'

Whittiker bristled beneath the viscount's contempt. 'Circumstances have changed.'

James had been incensed to learn that Elise Dewey and her sister had bolted. Of course, should he spill the beans, a furore would still erupt, but the damage to the Dewey family wouldn't be as potent. The fun of a scandal was in seeing despair crippling the prey when they were shunned and tattled about.

Arabella Dewey's antics had already besmirched the family's name and were another reason James feared his revelation might not have the required impact. The news of Elise's wanton behaviour might simply incite some muttering about *bad blood* running in families before people turned their attention to juicier *on dits* doing the rounds.

Since he'd last come to Upper Brook Street James had tested the waters, but sensed no undercurrent of fearful expectancy leaking out from the girls' kith and kin. On paying a visit on the Chapmans he'd found them to be no different, and the topic of the sisters' return home had prompted Maude to voice her regret at their departure and her hope that their aunt Dolly might persuade them to return to town.

James was ready to believe such people might still be in blissful ignorance of what lay in wait for Elise Dewey. But it was the viscount's attitude that really agitated him. Blackthorne was treating him as he had before the day he'd issued a threat to blackmail. Alex regularly turned up at White's and extended to him his customary weary courtesy before settling down to drink, gamble and converse with his friends.

James understood there was a possibility Blackthorne would flout the law and summon him to a dawn meeting. In that eventuality Whittiker knew he'd have no option but to attempt a humiliating withdrawal from the débâcle. The viscount's skill with weapons had been honed over many years in the military and far outstripped his mediocre talent with sword and pistol. James was counting on the noble fellow being as reluctant to risk arrest as he was of risking his life. But Blackthorne was playing his cards too close to his chest and James was sweating on the outcome of the game. He feared the whole episode might simply blow over with no gain made.

Thus he'd decided to make a premature visit to Upper Brook Street, to urgently discover what Blackthorne planned to do and with the intention of turning the screws if necessary.

Impatient to get rid of his unwanted caller, Alex prompted harshly, 'You said circumstances have changed. Elaborate or be gone if you please. I'm on my way out as you can see.'

'The Dewey sisters have left town,' James muttered.

Alex shrugged bewilderment. 'Were you expecting they might consult you before returning home?'

'If you think sending her away will dissuade me from pursuing this matter…' James hissed.

'Please excuse me, my lord…' Robinson had coughed loudly, then come into view to address his master. 'The curricle has been brought round. Shall I have your belongings loaded on…or send it back if you are to be a while?' He shot a pained look at Whittiker. When the fellow had turned up the butler had been in two minds whether to turn him away without recourse to his employer. But the viscount had been strolling the corridor towards him and had heard the bang on the door so there had been no opportunity to shoo the dumpy fellow down the steps. The viscount was a good and fair employer, but he demanded conscientious obedience in return for the generous wages he paid.

Robinson had read Alex Blackthorne's displeasure in his face when he broke the news of his caller's identity. Following the order to let Whittiker in and banish any servants from the hall while a meeting took place, the butler had set about attending to his master's travelling needs. Robinson had drawn some satisfaction from the fact that the viscount had denied the fellow an audience in his study.

'I'm ready to leave. Carry on with loading up if you please.' Alex approached his butler to take his coat.

'You're going out of town?' Whittiker sounded alarmed.

'I've estate matters to deal with. Robinson will show you out.' Without another glance Alex moved in the direction of the stairs, taking them two at a time.

Whitening in indignation, Whittiker stomped ahead of the butler to the great doors and affected not to notice the manservant concealing his contentment behind compressed lips.

Alex's expression, as he strode along the corridor in the direction of his chamber, was no less grim than Whittiker's had been moments ago. He hadn't lied to Whittiker: he was going to Blackthorne Hall. But he wouldn't be there for long. He intended spending no more than a day in Berkshire before heading towards Hertfordshire. He wondered if Elise would be as glad to see him as he would be to see her...

Chapter Fifteen

'The post has arrived, Papa.'

Beatrice had called out to her father then, twirling about by the front door with two letters in her hand, she hurried to his study to find him.

'There is one for you and I'm sure it is from Aunt Dolly as I recognise the hand.' Beatrice put the letter on the leather-topped desk. 'This one is addressed to Elise and is from Verity Chapman; I know her hand, too, you see.'

'Indeed, you are right about mine; this is certainly from my sister,' Walter confirmed, having scanned the writing and given his elder daughter a congratulatory beam.

'Who was hammering on the door as though they would break it in two?' Elise had been reading a novel in her chamber when the banging startled her.

'There is a letter arrived for you from Verity.' Beatrice proffered the parchment. 'Papa has one from Aunt Dolly.'

Beneath constricting ribs Elise felt her heart skip a beat. Had her friend and her aunt heard of an imminent scandal concerning them and simultaneously written to warn them of it?

Beatrice gave an exaggerated sigh. 'I should have liked a letter to open.'

The sound of the doorknocker again being employed brought three heads up.

'There you are, my dear,' Walter Dewey said, placing his letter back on the desk. 'The fellow is back with the one for you he forgot to deliver. And in a better frame of mind, I suspect, as the door's not taken such a battering.'

The summons to open up *had* seemed less forceful and Beatrice hurried back out into the hallway.

There was the sound of a muffled male voice, then moments later her sister reappeared with a gentleman at her side.

'Doctor Burnett has come to visit, Papa.'

'Ah…come in…come in, Colin, my dear fellow.' Walter pushed to his feet, flapping a hand to urge him forwards. 'Let me introduce you to my children, newly returned from the metropolis only days ago.'

Colin Burnett swung a smiling look between the young ladies. 'How fortunate you are, sir, to have such exceptionally pretty daughters.'

Elise glanced at her sister just as Beatrice gave the complimentary fellow a shy smile.

'My elder, Beatrice, let you in and this is Elise.' Walter held out his hands either side of him, proudly indicating the two young ladies. 'Now, shall we go to the parlour and have some refreshment?' He clutched at his stick leaning against the wall and came around the desk in a slow gait. 'The girls might be persuaded to entertain us with tales of their parties and balls in town.'

'I'll ask Mrs Francis to bring some tea, Papa.' With a little bob for the doctor Elise went ahead of them towards the kitchens.

She desperately wanted to open her letter rather than attempt a polite conversation with their guest, but instead slipped it into her skirt pocket. She knew she must wait until she could properly digest its contents and steel herself against dreadful news. Thankfully her father had abandoned his note unopened on his desk so they had some respite…at least until after Colin Burnett had left.

Elise felt guilty and selfish then for hoping the doctor would soon be on his way. Their life in the country was humdrum and before she'd gone to town she would have enjoyed a visitor calling on them. Her father and sister had both looked pleasantly surprised at the doctor's arrival. She purposely dwelled on him and how taken aback she'd been by his appearance. In her imagination the new doctor would resemble her first memory of the old one: a middle-aged fellow of dry character and spare build. But Colin Burnett seemed a congenial and cultured young man, perhaps in his late twenties, and was rather attractive in a bucolic way. Had she not known his profession she might have taken him for a country squire's son with his bluff complexion and shock of auburn hair falling forwards over one eye, causing him often to push it back with large square fingers.

'Ah…Miss Elise…I was going to find your father and ask what to prepare for supper, but I dare say you'll do as well as him.'

Elise had been on the point of entering the kitchen when Betty Francis had exited the pantry opposite, holding by the legs a chicken in one hand and a rab-

bit in the other. First one, then the other, lifeless crea-
ture was raised for Elise's inspection. 'My Norman will
pluck or skin it, so no problems in the choosing; you
may have whichever you fancy, or both if you reckon
Mr Dewey will run to it.'

'Chicken, thank you, and might we have some tea
brought to the parlour? Doctor Burnett has arrived.'

'Has he now?' Betty's eyes grew round. 'Quite a bit
of a to do going on in St Albans about him, you know.
When I was there the tongues were wagging nineteen
to the dozen...'

Elise blinked, then asked apprehensively, 'Why, what
has he done?'

'Nothing, so far as I know...apart from breaking a
few hearts since he arrived in the neighbourhood.' She
gave Elise a slow wink. 'But he is a rather strapping
handsome sort, isn't he? *And* a bachelor.' She pulled
a knowing face, crossing her arms under her ample
bust so the animals dangled below her armpits. 'The
vicar's girls have been hoping he'll come over for tea
with them and their mama. That saucy Victoria was
saying she'd break a leg if necessary to get him there.
I think she was funning. Well, seems you two young
ladies have beaten them all to it and not yet a week back
from town, are you.'

'He seems very pleasant.' Elise smiled. 'Might we
have that tea quite soon? I'm not sure how long Dr Burnett is able to stay.'

'Seeing as it's him, I'll break out the box of raisin
gingerbread I was saving for you all for Sunday after
church.' Mrs Francis ambled off towards the kitchen.

The mention of gossip in St Albans had made Elise's

heart resume pounding. She fingered the parchment in her pocket and was suddenly compelled to open the letter and quickly read it. If it contained the news she was dreading, she felt certain her aunt Dolly's missive would also distress her father. Since they'd returned home she'd noticed he seemed more tired and frail than usual. She was suddenly very glad that the doctor had come unexpectedly because he might sound her father's chest before leaving...

A loud rat-a-tat brought her head up sharply and with a quiet imprecation Elise thrust the letter back whence it came and marched towards the front of the house. Days went by when no soul came near nor by their front gate, she thought, as she turned the doorknob. Yet today, of all days, three knocks in the space of one hour...

'Are you going to invite me in, Elise?'

Elise snapped together her softly parted lips, finally conquering her astonishment and shaking some sense into herself. 'Yes...of course...I'm sorry...I was not expecting to see you...' she breathed.

Quickly she stood aside to allow Alex Blackthorne's large frame entry into the cottage. They faced one another in the narrow corridor, a sunbeam filtering through a high window, crowning her head with glints of gold. Quickly Elise pushed stray tendrils back behind her ears, wishing she'd not lain on her bed, crumpling her hair and clothes when reading earlier. Had she known he was on his way she'd have taken care with her appearance. But she'd not imagined he'd turn up out of the blue without first sending word to warn of his arrival.

'Why didn't you write and let me know you were coming?'

A sardonic smile conveyed better than words that there'd been no time to do so, and when Elise allowed herself a moment to study him she saw a fine film of dust on his rugged features as though he had travelled very fast without a stop. 'Have you brought bad news?' she whispered.

'I suppose that depends on how you take what I have to say.' Alex replied wryly.

'What have you come to say?' Elise murmured in a barely audible voice.

Alex looked about the hallway at the three doors leading off it. 'Is there somewhere more suitable for us to talk?'

The initial shock of seeing him had rendered her speechless, hence his need to prompt her to invite him inside. Once again he'd had to remind her of expected niceties. Her unintentional, yet reprehensible, lack of hospitality reminded Elise just how different were their circumstances.

Unkempt as he was from his journey, his bearing retained the unmistakable stamp of affluence and breeding. In her cotton clothes and rustic surroundings Elise was sure he saw before him a spinster who had attended fashionable town venues, garbed in the modest finery her father had scrimped to buy her, so she might catch a husband.

And, of course, it was the truth. A family of her own to cherish was no less appealing to Elise than to Beatrice, and had she attracted a suitor she could love, and trust to reciprocate her loyalty and affection… As she glanced at the handsome man just a hand span away from her, she was assailed by a wounding insight.

Her chin inched up. 'I should like to introduce you to my father,' she said proudly. 'We have another guest. The doctor is here.' Elise suddenly remembered the fellow's presence.

'Is somebody ill?'

'Doctor Burnett has come on a social call, although my papa has a cough. It is the time of year he says that makes his chest bad.'

Elise felt long fingers manacling her wrist, then Alex firmly led her to a door. 'Will this do?' He hesitated, primed to turn the handle on learning nobody was within.

She nodded. 'It is the morning room; the others are taking tea in the back parlour.' She remembered her manners this time. 'Would you like some tea, sir?'

Alex felt a smile tug at a corner of his mouth at the way she continued to address him. 'Perhaps later, Elise,' he said.

'I think we should leave the door ajar…'

'And I think it's a little late to worry unduly about etiquette.'

Inwardly wincing at his ironic tone, Elise clasped her hands behind her back to steady them out of sight of his hooded sepia gaze. 'You have come to tell me Whittiker has done his worst? Are people already talking about us?'

'Possibly.'

Alex's blunt answer drained the blood from Elise's cheeks.

'He came to see me yesterday and made it clear he

will not back down on this matter. Whether he has started to spread his poison…' Alex shrugged his uncertainty, strolling to the square sash and looking out at his curricle parked on a dusty track.

Already the racing equipage had drawn a few curious lads to circle it while sending glances towards the house. The tiger balanced on the back remained unflustered by their attention. Even in town, where top-notch carriages and horseflesh abounded, his master's various travelling stock drew admiration and envy.

'I don't believe Whittiker is bluffing, so if the news is not yet out it soon will be.' Alex turned from the window. 'He bears a grudge against me and has debts to settle. Now he has a means of extortion he's confident of killing two birds with one stone. His quarrel isn't with you, Elise. I have come here so we may discuss what to do to limit his spite.'

'Thank you,' Elise said with such heartfelt gratitude that it caused a smile to soften Alex's chiselled lips.

'You imagined I'd forget about the matter and allow him to do his worst,' he stated. 'Didn't you?'

Elise flushed indignantly, feeling that somehow she was being reprimanded. 'I'm not a fool, sir, and know this calamity might ruin my future and that of my sister.' She took a few paces to and fro. 'Whereas what awaits you?' A slender white hand gestured the injustice of it all. 'Clucking tongues and sly looks for a short while before you carry on much as before in all aspects of your life.'

Alex gazed at her relentlessly, making her avoid his penetrative eyes.

'I have suggested a solution to this dilemma, not at

a very appropriate time or place, I'll grant, but then we are in an unusual situation.' He paused, his mouth pursing while he studied her through narrowed eyes. 'I know you have turned me down once. I also realise you were in shock at the time and had little opportunity in Regent Street to properly consider every implication.' Again he paused, watching her. 'Have you given proper thought to my proposal, Elise?'

Elise swallowed. She'd feared him asking her again. And she knew now why that was. If only it was truly meant and incorporated the sentiment that should attach to such a vital moment, she might have relived that blissful calm that had bathed her when first he'd mentioned a way to defeat Whittiker. He was too gentlemanly to allow his tone of voice to reflect his regret at being pushed into a corner. In fact, there was nothing at all in his manner to indicate his feelings.

'I have thought about it, sir,' Elise began briskly, 'and will admit at first I thought you had spoken in haste and wished to reconsider.' She lifted golden eyes to his face, allowing him now to express that intention.

'I've no desire to withdraw my marriage proposal and, as we have most certainly run out of time, I should like to know your answer and speak to your father.'

'It is good of you to act honourably and try to protect me,' Elise said. 'But I think we both know that fine intentions are not enough to make a satisfactory marriage.'

'And what is?'

Elise shot a look at him, wondering if he was mocking her, but he returned her sparking gaze quite gravely. 'Love and respect and loyalty,' Elise uttered, edging up her chin again. 'I know such things are not always so important to people with wealth and land to protect and augment, but they are crucial to me.'

'You believe I am unable to meet your requirements?'

'Not all of them.'

'Will you tell me where I lack?' Alex asked after a tense quiet.

Elise met his gaze levelly. 'I have always found you respectful.' She glimpsed the beginnings of his sultry smile and her eyelids fluttered low at the memory of his passionate assault at Vauxhall. 'Following an initial lapse, that is,' she qualified her praise, pink cheeked. 'I understand why you at first thought me a…disreputable character.' She twisted away from him to shield her confusion. 'I don't blame you. You weren't alone in judging me unfavourably that night.'

'Oh?' The single word sounded perilous. 'Who else did, apart from Whittiker's doxy?'

'Every person I rushed past,' Elise admitted with a forlorn giggle. 'I got many hateful looks.'

'Unfortunately it's too late to remedy that, but I would if it were within my power.' He shifted so he could again observe her expression. 'So I now meet your approval as a respectful husband,' Alex noted. 'And as for the rest?'

Elise frowned, seeking a way to inoffensively convey she knew he'd be unfaithful. And why should he not spend his nights with a mistress he'd chosen rather than a wife foisted on to him by cruel fate? And as for love—did he love Celia Chase and had he intended to marry her before this calamity put paid to his hopes for the future? Aware he was awaiting her reply, she murmured, 'I'm sure you can guess at that.'

'I'd sooner you said what you mean,' Alex harshly demanded.

'I think, sir, you know very well what I mean!' Elise quietly exploded, exasperated at his persistence in playing this cat and mouse game. 'If a man has a mistress and little objection to committing adultery, pray tell me how his marriage might flourish in those circumstances.'

'I assure you many do.'

'But mine would not,' Elise snapped. From his muted amusement she deduced he found her attitude deplorably gauche.

Of course, she was aware that in the rarefied echelons of polite society many marriages endured despite the mercenary method behind the pairing. For such people assets and pedigree were priorities, not a vulgar prerequisite for love and affection between bride and groom. Elise knew she would never have the sophistication to live that way; neither would she want to.

'You live in a separate world to me and have been reared with different ideas,' she stated, striving to control her temper. 'I would not expect you to understand my silly sentimentality any more than I understand your lack of it.' Elise tore her eyes away from a dark glittering gaze.

'My parents were devoted to one another and I was glad to have been raised in a harmonious household.' Alex crossed his arms over his chest and lowered his face to study his dusty Hessian boots. 'I'm unsure why you imagine you know better than I what I expect from a wife and a marriage.'

It was a subdued set down, nevertheless Elise felt her face burning with mortification. He couldn't have made it plainer he thought her unfit to pontificate, given her background. Her mother had run off with her lover—his bachelor uncle—then when that liaison was over had transferred her affection elsewhere. Her father had been caught embezzling, so enslaved was he by his fickle wife. In contrast to her own, his parents seemed paragons of virtue, his childhood, blissful. She knew he'd not concocted for her benefit the story about his upbringing. It was the simple truth and she humbly regretted having spoken out of turn.

'Don't condemn me as a hypocrite because of my parents' failings.' Her words, though strongly spoken, held a hint of plea. 'It is precisely because they were so miserable that I crave something else for myself.' She sank small pearly teeth into her quivering lower lip to still it. 'Thank you for your proposal, but I cannot accept.' She twisted away from him and nervously plunged a hand into her pocket, wishing he would say something conciliatory, too, so they might at least part on civil terms. All she heard was a low muttered oath and whether directed at himself or her she was uncertain.

Suddenly her fingers fluttered against the letter in her pocket and she pulled it out, pivoting to face him. 'I have today received a note from my friend Verity. My father also got one from his sister Dolly.' Her eyes widened on Alex as she realised she might hold in her hand the awful proof that Whittiker had already set the rumour mill grinding. Because of their heated exchange she'd omitted to mention it immediately. 'The doctor turned up before we had time to read our letters. My father left his on his desk...but if both bear bad tidings...' Her shaking fingers broke the seal and she forced herself to read her friend's few neat paragraphs.

Chapter Sixteen

'Oh…it is good news!'

Elise's spontaneous sunny smile caused Alex to quizzically raise thick black brows.

'There is no mention of any scandal.' Elise suppressed an unladylike urge to whoop with relief. Her animated features lowered and she again scanned the script. 'Verity has let me know that Jago Clemence has proposed to her and she has accepted. He is going to speak to her father this week on Friday.'

'That's good…'

From beneath long curly lashes Elise flicked a look at the owner of that drawling voice. But she wouldn't allow his idle mockery to dilute her happiness for her friend.

'Yes…indeed, it is good.' Elise slipped the note again out of sight. 'I think it is high time I introduced you to my father before he discovers you have been in his house some while. Then I insist you have some refreshment before you leave. I shall ask our housekeeper Mrs Francis to fetch you some.'

Alex caught at a soft arm as she would have hurried

past towards the door. Slowly, deliberately he drew her back so she stood before him.

'Is there someone living locally you are fond of?'

'Someone?' Elise selected a word to echo back at him, her confusion genuine.

'An admirer,' Alex clipped out. 'I realise you accompanied your sister to London with the intention of finding her a husband rather than one for yourself.' He looked at the lone youth who remained by the curricle. 'Have you a sweetheart?'

Her eyes followed his and alighted on Danny, a well-built fellow, stationed beyond the front hedge. He was patting the flanks of an ebony thoroughbred harnessed to a sleek low carriage. Nice as Danny was, he was only about seventeen and Elise certainly didn't consider him a possible mate; she felt rather piqued that Alex appeared to. 'He is the blacksmith's son. His name is Danny…and if you are asking if he is my beau, the answer is no.'

'I didn't suspect he might be. He is somewhat unsuitable for a start.'

'He might be an apprentice smith, but he is a good lad. I like him,' Elise said stubbornly.

'But somewhat younger than you, I'd guess.'

Elise darted him a sparking look. She had no wish to be reminded by anybody, least of all him, that she and her sister were considered past their marriageable prime.

She pushed away such pettiness. The viscount had mentioned the fount from which all their problems had sprung: Beatrice's determination to go to London to find a husband. That in turn brought to mind the hazardous method her sister had used to attract suitors. Mr Best must take his share of the blame for the disastrous consequences of that clandestine meeting at Vauxhall, but it had been Lady Lonesome who'd started it all. Inwardly Elise cringed. She supposed she should be grateful he was too gentlemanly to fling that fact in her face.

With an amount of guilt Elise realised that since they'd arrived home she'd been too anxious over her own predicament to give much thought to Beatrice's disappointment over Hugh. Yet, oddly, she no longer regretted being a part of the drama, or of meeting Alex Blackthorne despite the heartache that fateful episode was sure to bring. But she did very much wish that something good for Beatrice had come out of taking such risks.

'How is Hugh? Has he sent word to Beatrice? I'm sure, in a moment when we join the others, she will ask you about him.'

'I've hardly seen him, but believe he is now quite friendly with the Chapmans and visits the family since Whittiker stopped bothering them.'

'Did Hugh know you were coming here?'

'I imagine he heard from his Aunt Edith that Dolly Pearson had provided me with your address in Hertfordshire.

'I see,' Elise said quietly. And she did see. Hugh was not missing Beatrice as much as a broken-hearted man should.

She surfaced from her depressing conclusion to become conscious of him watching her, but not as before when intelligently assessing her reactions during their heated exchange. A polite squabble had not increased the tension between them, making his jaw tauten and the depths of his narrowed eyes appear as if burnished by a smoky fire.

He still desired her, she realised, an ache beneath her ribs stealing her breath, and might be tempted to reach out and touch her…

She stumbled back a pace towards the door. If he again sent her into that blissful state where she clung to him, wanting his kisses and caresses never to stop, she would beg him to marry her. And where must such a marriage ultimately lead, based as it was on cruel necessity tempered with his lust and her love? In less than a year she would be a bitter, jealous wife, wondering where her absent spouse was…and whose bed he shared, during long lonely nights. She might end like her father, obsessed by someone who eventually would choose to stay away rather than live with the oppression of hypocrisy and deceit.

'You must come and have some tea.' Elise whipped towards the exit.

'Ah…there you are, miss; your father has sent me to look for you before the brew gets stewed. I've already brought a fresh pot, but that's going cold…' Betty Francis's voice faded as, over Elise's shoulder, she spotted the young woman had company. She gawped at the sight of an imposing gentleman standing at his ease by the mantel. The housekeeper could see from Elise's face that something was amiss and her lips formed a knot. She might only be an employee, but she'd been around Mr Dewey's daughters since they were knee high and believed she had a right to protect them from anything, or anyone, who might do them harm.

'I…we…were coming along to the parlour,' Elise said in a rush. 'Viscount Blackthorne has just arrived from London and will have some tea as well. Would you make a fresh pot, please, Mrs Francis, and bring more biscuits, too?'

The housekeeper was unable to immediately close her dropped jaw to answer. Young Dr Burnett and elderly Squire Thaddon were what passed for gentry in the locality and Betty tended to like what she knew and distrust the rest.

She'd noticed straight away that he was Quality…but a *viscount*? Proper aristocracy were not much in evidence in these parts until later in the year when they arrived in great processions and took up residence in the halls and manors nestling in lush Hertfordshire valleys. The routs and parties that went on through the autumn and winter months brought plenty of work for local people as guests arrived from far and wide to stay at the big houses. Then come spring they were all gone back to town to enjoy the London frivolities while the locals took a breather and pinched pennies for lack of employment.

Mrs Francis gave Alex Blackthorne's tall broad physique and darkly handsome face a sidelong look. 'I'll put the kettle on again, then, and get out the biscuit box,' she announced, turning on her heel.

'I do recall your family.' Walter Dewey took his spectacles from the arm of the chair and put them on, giving Alex a long, calculating look. 'I believe your mother was originally from Scotland and had a brother.'

'Viscount Blackthorne is a friend of Hugh Kendrick's,' Elise quickly interposed. 'I mentioned to you that we met that gentleman in town, Papa.'

'I recognise the name,' Walter confirmed. 'I recall he paid undue attention to your sister.'

'Hugh is the nephew of one of Aunt Dolly's neighbours.' Elise hoped to placate her father with a mention of his favourite relative. 'Edith Vickers moved from Mayfair to Hammersmith and has become good friends with your sister. Aunt Dolly likes Hugh.'

Elise flicked a sympathetic glance at Alex, a poignant glow enveloping her as his subtle smile thanked her for attempting to defuse the situation. It was obvious from her father's prickliness that he'd not forgotten the Blackthorne family ties and knew the viscount's maternal uncle had once been his detested enemy. She wondered if repayment of the monetary debt owed by Thomas Venner might improve her father's mood. Her eyes strayed to Alex's face, merging with his questioning long-lashed gaze. She answered him with a small nod. Now the memory of his old foe had lodged in her father's mind it would be a missed opportunity if Alex did not raise the matter and offer to repay what Thomas owed.

'I'm pleased to meet you, sir.' Having judged it a timely moment for formalities, Alex stepped forwards, extending a hand.

Walter hesitated momentarily before gripping the chair arms to lever himself upright. The upholstery continued to support him while he held out five thin, freckled fingers to be firmly shaken. The ritual over, he sagged back on to his seat.

'Please do sit down, Lord Blackthorne.' Elise indicated a chair close to the unlit hearth. 'Where is Bea?' she asked her father cheerily. 'Surely Dr Burnett has not already left.'

'They have gone together into the garden to look for feverfew and borage.'

Elise cast a startled glance her father's way as she perched on the edge of the sofa, hoping Mrs Francis would bring the refreshment and create a diversion to lighten the atmosphere.

'The doctor is a fellow who knows all about potions and lotions, you see,' Walter explained, peering over his spectacle rims at the viscount. 'My daughter Beatrice mentioned we have a physic garden and Colin expressed an interest in taking a look at our stock of plants. Feverfew and borage are what he is after, by all accounts, since the slugs and rabbits made a mess of his.' He peered lengthily at his younger daughter before again removing his spectacles and folding them neatly. 'Why do you not take your guest for a stroll and join them outside?'

'Perhaps in a moment we will; Betty is bringing us a fresh pot of tea, Papa... Ah...it has arrived.' Elise's grateful smile welcomed into the room the housekeeper bearing a tray.

Elise distributed the cups once the servant had poured and then placed a plate of raisin gingerbread on a table close to the viscount and sweetly urged him to help himself.

'I was sorry to hear of your father's demise,' Walter suddenly said before biting into a finger of cake.

'Thank you, sir.' Alex graciously dipped his raven head.

'He was a good man...astute. I found him to be a fine

judge of character,' Walter added darkly before rattling his cup back on to its saucer.

A corner of Alex's mouth twitched. He knew very well what lay behind the praise: his late father had openly loathed his brother-in-law and so had Walter Dewey.

'And how is your mother? Is she well?'

'I saw her just yesterday and she was a picture of health,' Alex truthfully replied.

'They were happy together, everybody said so...' Walter mumbled, more to himself.

Elise quickly finished her tea and stood up. She glanced at Alex, hoping he would understand the significance in her removing herself. She wanted to provide him with an opportunity to talk privately to her father about Thomas Venner's debt.

'I think I recall where the feverfew is to be found outside. It isn't in the physic garden at all, but up by the bonfire site. I shall show Bea and the doctor where to look while you finish your tea.'

'Your sister might not appreciate your help,' Walter remarked with the faintest of smiles.

Elise glanced thoughtfully at her papa, but a moment later slipped from the parlour.

'Help yourself to more if you would like,' Walter said after a few quiet moments, having noticed the viscount's cup remaining idle. He jabbed his pate at the tea tray. 'I'd do the honours, but as you've seen it takes me a while to get up and move about. By the time you had your tea it would be cold.'

'One cup is enough for me, sir, thank you.'

'I know...' Walter sighed, sloshing tea into his saucer

as he pushed it away. 'Truth to tell I'd had my fill of it before you arrived. Now, if I had something stronger close to hand, I'd offer you a glass. The port is in my study…' He sent the viscount a twinkling look from beneath wiry brows.

As Elise hurried out into the sunshine her head was crammed with a host of worries. The most pressing anxiety, of course, concerned that blackguard Whittiker and the havoc he might wreak. A short while ago, on reading Verity's letter, she'd been elated that gossip appeared not to have spread in town, but doubts were again creeping in. The absence of any mention of a scandal didn't mean the swine had changed his mind.

Then she had Alex's marriage proposal constantly tormenting her. She wished she could lock it firmly away, for no good could come of it…could it? If he asked her again, she might succumb to that wistful yearning that wouldn't quit niggling at her and accept him. Once married, her joy and relief would soon turn to ashes when the honeymoon was done. Unless… His scold that she knew nothing about his requirements in a wife and marriage meant he could grow to love her in the way she knew she'd come to love him. Did he hope to model their marriage on his parents' happy union? Elise sighed, throwing back her head to beg wisdom from the heavens. Was she allowing hope to blind her to sense and reason? Why would he give up his mistress—the woman who just a short while ago had travelled beside him, adoring him with her eyes—when he didn't have to…had not promised to…

Should she cede to a need to have him at any cost she

would be miserable and resentful, she decided, and constantly wondering whether she would not sooner have faced ostracism than endure a hollow sham of respectability. Yet dismissing salvation for her own sake was selfish; like rippling circles on a still pond her disgrace would spread widely and affect people she dearly cared about. With a pang she remembered the delightful news she'd received just a short while ago. The idea that her shame might taint her best friend's future happiness was intolerable. She prayed that Jago Clemence *would* be able to withstand gossip about his fiancée being friends with a woman ruined beyond redemption.

Overriding the muddle in her mind was one poignant certainty: she hadn't expected Alex to arrive today, but now he was here she didn't want him to go. She'd insisted he take some refreshment before leaving, as though the idea of his departure was of no consequence to her, yet she knew as soon as farewells had been said she'd be desolate.

Elise slowed her pace along the gravel path as she glimpsed her sister and Dr Burnett just ahead. Immediately she recalled her father's odd hint that Beatrice had already formed an infatuation for the doctor. Elise had thought her papa joking in view of her sister's obsession with finding a mate, but the scene in front of her was cosy and made her feel rather intrusive.

The couple were kneeling on the grass by a raised bed of herbs, absorbed in each other's company. Bea was teasingly dangling what looked like a frond of bronze fennel in front of Colin's smiling face. Elise had never known her sister show any interest in horticulture before, yet she appeared now to be digging out

a plant by the root with her bare fingers. They comple-
mented each other rather well, Elise realised: Beatrice
with her fragile fair loveliness and the doctor with his
capable sturdy body.

Snapping out of her dreamy daze, Elise stepped
closer. 'Papa said you were looking for feverfew and
borage.'

Colin Burnett sprung to his feet, clutching a wilted
stalk of greenery. Her sister got up more slowly, rubbing together her palms to remove soil.

'We have found some borage.' Beatrice smiled at
her sister, squinting against the sunlight. Unusually she
had come outside without a hat. Beatrice was normally
very conscious of her clear pale complexion being dark-
ened by the sun.

'You have forgotten your bonnet,' Elise said as the
three of them fell into awkward quiet.

'Oh…Dr Burnett says that rays from the sun benefit us.'

'When not too hot,' the doctor modified his advice
with a finger wag. 'Late afternoon such as this is ideal,
or early morning. It is best to avoid the midday heat and
a lengthy exposure. But I'm certain that sunlight cures
a multitude of ills.'

'As does feverfew and borage,' Beatrice piped up
with her new knowledge. 'Colin…Dr Burnett,' she hastily corrected herself with a blush at the familiarity, 'says
that chewing feverfew leaves cures a bad head.'

'But not too many or a sore mouth is the result.' He
smiled at his pupil.

Elise glanced at the collection of herbs arranged
neatly on the lawn. She couldn't spot a daisy-like plant

among them. 'I think there might be a small clump of feverfew up by our bonfire site. Oh…and we have another guest,' she continued casually, as they strolled together towards the rear boundary. 'Alex Blackthorne has arrived.'

That did make Beatrice stop and stare. 'Really? What a surprise!' She quite naturally slipped her hand through Colin's arm as he offered it, his other elbow extending for Elise to take. 'He is the important fellow I was telling you about who gave us a ride in Hyde Park in his landau.' Bea's eyes widened in emphasis. 'He is a viscount and very distinguished.' She brushed more soil off her stained fingers, sweeping the debris from the doctor's sleeve. 'We had a good time, in town, didn't we, Elise? But it is nice to be back home.'

Moments earlier Elise had been wondering how to break the disappointing news to her sister that Alex Blackthorne had arrived, alone, without even a message from Hugh. Now she was not sure that Beatrice would mind much at all, or even remember to ask after him. Bea had known the doctor for just hours, yet she seemed completely at ease with him. Elise slowed her pace to let them walk ahead, arm in arm, as the cinder path narrowed close to the bonfire site.

Chapter Seventeen

'I'll not pretend ignorance of my uncle's debts, sir, or the other wrongs he did you. I intend to do whatever I can to put matters right.'

Having made his opening gambit, Alex settled back in his wing chair with his glass of port resting on a knee. He gazed at the shrunken, elderly man dwarfed by the huge oak desk. As he noticed a suspicious gleam reddening his host's pale eyes Alex felt a surge of anger at Thomas Venner. He'd always liked his uncle, but at that moment he would have choked the life from him had he been present.

Walter drew out a handkerchief and made a show of polishing his glasses, giving inconspicuous dabs at his eyes now and then. 'I didn't imagine you would toe that scoundrel's line. I certainly didn't expect you to come in person to deal with the matter. I'm afraid you have made a wasted journey.'

'You knew of my uncle's plan to pass on to me his debts?' Alex asked, softly incredulous.

'My wife told me. It was the last conversation we had, shortly before she passed away. She thought it grossly impertinent of Venner to impose on you like that. It was odd for us to be in agreement upon something.' Walter gave a hollow chuckle. 'By then her infatuation with him had withered and Lord Reeves was her gallant of choice. But Arabella never could cut all ties with your uncle.' Walter swivelled his creaking chair so he might gaze out of the window and blink rapidly.

'It appears I didn't know him as well as I thought I did,' Alex said with a mix of regret and apology. 'When younger I considered my uncle Thomas a nice fellow. He would give me riding lessons or take me fishing in school holidays if my father was too busy to accommodate me.'

'You were young and he had a gift for turning the heads of innocents. My wife discovered that to her cost,' Walter stated with weary bitterness. 'I bumped into Arabella in town when I was on a visit to my sister. It was awkward, but we managed a civil conversation. I had my daughters with me, but before the girls spotted her in Oxford Street I sent them into a shop to buy some pretty fripperies. I don't know why I did that. They would have adored seeing her. Beatrice longed to join her mama in London.' An expectant quiet followed Walter's dreamy-voiced introspection, then he turned his head, fixing his watery eyes on Alex's face. 'Oh, I wasn't being wholly spiteful in denying my wife her children; I would have allowed occasional stays. But Reeves didn't like youngsters, so Arabella said.' His bony chest undulated in a grim laugh. 'I'm not sure my wife did either…not really; despite all her fulsome declarations her daughters bored her, inconvenienced her, just as I did.'

Walter frowned, becoming conscious that he'd revealed a great deal of his private thoughts to a man he'd never spoken to before. Oddly, he felt that he liked and respected this young fellow, just as he had his father before him.

'It seems such a long time ago…' He breathed out in conclusion and allowed the ticking clock and a chink of crystal to fill the silence. Having replenished his own glass, he pushed the bottle across his desktop towards Alex in wordless invitation.

'How much did he owe you, sir, if you don't mind me asking? I've no record of the sum.'

'In cash? Not a great deal. Fifty pounds, perhaps.' Walter closed his eyes and a soundless laugh puffed his withered lips. 'In every other way he took from me what was priceless.'

Alex got up and placed his empty glass on the edge of the desk. 'It is what is priceless that must be accounted for.'

'I want nothing from you,' Walter interrupted rather harshly. 'No money, no apologies. What happened was not your fault or your business.' Through the window Walter's eyes alighted on his fair daughters as they came into view walking with the doctor. A quiet smile curved his lips as he watched them. 'Even now he's dead and buried I can't escape Venner tainting my life. I won't have it, I tell you. You may tear up whatever papers you have relating to me. I wrote and told him to keep his damnable money when he started to send it. But still in dribs and drabs it arrived.'

Alex swiped a hand around his jaw, wondering how

best to proceed. And then he caught sight of the trio outside in the garden and his gaze softened, held steady.

He knew how he wanted to proceed with Elise if not with her father. He wanted her quiet grace and beauty always in his life because with a burst of wonderment he understood she held the key to his heart and his future happiness. He felt his mouth tilt wryly. All he had to do was convince her of it. And do so he would. It had taken just a kiss for him to lose himself to her. When her mouth and body had merged against his so naturally she'd stirred in him equal measures of desire and tenderness that had penetrated deep into his soul. Never before had a woman—even a mistress he'd allowed himself to grow fond of—affected him in such an immediate and explosive way.

Walter pushed to his feet and made a grab for his stick, making Alex rip his eyes from Elise and spring forwards to steady her father.

Courteously Walter removed his elbow from the younger man's grip and tilted his chin in a display of defiant independence. He looked up into Alex's dark features. 'You resemble your father…not just in looks. I know you are alike in other ways, too.' He nodded at the cane that lay on the floor. 'Would you be good enough to get that for me.'

Alex handed over the wooden stick. 'Will you allow me to escort you to wherever it is you are going?'

'I'm just off to stretch my legs in a turn about the room.' Walter smiled. 'Then I've a letter to read.' He tilted his head at the window. 'It is a fine afternoon. Why do you not join the young people outside for a breath of air.'

'I think I will, sir.' Alex hesitated at the door to watch for a moment as Walter started his ramble. A moment later he went out and closed the door quietly.

At first sight of his familiar dark figure striding along the gravel path towards them Elise had to curb an urge to hurtle to meet Alex and fling her arms about him.

Not that she'd really expected him to act impolitely and depart without saying goodbye. But she'd fretted over whether her frosty attitude might have made him think she'd sooner he left directly after his business with her father was done.

'Look! Lord Blackthorne is coming to join us,' Beatrice piped up, noticing the newcomer. Slipping a hand quite naturally around Colin's elbow, she urged him back along the path.

'Lord Blackthorne, I should like to introduce you to Dr Burnett,' Elise made the hasty introduction.

'It is a fine afternoon to be outside,' Alex pleasantly said, firmly shaking the doctor's hand.

'Indeed it is, sir, but I must soon be on my way.' Colin looked regretful. 'I have a patient to visit on my return journey to St Albans, so will make a diversion through the village of Woodley. I suspect a young lad might have contracted the measles.'

'The viscount has been troubled by that nasty disease spreading in the villages around his estate,' Elise spoke up.

'It can be hard to control if the afflicted are not quickly isolated.' Dr Burnett turned his attention to Beatrice. 'I shall collect those herbs we uprooted, Miss Dewey, and take them with me, if I may.'

'Would you mind checking on our papa before leaving, sir?' Elise interjected. 'He was coughing earlier and seems unusually pale.'

'The pollen affects his lungs, I believe,' Dr Burnett said. 'But certainly I'll examine him and see if he has a fever.' He hesitated, turning solemn. 'I don't think he would mind me telling you that I have taken his pulse on a few occasions and found the rhythm irregular and weak. He maintains he is as fit as a fiddle, but I have to disagree on that. I don't want to worry you unduly; it is to be expected that the health and vigour of a man of his age will decline.'

Elise and Beatrice exchanged frowns of concern. 'I appreciate you telling us, sir,' Elise said quietly.

'But he is so very stubborn about accepting help,' Beatrice chipped in, pulling a face.

'I've noticed he is a fellow not naturally given to taking advice or assistance,' Dr Burnett agreed, his expression rueful. He gave Beatrice's arm a gentle, comforting pat.

'If you come back and dine with us later, you could collect your plants then,' Beatrice blurted. 'I will pot them in soil so they don't wither in the meantime.'

Elise shot her sister a cautionary glance. Before issuing an invitation it would be wise to check that they had enough to feed everybody. Their father was a proud man. She knew he would sooner forgo company than serve up meagre portions.

'It is most kind of you to offer, but I would not like to impose at short notice...' Dr Burnett flicked a glance between the sisters. His unsuspecting host was obviously oblivious to his elder daughter's generosity. Nevertheless his expression made it clear the invitation was appreciated and welcome.

'You also must dine with us, Lord Blackthorne,' Beatrice extended the invitation.

'It is a kind offer, but my reply must be the same as the doctor's.'

'Oh, Papa will be delighted,' Beatrice encompassed them all in a sunny smile. 'He likes nothing better than to take port with gentlemen after dinner. When we have had the vicar and his wife and daughters over in the past he has got quite merry.'

'Oh…here is Papa now…' Elise frowned as she caught sight of their father looking anything but merry. She knew only a matter of some urgency would bring him out of doors to find them. Elise felt her heart plummet on suddenly noticing he seemed to be struggling to run rather than take his time in a pleasant stroll. He stumbled, despite employing his walking stick to aid his poor bent legs, and at once Elise hurried towards him.

'So you are not your father's son, after all, but more like that blackguard of an uncle of yours,' Walter cried out as soon as he was within earshot. He jostled a path past Elise, his face tense with fury, and limped on towards Alex, waving a parchment in a fist.

Elise pivoted about to watch, her complexion draining of colour. She'd guessed her father had in his hand Aunt Dolly's letter and his irate reaction to having read it could mean only one thing…

'You came to offer me recompense for what was priceless!' Walter thundered. 'What had you in mind to pay for? The loss of my wife's virtue, or my daughter's?'

'Please…Papa…do not blame the viscount! He has has

come here not only to speak to you, but to me, too.'
Elise darted after her father and clutched at his thin,
quivering arm.

'Has he now!' Walter snapped, his weak eyes sav-
agely attacking the viscount's face. 'And what was your
answer to his damnable impertinence? What's he offered? *Carte blanche?* I believe that's what his uncle
offered your mama, yet the wretch could manage no
more than a seedy room and a few cheap clothes.' He
shook the letter in Elise's face. 'This fellow will treat
you better, do you think, just because he has the where-
withal and you are a maiden?'

'I think we should go inside and finish this,' Alex
said with quiet authority. His features were taut, yet ex-
pressionless, and he extended a hand as though inviting
the others to precede him.

'I'll not have you again in my house, sirrah!' Walter's apoplectic fury came to an abrupt halt. He sagged
against his stick for support, prompting Alex to easily
bear the weight of his limp body. Walter roused himself and weakly shook off his saviour.

'You must calm yourself, sir!' Doctor Burnett had
swiftly drawn close, replacing Alex's assistance with
his own by firmly gripping Walter's arm to prevent
him wobbling. 'Come…do as his lordship says and repair indoors where you can sit down and debate in a
sensible manner.'

'He has seduced my daughter! How can a man be
sensible on knowing that?' Walter again raised the letter
in vibrating fingers. 'My sister has given me the news,
and if Dolly has heard the rumours in Hammersmith,

so has every confounded fellow and his wife from Mayfair to Cheapside.'

Elise used the heel of a hand to smear away tears
that had trickled on to her cheeks. She knew her father wasn't exaggerating the way scandals could spread
like wildfire. She noticed that Beatrice's pretty features
were frozen in shock and bewilderment at this alarming turn of events. Wearily Elise realised that her sister
had no idea this calamity had resulted from her stubborn determination to go to London and masquerade
as Lady Lonesome.

'I would not have advertised in the gazette if I'd
known how it would end!' Beatrice whimpered, scrub-
bing at her eyes with her hanky.

'I know,' Elise soothed her sister, attempting to
quieten her crying. But her memory was not so short
that she could not recall warning Beatrice time and
again of the perils associated with such a harebrained
scheme to get a husband.

As soon as they'd re-entered the house Mr Dewey
had ordered both his daughters to go to their room. Elise
hadn't immediately obeyed; she'd attempted to defuse
the situation by again impressing on her father that Alex
Blackthorne's proposition wasn't what he thought. But
her father would not listen, and the more determined
she was to stay and defend Alex, the more Walter's agitation increased. Like her mother before her she was
too far under a rogue's lecherous spell, her father had
roared, at which point Dr Burnett had swiftly inter-
vened, drawing Walter aside to calm him down. Alex
had stayed just outside on the small terrace, as her fa-

ther had denied him entry to his house. Elise had felt in equal part mortified and outraged at the injustice of his shabby treatment.

Elise had ushered Beatrice towards the stairs, knowing that further appeals to her father would only end in him becoming more overwrought.

Halfway up the treads Elise had glanced over a shoulder to see Alex watching her through the open back door. His smile of comfort and reassurance had crumbled her composure, making a huge sob swell in her chest. By the time they reached their chamber her tears were flowing as fast as her sister's.

Once they had quietened down and had a chance to compose themselves Elise had explained to her sister the circumstances prompting their father's distress and how Aunt Dolly's letter was the catalyst to it all.

Beatrice had blinked in astonishment for a full minute before flinging herself back on to her bed in a renewed fit of hysterics. Now she used an elbow to get herself upright, raising bleary bloodshot eyes to Elise. She'd picked over some of the bones of the tale and was ready with questions. 'Does Hugh know that *I* was his Lady Lonesome?' she croaked. 'Does he know that at Vauxhall you went off to meet Mr Best instead of me?'

'I suspect Alex has not told him anything much, but can't be sure, of course.'

'And Papa…does *he* know the whole dreadful episode came about because of what I'd done? Will I be blamed for everything do you think?'

'I don't know…' Elise gave a hopeless shake of the

head. 'I don't know if he will allow the viscount an audience so he can explain. Oh…I don't know what might come of it all, Beatrice. Papa might have already sent Alex on his way.'

Elise wandered to the window and looked out at the afternoon sunshine gilding the grass and the shrubbery where just an hour or so ago she and her sister and two handsome gentlemen had walked in pleasant harmony. Then, just for a fraction of time, she had deemed it possible that this might be one of the happiest days of her life; now her dreams had turned to dust. Her fears for her papa's health were overriding every other anxiety whirling in her mind. She felt terribly guilty and that was frustrating because all of her actions in this dratted melodrama had been carried out with the purest of motives. The irony, of course, was that, had she simply curbed her boredom for a few months more, Beatrice would have been at home on the first occasion that Dr Burnett came to call on them.

'Papa will never forgive me for getting you into trouble.' Beatrice lifted her whitening face from a mopping hanky. 'Are we *all* to be ruined?' she whispered, aghast. 'Will nobody ever want to speak to any of us again?'

'No…don't be silly…it won't come to that,' Elise promised in a heartening voice.

'Why does the viscount not just pay Whittiker his money?' Beatrice squeaked. 'He is very rich and can afford it, I'm sure.'

'Because it will not do.' Elise sighed. 'You know it will not. Alex has done nothing wrong other than agree to act as his friend's proxy and meet Lady Lonesome.

Besides, a blackmailer should be exposed and punished, not rewarded for his wickedness.'

Elise could tell that her sister was panic-stricken over the dreadful consequences of ostracism. Quite rightly Beatrice feared that her budding friendship with Colin Burnett might wither before blooming.

'*I* didn't go off to meet Mr Best. I don't know why you thought I would.' Beatrice sniffed. 'I promised I would not go that night. You should have believed me, then none of this would have happened.'

Elise sank wearily on to the edge of her bed, her face dropping to rest in her cupped palms. How easily the finger of blame could spin and point away from its source. But there was truth in Bea's accusation, too.

The sisters swivelled towards the door as they heard the light knock.

Betty Francis's lined face and grey bun appeared before the woman stepped into the room. 'Well…what a to do and no mistake.' She puffed out her lips and shook her head. 'I'm not about to pretend I've turned deaf…or daft. I've heard enough of your papa's ranting and raving to get the gist of what's gone on.' She cast a gimlet eye on Elise. 'The tall good-looking fellow… the viscount…he's the one your father's mad at, I take it?'

'He's done nothing wrong…'

'That's what they all say, Miss Elise.' Betty crossed her arms under her bust. 'Handsome is as handsome does.'

'Is Lord Blackthorne with my father?' Elise asked, rather fearful of hearing the answer.

'He isn't, miss.' The housekeeper noticed the immediate flash of distress in Elise's eyes and reassured, 'Don't you fret. He's not gone away; he's outside somewhere. Mr Dewey wants you to attend him in his study. That's what I'm here to tell you, miss.'

Chapter Eighteen

From the landing Elise spied the top of Colin Burnett's auburn head as he closed the door of her father's study. Immediately she flew down the stairs to demand in a breathless whisper, 'How is he, sir?'

'I have given him a soothing draught and checked his pulse. He seems quite relaxed.' Colin steered Elise away from the door to ensure his patient would not overhear them. 'I tried to persuade your father to retire to bed for an hour or two, but he insists he is comfortable where he is in the large wing chair.' He hesitated, tapping a blunt finger against his lips. 'He wants to speak to you and the viscount. But whether together or separately…' Colin's warning grimace terminated in a sympathetic smile.

'Where is Lord Blackthorne?' Elise asked, feeling a trifle breathless at mentioning him.

'I believe he went outside to talk to his tiger. I expect the lad is getting hungry and stiff if he has been balanced on his curricle for a time.'

'Oh, would you let Mrs Francis know of his presence? I'm sure she'll gladly fetch the boy a drink and a bite to eat.' Elise felt guilty for only belatedly seeing to the tiger's comfort; she'd seen him outside when she'd been with Alex in the morning room. It pleased her that Alex had been less short-sighted, proving himself a caring master.

Colin nodded acceptance of her errand. 'Then I must set off and see my patient in Woodley.' He took out his pocket watch, briefly consulting it. 'I will be back later to check on your father…but not to dine, that was not my intention in mentioning my return,' he added hastily.

'It would have been nice to have you as our guest,' Elise said simply. Even on short acquaintance she knew she liked Colin Burnett. 'I'm sorry you witnessed such…unpleasantness earlier.' A wry smile pulled down the corners of her mouth. 'We are usually a very sedate household, you know. Too sedate, we might have said… up until today…'

Colin gestured away her apology. 'You would be surprised how often I minister to people with ailments arising from family upset. It is all part of life's rich tapestry.' He cleared his throat, levity vanishing on asking, 'Has your sister been very distressed by what has gone on?' He glanced towards the stairs rather wistfully, as though hoping Beatrice might appear and put his mind at ease.

'She is calmer now the shock has passed.'

'Would you let her know I said not to bother herself with potting the plants we dug out, but that I shall certainly return later.'

'I'm sure Beatrice will like to see you.' Elise smiled before turning apprehensive eyes on the door of her father's study. In response to her wordless plea for encouragement Colin put a hand on her shoulder. 'Go on,' he urged gently before turning away and setting about his business.

'I'm so sorry, Papa, that you have found out this way.'

'Did you think such shameful behaviour wouldn't eventually reach my ears?' Walter demanded in a thin voice.

'I hoped it would not.'

'Well…at least you're honest with your father.' Walter ground his head fitfully against the chair back, patting his palms in a restless rhythm on his knees. 'What were you thinking of? Have you learned nothing from your mother's mistakes?' he cried in muted anguish.

'It is not the disaster it might have been.' Elise moved swiftly closer to soothe her father with an explanation. 'The viscount came here to speak to you and to me. He has asked me to marry him, Papa…and I intend to accept his proposal.' There was barely a wobble to her voice hinting at the momentous decision she'd made, but her conflicting feelings were mirrored in her father's face.

'Well!' Her father's gruff incredulous snort accompanied the barked word. 'He did *not* speak to me on that matter. And I'd sooner have any good intentions from the person promising them. He mentioned debts outstanding to me. You can't blame a father for believing a rich fellow might tender cash as a remedy for disgracing a poor man's daughter.'

'You're wrong, Papa, he isn't like that…he's an honourable gentleman.' Elise shook her head, nervously clasping then unclasping her hands so they might flutter to emphasise her convictions. 'The viscount has said nothing to you about his marriage proposal because… I've already refused him.'

Walter's jaw sagged towards his chest. 'You've *refused* him?' He raised a limp wrist in exasperation. 'You said a moment ago you intend to accept him.'

'I've changed my mind and will agree to marry him now.'

Walter tipped up his tilted head, peered judiciously down his nose at his daughter. 'Ah…I see…you do not love the fellow, but realise you are backed into a corner and can see no other way out.' Walter shook his head and sighed. 'I can see few alternatives either, miss, but if you need proof of where a lack of affection in a marriage might lead you need only cast your mind back on your own parents' *mésalliance*.'

His colourless eyes softened on Elise, his expression altering in a way that merged all his past misery and humiliation into a sad little twitch of the lips. 'I loved your mother dearly, but she merely tolerated me for as long as she could. So I shall not lecture you on which road to take as, once you set on it, it will be a long one. It must be your decision, my dear, and you need to decide whether to make it with head or heart. Of course, you have your sister's future well-being in the palm of your hand. But choose wisely for yourself, too, for rancour and regret strengthen with the passing years and become a horrible burden.'

Elise's chest tightened until it seemed her heart might shatter. Her father's counsel had been a raw and personal account of the torment he'd suffered during a marriage of terrifying loneliness.

As Elise dipped her head, employing her fingertips to dash away tears, Walter reached for the bell on the edge of his desk and gave it a shake. 'Let's see what the fellow has to say for himself.' Walter returned the brass implement to rest on wood. 'Seducing a damsel comes at a price and I'd like to hear from his own lips that he's prepared to pay it. After that it is up to the two of you what ensues.' Walter clutched the chair arms and leaned forwards, an intense expression shaping his withered features. 'But if you decline him, then discover you need the protection of his name, after all, because you are with child, and he attempts to wriggle free, viscount or no, I'll hound him till the day I die with every breath I draw.'

'He did not seduce me, Papa. I swear he didn't… he did nothing wrong at all…' Elise darted forwards to ease her father back in his chair as his agitation increased.

Walter allowed his daughter to settle him, drawing two deep breaths. A moment later he opened his eyes and hiked a grey eyebrow at her. '*Nothing* wrong at all…?'

Her father's scepticism indicated he'd spotted the blush heating her cheeks, so Elise rattled off, 'He kissed me…that's all…'

'Indeed…did he now…the prelude to seduction, as I recall,' Walter remarked exceedingly drily.

Her next attempt to champion Alex was held on the tip of her tongue as Betty Francis appeared on the threshold.

'Would you ask Lord Blackthorne to join us please, Mrs Francis?'

The woman obeyed with a bob, slanting an encouraging glance from under her eyebrows at Elise as she backed out of the study.

'Lord Blackthorne is innocent of wrongdoing, Papa,' Elise stressed quietly as she moved towards her father to sink on to her knees by his chair. She didn't want Alex to enter to a barrage of unjust accusations.

Walter gazed into his daughter's soulful amber eyes. 'So you have said.' He plucked up one of her hands, cradling it between dry palms before holding it on his knee. 'You seem mightily keen, my dear, to protect this fellow you do not love or want to marry.'

'He is a good man.'

'And how did you and this *good* man come to be spotted alone together at Vauxhall, in a dark walkway?' He picked up the letter from Dolly reposing by the bell on his desk. 'I expect my sister exaggerates the matter, but naturally she is most concerned about repercussions for everybody, including herself.'

Elise massaged her throbbing forehead with a thumb and four quivering fingers. She didn't want to get her sister into trouble. Neither did she want to lie. 'On the evening we visited Vauxhall I lost sight of Beatrice when we were by the stage listening to the music,' she started in a voice so husky it was virtually inaudible. 'I panicked and thought she might have got lost and be unable to locate us all in the throng, so went to look for her.'

'Why did you not seek help from Anthony Chapman? I'm sure he would have scouted for her, had you explained,' Walter argued.

'I didn't want to worry anybody else or spoil their

enjoyment. We were all having a nice time. It seemed… not the right thing to do.'

'And the viscount? Was he helping you to look for your sister?'

'Not exactly, Papa,' Elise murmured. 'But he, too, was on a mission to find somebody and we met by chance. It was not arranged between us…but we were seen together.' She abruptly bowed her head, causing a thick wave of honey-blonde hair to curtain her pink cheek. 'The vile man who has spread this gossip is Lord Blackthorne's enemy. James Whittiker tried to extort money from the viscount in return for keeping quiet.' She snapped up her face, revealing eyes alive with anger. 'Alex refused to be blackmailed, but we know now the villain was not bluffing. He has gone ahead and done his worst from greed and spite.' Her impassioned words died away, but fury was still evident in the small fingers forming fists in her lap.

'James Whittiker, eh?' Walter nodded slowly. 'Well, I know in describing him you do not malign his character. I remember that young pup at the age of about eighteen. He was remarkably snide and bumptious even then—'

Walter broke off on hearing the knock on the door. He immediately gave the call to enter.

Elise stood up slowly, smoothing crumples from her skirt and fidgeting tresses behind her ears, as Alex entered, closing the door behind him. Her heartbeat quickened as he turned and took that first look at her. He appeared tired, she realised with a pang that made her want to rush to comfort him. He had travelled for hours to see her and ask her to marry him. He'd also graciously offered to repay her father's debts…debts that he'd no legal obligation to settle. For his pains he had received a cup of tea and vilification. Elise tried to signal with her beautifully expressive eyes that she was sorry, that she still needed his assistance in finding a solution to the woeful predicament in which they found themselves.

'I have spoken to my daughter,' Walter began without preamble, 'and she tells me you have asked her to marry you.'

'I have, sir,' Alex confirmed in a low baritone that betrayed none of his feelings.

'And why is that?' Walter asked.

Alex's dark eyes slid again to Elise, bathing her in a velvety intimacy before courteously returning to her father. 'Your daughter has been compromised by me. I understand your sister has written to tell you about it now gossip has started spreading in town.'

'That's exactly it,' Walter confirmed. 'So...had you not been spotted together in awkward circumstances at Vauxhall there would have been no proposal?'

'Papa...' Elise whispered, wondering where this was leading and which of them was to be most embarrassed by her father's line of questioning.

Walter raised a finger to his daughter, begging her silence and obedience.

Alex shifted, resisting the urge to plunge his hands in his pockets. He glanced down at his boots, concealing a reluctant smile and subduing an urge to polish the dusty toecaps on the backs of his breeched shins. He felt like an errant pupil summoned to an audience in a headmaster's office; he also felt a surge of the utmost respect for Walter Dewey, despite realising the old fellow was not about to make anything easy for him.

He might have done the decent thing by proposing to Walter's daughter, but Walter wanted more than his title, his estates, his millions of pounds for Elise. He wanted to know she'd be cherished. In the not-so-distant past he'd been approached by a marquess willing to sell a daughter to him for the price of a short lease on a Mayfair town house. Alex knew which of the two gentlemen he admired and which he'd like as his future father-in-law.

Alex had made a few enquiries and knew Walter Dewey was impoverished. He had nothing other than this rented house, a small private income and his two beloved children. Yet future scandals held no fear for Walter; he'd charged those demons years ago and lost, emerging battle scarred. Just hours ago Walter had proved his contempt for compensation by rejecting Thomas Venner's conscience money. The purpose of this interrogation was to allow Elise to listen and learn from his answers and his conduct whether she could trust him as the father of her children, the keeper of her heart.

'Are you to answer me, sir? Or might I draw the conclusion that you have nothing further to add.'

'I have something to add,' Alex said. 'There would have been no proposal…just yet.'

'Ah…I see…' Walter nodded. 'Expand on *"just yet"* if you please.'

Alex's eyes moved and merged with a wondrous golden glance before she whipped her eyes away. He observed her frown, her uncertainty before she once more fixed her eyes on her father.

What had Elise needed from him? Alex brought to mind her three vital requirements for her marriage: love and respect and loyalty... He'd vow each one and more besides if she'd let him.

'It would have been too soon to expect your daughter to believe me sincere when promising her my love and respect and loyalty.'

'I see...' Walter said, glancing at his daughter just as Elise averted her face to conceal a bright sheen in her eyes. 'It seems your acquaintance was not so short that you deemed kissing her in the shrubbery might be inappropriate—' He broke off as he heard his daughter's muffled protestation. He squeezed her hand, patting it in apology and consolation at breaking that confidence.

'Well...*I* believe you sincere,' Walter said, cocking his head at Alex. 'I can tell my daughter might need some persuading. So...I think it best I leave you alone so you might do what a fellow must in these circumstances.'

Walter gripped the upholstered arms and pushed. He grimaced, lowering himself back into his chair. 'As it is easier for you young people to get about, perhaps *you* should remove yourselves.' He squirmed again into a comfortable spot in his seat. 'Why not go outside and enjoy the last of the sunshine while you talk?' he suggested.

Elise darted glossy golden eyes at Alex, her heart thudding like a drum. He held out a hand and it seemed the most natural thing in the world to go to him, to feel the hard gentleness of his long fingers at the small of her back, guiding her to the door.

Walter watched from his vantage point as the couple emerged on to the terrace. Not arm in arm yet, but close enough to make him contentedly close his tired old eyes.

He wasn't surprised his Elise had caught herself such a noble gentleman. He'd seen early her beauty that went beyond looks and eclipsed her older sister's prettiness. But Arabella had been blind to it. When Elise was little more than a toddler his wife had been disappointed that her younger child's hair wasn't fairer, her eyes not china blue, but turning a hue that hinted at autumn leaves. She'd wanted a twin for Beatrice and another tribute to her own image rather than a daughter who resembled the man she'd agreed to marry when in his prime. A man she'd henceforth found it impossible to love.

The viscount was a smarter fellow than he, Walter acknowledged with an inner chuckle. He wouldn't allow himself to be led astray by a vain beauty who fluttered her eyelashes at every fellow in the room the moment her spouse left it. Oh, Walter had heard of his reputation and knew Blackthorne was a wealthy aristocrat with a penchant for the petticoat set. He knew, too, that he could easily negotiate a marriage contract within the aristocracy. But the boy was made in his father's image and required a wife and a marriage that would remain steadfast through life's ups and downs, and Elise with her grace and wit would challenge and charm and suit him perfectly till the day he died.

As soon as Alex Blackthorne had come into his study and Walter had witnessed the two of them together he'd known. A short acquaintance, maybe, but they were in love, yet each too proud or stubborn to yield and declare feelings when fate seemed set against them.

Walter chuckled softly to himself. One down…one to go…

But he was optimistic on that score, too. The doctor was well within his rights to give the Dewey household a wide berth following the scandalous uproar he'd witnessed earlier, yet Walter had an inkling that Colin Burnett would return later, and primarily to see Beatrice rather than to fuss over him.

Chapter Nineteen

'I'm sorry my father has…' Elise's courage deserted her along with her voice. She had no idea how to carry on, but had felt compelled to blurt out something to shatter the wall of tension that seemed to be building between them as they walked side by side.

She indicated a path that opened on to a small rectangle where a bench was situated beneath an arbour smothered in ramblers. The rose garden faced west and the golden warmth of the sun clung to the mellow red-brick walls enclosing it. The early evening air had turned fresh and Elise crossed her arms, absently rubbing at their tops.

'Are you cold?'

'A little…' She gave him a fleeting glance, glad he had spoken at last.

He slipped off his jacket, settling the fine garment about her hunched shoulders. Elise smiled her gratitude as sandalwood and a faint aroma of port and tobacco enveloped her. She nestled into the coat bearing his warmth and musky scent.

'I'm sorry my father made such a scene in the garden

earlier,' she began quietly. 'Please make allowances for how dreadfully overwrought he must have been after reading Aunt Dolly's letter.'

'It was an understandable reaction.'

'And I'm sorry he has engineered this awkward situation and has made you…' Again Elise faltered, gestured with a hand as she approached the ancient wooden bench and sat down, an inaudible sigh shuddering up from deep within.

'Sorry your father has made me…?' Alex prompted,

'Oh…I think you know what I'm trying to say!' she cried in muted frustration. 'He has made you say things…indicate things you don't mean and from embarrassment, or good manners, you have gone along with it.'

'I've not humoured your father,' Alex countered mildly. 'You seem to assume that I know your thoughts, Elise. More often than not I'm simply optimistically guessing at them, wishing your feelings to reflect mine.' His expression turned wry as he sat down beside her. With a weary sigh he sat forwards, resting his elbows on his knees. 'Despite you assuming I'm a practised womaniser, I'm as clumsy as the next novice suitor attempting a courtship. Attempting a *proper* courtship,' he qualified ruefully, sensing her narrowed eyes leap to his profile.

Elise quelled an urge to snap that he'd been skilful enough to gain his mistress's blatant adoration on the afternoon she'd seen them together in his phaeton. As he turned towards her, she squinted against sunlight that shadowed his features, yet lit hers to his slow scrutiny.

The vague amusement in his eyes transformed to

a gaze of passionate tenderness as he took her slender pale fingers, slowly raising them to his lips in a reverential salute. He lowered her hand to her lap, allowing his fingertips to continue the caress.

'Did you intend to say that you're sorry your father manoeuvred me into declaring my proposal was heartfelt, but premature?' he asked with studied solemnity.

'Yes…' Elise croaked, intensely aware of the sensation of his skin stroking on hers. Involuntarily she unfurled her fingers to allow more of his seductive touch. 'Yes,' she repeated, having cleared her throat. 'I'm sorry you had to do that.'

'I didn't have to do it. I just found the courage, somehow, to lay bare my soul, despite not knowing how you would take hearing that I love you and respect you and will remain faithful to you.'

Elise's dusky lashes lowered in confusion before flicking up so she might search his face for a sign he was teasing, or, worse, continuing to be dreadfully polite. But a glimmer of wonderment began rippling through her as his eyes remained steady despite self-mockery clouding their depths.

'You will promise to give up your mistress for me?' Heat spontaneously suffused her cheeks; the thought that had been spinning in her mind, making her jealous and miserable, had spurted forth from her lips of its own volition.

'Of course…I already have. Did you seriously think I would not?' His hands cupped her face, tilting up her chin so she must look at him. 'I take my marriage vows seriously, Elise, that's why I've not yet felt inclined to utter them.'

'Neither have I,' Elise whispered. 'I know as a good daughter I should marry and not be a burden on my papa, but I'm glad I've not been asked as there's been nobody that I've liked enough…until now.'

He smiled crookedly at her while brushing a thumb over her full pink lips. Instinctively Elise parted her mouth, touching moisture to soothe the sensitivity he'd trailed in his wake.

Alex dipped his head, ready to plunge his mouth on hers following her innocently erotic teasing.

'What will become of her?' Elise asked when their lips were merely a hair's breadth apart. Her small palms caught either side of his abrasive jaw, tightening fiercely to hold him back. 'How did your lady friend take knowing you are to be married?' Elise knew she was being brazen in mentioning Celia Chase at all. A genteel young lady did not acknowledge the existence of a gentleman's paramours; she certainly didn't quiz him over them, even if she considered herself to be his future wife. Of course, in the eyes of the *ton* she was now sullied and need not adhere to their hypocrisies, she reminded herself, so promptly repeated her question.

'I believe she is adequately supplied with admirers and will soon find another gentleman friend.' Alex kept his tone neutral, his eyes on hers despite the temptation to let them fall to her alluring lips.

Elise was not content with that answer. How did she know if *he* might still number among Celia's admirers? The thought of her husband secretly lusting after another woman pricked her pride. 'Can you so easily suppress your feelings for Celia Chase?' she demanded huskily.

'Yes.'

'And if I should decline your proposal?'

'Then perhaps she would remain my friend… Who knows?'

There was a subtle challenge in his voice and velvet-brown eyes that was not lost on Elise. 'So you *do* still love her and want to sleep with her…' Elise's brittle conclusion terminated in a gasp as Alex shifted alarmingly quickly, looming over her and trapping her back against the bench's slats.

'I don't love her, Elise, and as for sleeping with her…I have no more desire to do so if we are to be married. I am not an adulterer. As I have told you.' He dipped his raven head, smoothed his cool mouth against one of her flushed cheeks. 'I love you, Elise. I want you…but if you were to reject me…not want me…you'd have no right to blame me for turning elsewhere.'

'I do want you…' Elise breathed. 'I really do…'

Inwardly Alex smiled as he nuzzled her neck, causing her to blissfully sigh. She did love him and all that stood in the way of her trusting him was her wrongful perception of Celia Chase's part in his life. How was he to explain that a man's mistress often was no more important or useful to him than his tailor? In the way a gentleman might tire of a particular cut of clothing, so might he decide he'd outgrown his current paramour and look elsewhere for female company. He didn't feel guilty or callous because of his point of view; he liked women he knew treated their role professionally and who were keen to benefit from the transaction. Alex knew fellows who had fallen in love with their mistresses and married them, but it had never occurred to him to seek more than shared passion and companionship from the women he bedded. Until he'd met Elise he'd not been sure that any woman could completely satisfy everything he needed from a wife.

'*Coup de foudre*, I believe it's called,' Alex said softly. 'From the moment you marched over to me to confront me at Vauxhall I was smitten even though I thought you were scheming Lady Lonesome. After you ran off I started scouring the crowds for a sight of you almost immediately.' He twisted a smile. 'I couldn't believe my luck when I saw Hugh had joined your group and I realised I had a reason to approach you.'

'I think I fell in love with you almost at once as well.' Elise tilted her face to welcome the hand that had cradled her cheek at her shy declaration. She closed her eyes, letting out a soft sigh as Alex pulled her roughly towards him on the seat.

'Perhaps Whittiker has done me a favour rather than a disservice,' Alex said, his lips smoothing over satiny skin close to her brow. 'But for him I might still be too proud to admit to what I've known for some time. I might invite him to the wedding reception.'

'Don't you dare!' Elise giggled, nestling against his shoulder.

Alex pulled his coat away from Elise's body by a lapel. She watched his long fingers disappear close to her breast, felt the nudge against tingling flesh as he withdrew the hand clasping a small box.

'So, Miss Dewey…will you marry me?' Alex asked with a gravity that wasn't wholly playful as he went on to bended knee by her side.

'I will be greatly honoured to do so, sir.'

He snapped open the small leather casket, turning it so she might see the jewel inside.

Elise stared at the ring for a long moment before raising astonished eyes to his face. 'You brought this with you for me?'

He nodded. 'It was my grandmother's engagement ring. My mother had it in her safe keeping, so I called on her before heading towards Hertfordshire.'

Elise touched the huge sparkling diamond with a hesitant finger. 'It's so very beautiful…I've never seen anything so grand…' she murmured, awestruck.

'And it's yours if you'll do me the greatest honour, make me happier than I've ever been…and say you'll marry me.'

Instead of reaching for the ring Elise joined him on her knees on the ground, hugging him tightly about the neck. Joyous tears dribbled on to her cheeks, wetting his hair. 'I've never felt so happy either, Alex,' she sniffed.

'You like your gift,' he noted with gentle humour, drawing her up to sit beside him. 'I'm very glad…so would my grandmother be to know it goes to someone as fine and beautiful as you; my mother will adore you.' He chucked up Elise's chin as she dried her eyes with her knuckles. 'She has given me firm instructions to introduce you to her the moment we return to town.'

Alex wriggled the gold shank free of its velvet nest and, taking her left hand, slid it in place.

The unaccustomed weight made Elise carefully lift her fingers so the dying sun might fire the magnificent diamond to rainbow brilliance. 'It fits me very well.' She gave a beatific smile, spinning the ring and turning her face up to his.

It was the opportunity Alex had been waiting for. His lips seized hers with hungry heat, sliding silkily back and forth parting her lips. With an inaudible gasp Elise's hands coiled about his neck and she kissed him back, luxuriating in the way her response made him widen her mouth to the touch of his tongue. It was the same as the first kiss he'd given her, but so much better, imbued with a wooing sweetness that had been lacking when he'd thought her a mercenary harlot.

'God...do you know how long I've waited to do that again?' Alex groaned against her hair when their lips finally unsealed.

Elise nodded, crumpling her loose silken hair on his jaw's stubble. 'Far too long...' She sighed.

Alex pulled her on to his lap, ignoring her squeal of protest at the immodesty of it and again captured her mouth in a drugging kiss.

'I want you!' It was a rasping, half-laughing apology for his lack of control. 'I want you, Elise...right now...I feel as though I could devour you...'

He sounded agonised and she held him in comfort, his mouth steaming against her heavy sensitised breasts covered by the wool of his coat. She arched her back, dropping back her head as exquisite sensations streaked from her nipples to the core of her femininity. Instinctively her hips squirmed against the hard heat pressed against her buttocks and the small groan grazing his throat turned feral.

Alex sprang to his feet, carrying Elise in his arms as though she were featherlight as he strode urgently towards the screening shelter beyond the brick wall. But just a few paces away from his destination a frustrated curse burst through his teeth and reluctantly he put Elise down.

Norman Francis goggled at the couple from beneath his low forehead. In his opinion, if one of the girls took after her mama it was Miss Beatrice, not the quieter one…or so he'd thought.

He'd heard from his wife just half an hour ago that a right to do had gone on while he'd been away in town collecting a few provisions. She'd given enough details for him to know a scandal was again brewing for the Dewey household.

Norman thought that the *to do* would be far worse if Mr Dewey discovered his younger daughter was again allowing herself to be ravished by a Mayfair rake before the fellow had put a ring on her finger. He took a cautious glance at the fellow's broad shoulders and thunderous expression. He knew what he'd seen; but he'd pretend he hadn't, he decided. His wife had said that an engagement might be announced before the day was out. It was obvious Miss Elise hadn't been putting up a fight.

'Umm…yer pa wants to know whether you'll want your guest staying for dinner, Miss Elise. Rabbits need skinning and two more chickens need wringing 'cos seems the doctor'll be coming back and might want dinner 'n' all.'

The hand gripping hers in the folds of her skirt tightened. A thumb slipped to and fro against Elise's soft palm, causing an oddly arousing sensation to weaken her knees.

'Lord Blackthorne would very much like to stay to

dine as he's very hungry, thank you, Mr Francis,' Elise said impishly, but she avoided looking at Alex even when his stroking became unbearably sensual.

Norman tugged at his cap and turned to meander back the way he'd come.

'Come, we must go in to see Papa. He'll be waiting for our news.' Elise had seen rekindling desire closing Alex's eyes to sleepy slits. 'It will not do to scandalise the servants,' she squealed as his mouth chased hers, claiming another slow honeyed kiss. Despite her fine words she sagged against him, her small hands splaying over white cambric covering hard ridges of a muscled chest.

'I think we should be married here before the week's out,' Alex murmured against her cheek. 'I can't wait longer for you, I swear. I'll get a special licence easily enough. Please don't tell me you want a fancy affair in town.'

Elise gazed up at him, shaking her dishevelled blonde head. 'I don't. I think a quiet country affair sounds perfect.'

'We can honeymoon for a couple of days in a hotel in St Albans, then have a wedding reception in town when we've had time to arrange things. In the meantime I'll arrange for an announcement to be immediately gazetted in *The Times*.'

Elise sprang on to tiptoe to kiss his cheek in a show of love and gratitude. She clasped his face with her hands, as she had earlier, keeping his eyes merged with her glowing golden gaze. 'I love you very much, Alex.'

'I know, sweetheart,' Alex said softly, soothing her bashful blush with a leisurely stroke from a cool finger.

Alex started along the path, his strong grip enclosing Elise's fragile fingers as he led her back towards the house.

Chapter Twenty

'It is wonderful…' Beatrice's eyes were fixed on the sumptuous stone sparkling on Elise's betrothal finger. 'I'm very happy for you both.'

There was wistfulness in her sister's congratulations and Elise withdrew her hand, feeling rather awkward. Much good luck and happiness had been showered on her in a few hours, whereas for Beatrice there presently seemed only the prospect of being pitied and overlooked as the spinster older sister of Viscountess Blackthorne. Unless… Elise studied Bea's face, recognising dreaminess in her expression. She realised that perhaps her suspicions were to be proved correct and Bea had really fallen for the doctor. It seemed unbelievable on such a short acquaintance…yet Elise knew it had taken her no longer than a few moments in Alex's company for exciting, untasted emotions to overwhelm her.

Alex had left immediately to start making arrangements for the wedding at the village church once Walter had expressed his delight at being informed of the happy couple's decision to get married. But her new fiancé had said he would be glad to return later to dine with them. Elise's own excitement at the imminent change in her life had been deliberately muted, acutely aware as she'd been of Beatrice's disappointment at having gained nothing from their trip to town to get the husband and the family life she craved. But now Elise was wondering if Hugh figured much at all in Bea's thoughts.

'Have you forgotten all about Hugh?' Elise asked softly. She picked up the hairbrush from the dresser and gently drew it through her sister's long pale locks, tilting her head to read Bea's expression reflected in the dressing table mirror.

'No...I haven't forgotten him.' Beatrice glanced at her hands, folded in her lap. They fluttered a gesture. 'I liked him very well, but...' She sighed. 'I accept now that nothing could ever come of it.'

'Do you blame him for leading you on?'

'Perhaps I should, but I can't claim ignorance of Hugh's financial situation. His aunt mentioned it to us at Vauxhall even before he'd turned up to be introduced. I knew he must marry an heiress, yet still made it clear to everybody that I had set my cap at him.' A wry smile tilted her lips. 'I would have felt dreadfully miffed if he'd not responded to my pursuit.'

'And respond he did!' Elise chuckled. 'There was no doubt he was equally smitten.' After a pause Elise continued. 'Alex mentioned that Hugh has been visiting the Chapmans.'

Beatrice met her sister's eyes in the glass. 'I'm not surprised; Verity is now spoken for, but Fiona is not. And they are very nice people.'

Elise nibbled at her lower lip. The same thought had

occurred to her: that Hugh might turn his attention to
Fiona and her small inheritance once all hope of marrying Beatrice had gone.

'Don't look so glum,' Bea rallied. 'He needs a wife
with a dowry; it was silly to expect we could survive
on love alone.'

'Did you really love him?' Elise asked, the hairbrush
remaining idle in her hand while she awaited her sister's answer.

'I expect it was just infatuation. I so wanted to find a
nice attractive gentleman who I knew would be kind to
me and our children. Hugh met my requirements, you
see, and I forgot that money is so very important, too.
But constantly fretting over bills would have made us
argue, then we'd have grown to hate one another, and
that would have made our children sad.'

Elise knew that her sister was recalling how they
had suffered from living in a cold home atmosphere
when young.

'Hugh didn't send word with Alex, did he?'

'No,' Elise finally said. 'I'm not sure Hugh realised
Alex was coming to see us in Hertfordshire.'

'I am.' Beatrice's huffed a laugh. 'It doesn't matter.
That day at the park Hugh said it would be best if we
made a clean break. At the time I thought him heartless. Now I see he was right.' She stood up, gathered her
lemon gown from the bed and held it against her figure. 'I shall wear this for your engagement supper this
evening. I wish now I had done as you said and stitched
my new turquoise ribbon about the hem.'

Elise enclosed Beatrice in a fierce hug. 'Thank
you…'

'For what?' Bea asked, chuckling.

'For being a good sister…for agreeing to be my bridesmaid…oh…for lots of things.'

'I shall want you as my maid of honour when I wed, viscountess or no.'

'And you shall indeed have me!' Elise pulled back, looking deep into Bea's blue eyes. 'Colin Burnett likes you and you've not yet known him one full day.'

'I know.' Bea's lips twitched in a private little smile. 'And I like him. But as you say, I've not known him very long at all.' She turned to her reflection, assessing the dress against her body. 'I am determined to henceforth be sensible and take things slowly so I don't raise my hopes, or Papa's.' She suddenly grinned, in the excited way that reminded Elise of the old Beatrice who was never at all sensible about gentlemen admirers. 'Colin is very well situated. He has told me his uncle is a baronet and he is his heir…and he is very interesting to talk to. He knows a good deal about lots of different things besides the work of a physician—'

'Are you two young ladies ever coming below stairs?' Mrs Francis had poked her head about the door, interrupting Beatrice. 'The gentlemen have arrived. The doctor came first on horseback and is joining you at the table. He was pleased to see your father looking so well. The viscount turned up a few minutes ago in a carriage. They have all been having a jolly talk and a drink before dinner while waiting for you to join them.' Mrs Francis closed the door behind her as the sound of their father's laughter was heard. 'All getting on fine and dandy they are.' She wagged a finger. 'But you know how your papa is with a few tots inside of him.'

Elise and Beatrice exchanged a rueful look at that caution. Indeed, they did know how easily their papa could overindulge and empty a decanter.

'Get dressed and come down quickly so I can serve up,' Mrs Francis instructed. 'You won't want your father ending up with his head in his soup bowl, will you?'

'Capital!' Walter raised his glass in a toast. 'I think Friday is a fine day for a wedding.' Having just heard from his future son-in-law that he had made the necessary arrangements for the end of the week, Walter beamed at his blushing daughter. 'What say you, my dear? It will suit us all, won't it?'

Elise nodded, smiling at Alex as he picked up his wine to join his host in toasting their forthcoming nuptials. 'I hope it will not rain,' she blurted, holding her own cool goblet momentarily against a hot cheek to soothe it. She felt she might burst with excitement and happiness knowing in a few days time she would be Alex's wife. Through the wavering tapers on the dining table his eyes caressed her and he tipped his glass, a small private salute just for her.

Colin Burnett glanced at Beatrice and, noticing her glass was almost empty, courteously poured her a small drink from the carafe. The couple then held their wine aloft to complete the circle of crystal reflecting flames from the candelabra.

'To my daughter and her fiancé and wishing them every future happiness that is most richly deserved!' Walter boomed, then swallowed a good amount of claret. 'I believe we have some champagne in the cellar. I have been saving it for a special occasion. I will call for it to be brought up later—'

'Perhaps we might have that on Friday, Papa,' Elise interrupted quickly. Her eyes swerved to Alex, reading from his mild amusement that he could also tell her father was very tipsy. Walter had had a hearty appetite for his dinner, but, despite the amount of good food eaten, the alcohol seemed to have gone straight to his head as Mrs Francis had predicted it might.

'I should like a taste of that champagne on our wedding day, sir, when I might appreciate it to the full,' Alex tactfully said. 'Tonight I must drive back to my lodgings in St Albans and arrive in one piece, you know. There are many more arrangements to make tomorrow.'

'Yes…yes…I suppose so. It is a shame we are so cramped for space or you two gentlemen would be most welcome to overnight here and take a nightcap with me once the girls are tucked up in bed.'

'That is kind, sir,' Colin replied smoothly, taking up the task of dampening Mr Dewey's eagerness to over-imbibe. 'But I have to return home, too, as I have an urgent appointment with a patient first thing in the morning.' He put down his glass and swung a smile between the newly betrothed couple. 'I wish you good luck and a fine day at the church on Friday.'

'Actually…I was wondering if you'd act as my groomsman?' Alex asked.

'I'd deem it an honour,' Colin returned with a beam of surprise. 'I'm not sure I have a suitable set of clothes.'

'Neither do I.' Alex grinned. 'But I'm sure we'll pass muster.'

'I'm to be Elise's bridesmaid,' Beatrice announced,

turning to Colin. 'I'm wearing one of my new gowns that I had made in town.'

'The one you have on is very becoming.' Colin glanced at the taut pastel material rippling prettily over Beatrice's pert bosom.

Beatrice dimpled at his warm admiration and to spare her further blushes Colin gallantly turned to his host to thank him for the fine dinner they'd just eaten.

Alex echoed that sentiment before draining the wine in his glass. 'What will you wear sweetheart?' he asked softly as his fingers found Elise's under cover of the tablecloth.

'I have a fine new dress, too, that Papa bought for me while we were staying at the Chapmans.'

'The one you wore to the Clemences' ball?'

'Do you remember it?' Elise asked, surprised.

'Of course…it's not white, it's the colour of your eyes.'

'I don't care what people make of it, if you don't.' Elise chuckled, emboldened by the wine she'd drunk. The warm glow inside seemed to be as intoxicating as the smouldering dark gaze bathing her face.

'If only we had the time I'd engage a dressmaker for you. When we return to London I'll buy you everything your heart desires,' he murmured with a hint of apology.

'I have everything my heart desires,' Elise whispered back, her soulful tawny gaze signalling that she didn't give a jot for material possessions. Her small fingers turned within his cradling hand, tightened in emphasis. She hoped he understood she'd gladly take him as plain Mr Blackthorne and would live with him in a cottage in the countryside if it ever came to pass that that was all they could afford.

Aware that their papa had been quiet for some time, the sisters simultaneously turned their attention from their admirers to the head of the table. A snuffling sound confirmed their suspicions.

'Oh…he has fallen asleep.' Elise gasped a tiny giggle as she fondly surveyed her father. He was leaning back in his carver with his head lolling awkwardly on a shoulder. 'I shall find Mr Francis and ask him to get Papa upstairs.'

'There's no need to do that.' Alex's warm fingers arrested Elise as she would have stood up. 'It's no trouble for me to put him to bed.'

'I'll gladly give you a hand in getting him out of his clothes,' Colin immediately offered. 'Then might I ask for a ride with you back to St Albans? I fear it has come on to rain.' A hiss of water splashing on to the embers in the grate proved the doctor's suspicions correct, likewise a pattering against the windowpanes.

'Of course, I'll be happy to take you. You can tether your horse behind the carriage.' Alex pushed back his chair and stood up.

As the gentlemen carefully eased their father from his seat Elise and Beatrice went to find Mr and Mrs Francis to thank them for the fine job they'd done of providing good, ample fare at such short notice. The pea soup had been wonderfully thick and tasty and the chicken and rabbit main courses, served up with plenty of dishes of vegetables and several spiced sauces, had been very well received. The puddings had consisted of a creamy syllabub and sweet tarts of dried fruit steeped in brandy. And, of course, their father had insisted that each course be accompanied by various bottles of wine.

'Is he still fast asleep?' Elise whispered.

'Snoring,' Alex confirmed on a chuckle as he descended with Colin close behind.

The sisters had waited at the bottom of the stairs for the gentlemen to come down after settling their father in his bed. Beatrice and the doctor diplomatically disappeared towards the back hall with a mention of fetching coats and hats, allowing the newly betrothed couple a little time alone.

'Thank you,' Elise said simply, raising herself on to tiptoes to kiss Alex. She suddenly curled her arms about his neck, slipping her soft lips from his cheek to his mouth. He tasted of sweet wine and musky masculinity and, remembering how earlier in the garden he had caressed her mouth with his tongue, she shyly returned the seductive salute.

Alex seized the delicate wrists gripping his shoulders. 'God…don't, Elise,' he groaned, forcing her gently away. 'It's torture wanting you, yet knowing I must still wait some days and nights.'

Elise flicked up her lashes, her confusion at being rejected softening into an expression of wonderment. She hadn't realised she wielded such power over him. She buried her head against his shoulder. 'I can't wait either,' she said softly, although in truth she didn't exactly know what it was Alex anticipated doing with her when they were alone in bed that caused such a self-composed aristocrat to be agonised by frustration.

'What can't you wait for?' he teased, feathering a kiss on her soft brow. 'Tell me…'

'Whatever it is you want,' she said sweetly. 'I'll do my best to please you, I promise.'

He backed her against the wall, lifting her till their faces were level and she was pinned in place by his long hard body. 'And I'll do my best to please you and cherish you and love you every day of your life. Don't be scared about our wedding night, Elise, even a little bit. I'll make it wonderful for you, I swear.'

Spontaneously she thanked him with a kiss, then remembered and jerked away. 'Sorry…'

'Don't be,' he growled. 'Don't ever be sorry for kissing me or loving me—'

A cough preceded Colin's arrival in the hallway, Beatrice hovering just behind him.

Alex allowed Elise's feet to touch the floor, sliding her body against his despite the torment it aroused.

'Shall I help you put up the hood on your curricle?' Colin blurted in a jolly tone.

'I hired a carriage this evening and left the curricle and my tiger behind at the Red Lion as it looked like rain.'

'Ah…' Colin mumbled. 'Goodnight, then, to both you ladies and please thank your father for a most pleasant evening.'

'Goodnight, Elise…Beatrice,' Alex said with teasing formality. 'I shall call on you tomorrow.'

The sisters waved as the gentlemen went outside, closing the door quickly against a gust of wet wind that would have sent the panels crashing back against the wall.

'I feel…quite content,' Beatrice said softly, gazing at her sister through dusk illuminated by a wall sconce and a stumpy taper burning on the hall table.

'So do I,' Elise breathed dreamily. Lifting the candle, she lit the way to the stairs.

Chapter Twenty-One

James Whittiker spat out a curse and slammed down his losing cards.

'No luck?' It was a question from a rival gamester seated on the opposite side of the baize-topped table.

James knew the fellow's sympathy was as false as his smile: both held a hint of vicious satisfaction. The pot was large and many pairs of eyes were avariciously lingering on it. The atmosphere was becoming increasingly hostile as slowly individuals withdrew from the contest for want of funds, or courage to continue bluffing on a hand that lacked royalty.

James shoved back his chair, stalking off to find a steward to fetch him a cognac, hoping he wasn't about to be embarrassed by a refusal because he'd not yet settled a long-overdue shot. An ugly grimace hiked up his top lip at the thought.

Not long ago he'd been confident that Blackthorne would come up trumps and protect Elise Dewey's reputation with his cash. But Whittiker hadn't received a penny. Neither had he received any response to the two coded threats he'd sent to Upper Brook Street so he had gone again in person. The insolent butler Blackthorne employed had told him the viscount was still out of town and when he might be back was unknown.

Robinson's curt dismissal had prompted Whittiker to act rashly while fired by Dutch courage and a burning resentment. By the next morning the gossip he'd started in the Palm House—a den of iniquity for gentlemen who liked to gamble and whore under the same roof—had spread far wider than he'd anticipated. Despite his thumping hangover twinges of doubt had immediately set in…not from conscience, but because he questioned his own tactics.

He now knew he should have waited longer, allowing Alex Blackthorne to return so he might again inveigle him for cash. If nothing else, he'd hoped Alex might agree to give him a few hundred pounds simply to get rid of him.

Yesterday James had bumped into Dolly Pearson and Edith Vickers in Pall Mall and had deduced from twin despising stares that they'd heard the gossip and knew who'd started it. James realised there was now nothing left to gain from the débâcle other than revenge, and even that advantage was turning sour. Usually the *beau monde* loved nothing better than to topple heroes from pedestals and eject damsels from ivory towers, but it seemed Alex Blackthorne and Elise Dewey had steadfast friends who were dousing the flames of the scandal before it could spread. James had not been fêted, as he'd hoped, for unearthing a juicy titbit concerning the eminent viscount and the country miss, but rather shunned.

'Whittiker…'

James pivoted about on hearing the shout. Hugh Ken-

drick was bearing down on him, a paper in one hand
and a tumbler in the other.

Hugh clapped a hand on James's shoulder. 'Just the
fellow I wanted to see,' Hugh exclaimed, then took a
swig of brandy.

James's eyes narrowed suspiciously. He knew very
well that Blackthorne's friend disliked him as much as
the man himself did.

'Have you heard the wonderful news?'

'News?' James parroted. But his mind was agile and
he speared a glance at the gazette under Hugh's arm.

'Here, have my copy and read all about it,' Hugh said,
all generosity, whipping out the paper. 'See…I've even
turned it to the right page for you.' Having despatched
his drink in a single swallow, Hugh started on his way.
'Can't stop; I'm off to my tailor to see about a suit of
wedding clothes. There's bound to be a grand reception in due course.' A gleeful bark of laughter flowed
back over Hugh's shoulder, but he didn't turn around.
Had he done so, he would have seen Whittiker's teeth
snap together in a snarl of frustration because he'd lo-
cated and digested a paragraph Hugh had boldly cir-
cled in black ink.

James tossed the paper on to an empty table on striding to the door. He now knew what, or rather who,
had been keeping Blackthorne out of town. He also
knew where the viscount was sure to be found: St Albans in Hertfordshire because that was where the confounded chit he'd seduced lived with her father and her
sister. Hugh Kendrick's delight about the forthcoming
marriage had been genuine and Whittiker felt livid at
the idea that instead of causing Blackthorne great inconvenience he might have precipitated the fellow's
wedded bliss.

* * *

Whittiker wasn't the only person to feel cheated on reading that Viscount Blackthorne and Miss Elise Dewey were shortly to be man and wife. The groom's mother seized her lorgnette and employed it for several minutes, reading and rereading the notice that announced her son's nuptials in a few days' time. Finally she pushed the paper away and returned her attention to her buttered toast. 'Well, really, Alex,' she sighed, taking a dainty bite and swallowing. 'Just because I told you I approve of the girl doesn't mean I wouldn't have liked an invitation to the wedding.'

Another woman was not quite so prepared to be philosophical about the whole affair. Celia Chase ripped the offending page in two on reading that Alex Blackthorne was to be married. Having screwed the newsprint into a ball, she hurled it as far as she could, then slumped into a chair and burst into furious tears.

Everything had suddenly become very clear to Celia. On the day Alex had left town she had received a short note from him ending their liaison. In the same post had come a letter from his attorney detailing her generous settlement.

Celia had been incensed to know she was being pensioned off, having only briefly enjoyed the advantages of being the mistress of the *ton*'s most popular bachelor. Not that she'd expected him to propose, but she would have been content to remain his paramour whether or not he took a wife. Now she wished she'd made that perfectly plain to him because she wanted back the life he'd shown her. She was young and ambitious. Pensions were all very well, but they didn't provide intense sensual pleasure or an entrée to the circles where rich and influential people congregated.

Alex's good looks and raw virility had drawn Celia to him like a moth to a flame. She'd been delighted in his skill as a lover. As equally satisfying had been putting out of joint the noses of ladies who were keen to impress on her their superior status. Her betters, maybe, but their contempt could never disguise their jealousy. Celia knew every one of them craved replacing her in Viscount Blackthorne's bed.

Celia was sure Alex must still desire her voluptuous body and was hoping she could coax him to have her back. She'd heard the gossip, spread by one of Alex's enemies, about the viscount compromising a lady, and had dismissed it as irrelevant. The reason why he'd ended their affair now became apparent to her. He'd feared her being hurt by him taking a wife…a wife he didn't truly want, but had been burdened with from social graces.

Having been raised in straitened circumstances by her milliner mother, something as twee as etiquette was absurd to Celia. A pampered life and the respect and envy of her rivals were what were important to her. Many months ago, on the same day she had eagerly agreed to Alex's proposition, she had turned down a similar offer from a coal merchant. She was confident she'd still have that fellow twined about her finger. So, to her mind, Alex Blackthorne *owed* her another chance to prove to him he'd no need to look elsewhere for his pleasure.

Celia dabbed at her tears with a handkerchief. Her pretty features hardened and a moment later she tossed the soaking linen towards the table where it landed on what remained of the crumpled newspaper. She was determined to get what she wanted just as she had when, at the age of sixteen, she'd escaped a miserable life as her mother's apprentice by warming the bed of a local magistrate.

Springing up from her chair, Celia paced to and fro, her fingers clenching and unclenching as strategies darted in and out of her mind. All she needed was an opportunity to tell Alex she could be trusted to be discreet and they could carry on as before. And she needed to do it immediately, before he got another woman to take her place. Like most men of his wealth and class he would keep a mistress, perhaps even before his little wife's belly started swelling.

Celia took a deep breath, feeling quite better now she'd decided on a course of action. She knew who might be useful in her scheme and had no qualms about the method needed to persuade him to help her.

Having approached the mantelpiece, Celia clattered the little bell that reposed on its marble shelf. While waiting to be attended by her maid she studied her creamy complexion in the mirror that soared up almost as high as the ceiling. A plump white finger fussed at the dark curls on her forehead before she stared deep into slanting dark-blue eyes, lively with intrigue.

A tiny French woman appeared on the threshold and bobbed her mobcap.

'I have an errand for you Paulette.' Celia turned slowly about.

'Madame?'

'I should like you to discover the location of a

certain gentleman. I wish to make his acquaintance, but unfortunately I do not have his whereabouts, you see.'

Paulette raised her thin face and frowned at her mistress. ''Ow shall I do it, *madame*?'

'Make some enquiries,' Celia answered a trifle impatiently. 'The butcher's boy, for example…he might know of the fellow's direction if he is a resident in the neighbourhood. Or…try at a coffee shop…or tavern… the sort of places fellows frequent besides their fusty clubs.' Celia clapped her hands. 'Of course! The clubs along St James's! He is a well-bred gentleman and a patron of one or other, I'm sure.'

'I cannot enter…I will be thrown out, *madame*,' Paulette whispered, scandalised at the very idea of attempting to breach one of those male bastions to pimp for her mistress.

'Wait outside, then, and ask after him.' Celia flicked an imperative finger, turning away to find a scrap of paper and a pen. Quickly she wrote her name and address, folded it and handed it to her maid.

'And *his* name, *madame*?' Paulette asked sarcastically, having looked at the parchment.

Celia pivoted about. 'Ah…yes…his name is James Whittiker and when you find him you may give him the message that I should like him to call on me at his earliest convenience.'

Paulette was glad she'd had no need to traipse all the way to St James's and loiter about accosting gentlemen like a trollop. The butcher's boy had, after all, known of James Whittiker. The cheeky scamp knew the fellow because his older brother was a tailor's apprentice and the tailor had been dunning for unpaid goods a certain James Whittiker. He was a little puffed-up fellow who lived on Cranley Street, the boy had told her. That information had made Paulette frown. Her *madame* liked distinguished gentlemen with plenty of money. It was a mystery to Paulette why she would be interested in a debtor living in a seedy district.

Paulette alighted from the cab, paid the driver then huddled into her cloak. She stood at the top of Cranley Street outside a pawnbroker's shop, glowering and muttering to herself a promise that on the morrow she would go to the agency and seek a new position once she'd found this ugly fat fellow called Whittiker.

Celia covered her naked body with a silk robe, then slid off the crumpled bed. She walked away without a glance at the snoring fellow. Once she had washed and dressed she would wake him and eject him from her house. He had served his purpose; she now knew where Alex was to be found. She pivoted about, knotting the silk belt about her waist. With mild disgust she eyed James's flabby torso displayed beneath crumpled sheets. His short soft body was nothing like Alex's big, hard physique. The contrast in their looks and wealth made her ever more determined to get back the life she'd had. But bedding Whittiker hadn't been such an ordeal; he had little stamina and the wine he'd drunk had quickly sent him to sleep after a thankfully brief performance. She had endured worse in the four years since she'd started her career as a courtesan. But Celia knew that she'd never improve on a gentleman like Alex and that was why she was not going to let him slip between her fingers…

'I've heard that the Red Lion cater for parties. I'm sure they would gladly provide a small wedding breakfast.' Colin grinned at Alex. 'Would you like me to enquire and make arrangements?' He thrust his hands into his pockets. 'As you've done me the honour of asking me to be your groomsman, I feel I ought to make myself useful before the big day.'

'I've already enquired,' Alex replied. 'The landlord is setting aside two rooms and will do his best to supply us with a good spread at short notice.'

The two men had met by chance in St Albans. Colin had been about to visit the apothecary shop when he'd seen Alex's tall figure striding along the street towards his sleek vehicle. He'd quickly diverted to speak to him before he could spring into his curricle and race off.

'You're a lucky man,' Colin congratulated gruffly. 'I've not known the family very long, but have found them very nice people.'

'I feel blessed to have Elise, but wish circumstances had been different so she might have had the celebration she deserves.'

'Sometimes spontaneity can be a good thing,' Colin murmured, looking thoughtful.

'Indeed…' Alex encouraged with a private smile. 'A man should follow his instinct. You are not long in the area, then?' he asked.

'A matter of months only, but I think I shall like it here.'

'I'm sure you shall.' In Alex's opinion it was obvious to all but a blind man that, short acquaintance or no, Beatrice Dewey liked the doctor and he was equally under her spell. Alex was glad Elise's sister seemed to have quickly recovered from her ill-starred romance. Despite understanding Hugh's predicament, he'd been annoyed to discover that his friend had started squiring the elder Chapman girl about town with indecent speed following Beatrice's departure.

'I must get going. I have to purchase a wedding ring for Elise.' Alex sprang aboard his carriage, aware of the day passing.

'There is a goldsmith in St Albans,' Colin offered helpfully. 'But I'm not sure if he has ready stock.'

'I know of a fine craftsman in Enfield who keeps a good selection of pieces of jewellery. It is a bit of a trek, but I should be back by nightfall.'

'Are you *sure* we will be welcome, Dolly?'

Edith Vickers leaned forwards to converse with her travelling companion as the vehicle bumped over a rut. A buxom matron seated beside her with a child on her lap used the opportunity to elbow some more room on the cramped seat of the mail coach.

'Of course—my brother will be delighted to see us!' Dolly Pearson flapped a hand and Edith squashed herself back against the upholstery.

'I shall be glad to get off this confounded contraption,' Edith complained. In her heyday, when her husband had been alive, she had been used to travelling in style.

'We allus makes a stop just up ahead at the Crown

at Enfield.' The fellow wedged in the corner next to Dolly helpfully supplied that information in his country brogue.

'Thank heavens!' Dolly murmured as she eased a small space between her bombazine coat and his musty tweeds.

'Are you certain it won't be an imposition on your brother if we turn up without warning?' Edith took a sip of her coffee. The two ladies were seated in the Crown tavern's snug, enjoying some warming refreshment, while the horses and driver took a well-earned rest before the final leg of the journey. It was midsummer, but cloudy and with a brisk wind cooling the air, making people huddle inside.

'Walter will be delighted to see me,' Dolly asserted. 'He will be glad that I have come to take charge. With no mother to advise the girls on such important matters as wedding day…and *night* matters,' she mouthed delicately, 'my brother will be grateful for my assistance.'

In truth, Dolly's determination to attend the imminent nuptials of her younger niece was not quite so altruistic. The momentous occasion of one of her relations joining an important aristocratic dynasty was likely to present itself only once in her lifetime and she'd no intention of missing it.

'Well…if you're sure Mr Dewey will have the room to accommodate us.' Edith sounded doubtful.

'We *might* have to put up at a local hostelry. My brother doesn't keep a large establishment,' Dolly owned up. She had kept that vital bit of information to herself when persuading her friend to accompany her to Hertfordshire. She'd not wanted to travel alone and Edith had, at first, seemed keen to be part of the big day. But Dolly could tell that her friend was now having second thoughts about the wisdom of agreeing to gatecrash the rushed affair. To soothe her friend's nerves Dolly exclaimed, 'Oh…it is a grand adventure, Edith. You cannot say it is not.' She clapped her gloved palms in excitement. 'Not an auspicious start to the romance, I'll agree. But look how it has ended! My dear Elise is to become a viscountess! I knew from the first moment I saw them together that Alex Blackthorne was utterly smitten by her sweet nature and pretty face…' Dolly's reminiscence faded as she noticed she'd lost her friend's interest.

Edith was frowning through the square-paned window into the tavern courtyard. 'Good heavens, Dolly… look! Celia Chase is alighting from that carriage.' Edith's chin was sagging in astonishment.

Dolly gawped through the window, her eyes becoming slits at the sight of a familiar brunette straightening her stylish velvet hat. 'I think I can guess what the troublemaking hussy might be doing so far from home, on the road to Hertfordshire.'

Edith inclined towards Dolly across the tabletop to hiss, 'You surely don't think the groom's mistress would try to spoil things for the bride?' She blinked in astonishment. 'But that would be so…uncouth.'

'I doubt good manners are that one's forte.' Dolly surged to her feet. 'I'm happy to give the brass-faced baggage a much-needed lesson in etiquette.'

Before Dolly had moved a foot, Edith was dragging on her sleeve.

'Wait! Look!'

Dolly dropped back into her chair, goggling in the direction of her friend's pointing finger.

'Oh dear! That is the viscount's curricle, pulling in over there, Dolly, I'm sure I recognise it, and him.' Edith's voice was brimful of pity.

The two women craned forwards to watch the riveting scene unfolding through the window.

An athletic male figure jumped down from the racing equipage then suddenly, called from behind, the viscount pivoted on a heel, frowning. Grabbing at her skirts to keep them free of her flying feet, Celia hurtled over gravel. Having launched herself at Alex, she wound her arms about his neck and kissed him full on the lips.

It seemed that the viscount was aware of the impropriety of such behaviour in broad daylight even if his paramour was not. In an instant he was propelling Celia by the elbow towards her vehicle. A moment later they disappeared from sight behind its coachwork.

Edith turned saucer-wide eyes on her friend. 'Well… what do you make of that, Dolly?' she gasped.

'Nothing good,' Dolly muttered. 'Nothing good at all.'

'It seems we are witnessing an assignation. Shall we turn about and go home?' Edith ventured. 'Perhaps there might be no wedding, after all…'

'Indeed we shall not!' Dolly pulled herself up in her chair. 'There *will* be a wedding.' She pursed her lips. 'We must not let them know…or anybody else know, for that matter…what we have seen. That hussy is sure to report this secret tryst to all and sundry in an attempt to break my niece's heart. She'll have no corroboration from me, or you, to help her do it.' Dolly sighed in deep disappointment. 'Perhaps it is a farewell meeting between them—who knows? Even so I can tell you that that fine gentleman has plummeted in my estimation.'

'Should we let the viscount know we are aware of his true colours?' Edith suggested.

A forceful shake of the head answered her.

'We shall let him know nothing of our opinions on his character till after he's put a ring on Elise's finger,' Dolly said firmly. 'Come…it is time to get back on the coach.'

'It seems he was not as smitten by Elise as you thought,' Edith said, following her friend to the exit, oblivious to the glower Dolly sent over a shoulder at the mournful remark. 'The viscount might be doing the right thing by your niece, Dolly, but you'd have thought he would have kept his *chère amie* at home in London at least till after the honeymoon.'

Chapter Twenty-Two

Walter had been taken aback by his sister's uninvited visit, but had nevertheless welcomed her and her friend cordially, as befitted a gentleman of good breeding.

Now he wished he'd turned them away and had stayed in blissful ignorance of the news they'd brought with them; because of it he had a harrowing task ahead of him. With the aid of his cane he proceeded along the passageway towards his study, his sister's reluctant footfalls dogging his steps. Walter swallowed down wrathful tears, rallying his courage. Once he'd done questioning Dolly he would wait for his daughters to return home from their shopping trip, then speak to his beloved Elise. His report was sure to make her inconsolable. But do it he must…

In his daughters' absence Walter had slowly busied himself in going to the kitchen to arrange refreshment for their guests. After speaking to Betty, he had gone back to his sanctuary to fortify himself with a nip of something stronger than tea before belatedly joining the ladies in the back parlour. He had been on the point of entering the room when he'd sensed, from a sibilant whispering from within, that he might be intruding on a delicate female conversation. Out of respect he had hesitated behind the door, awaiting an appropriate pause.

What he'd overheard next had not embarrassed him, but wounded him like a blow to the guts. *The dreadful spectacle* the ladies had encountered on their journey, and were picking over in scandalised murmurs, had precipitated Walter across the threshold. No amount of flummery from Dolly would convince him that his ears had deceived him. The ladies' dismay at knowing he'd learned of the tale was proof enough of its authenticity.

Walter was not a prig; of course, he knew wealthy fellows kept mistresses and bastards, as well as wives and heirs, and considered it a matter for their own consciences. What he could not abide was the hypocrisy and lies concocted by the wretches as a smokescreen to their sordid carryings-on. Had he the legs and energy to carry him he would have called for a pistol and a carriage pointed towards Enfield, and gone after the scoundrel.

Lord Blackthorne had vowed to remain a faithful husband to Elise, just as he'd promised to cherish and honour her till the end of his days. Walter had had those statements from the man himself on the afternoon the couple had come to see him to announce they were in love and wanted to be married. But now it seemed that the fellow was a callous fraudster, after all, who had no intention of giving up his paramour. If he could keep an appointment to sleep with another woman on the eve of his wedding, Walter knew he would certainly be tempted to do so again when the honeymoon was over. So…it was his duty to make Elise aware of Blackthorne's deceitful character before she tied herself to him. After that, her future was hers to decide…

But first he must make absolutely sure of his facts. Having reached the study, Walter turned the door handle, allowing Dolly to precede him, then with heavy heart he followed her inside.

'Why…Mrs Vickers…what a surprise to see you.' Elise came into the room with Beatrice just behind. Flustered, Edith shot to her feet.

'Is my aunt with you?' Elise asked pleasantly.

Edith's affirmative manifested itself in a tiny vibration of her head.

'Where is she?' Elise prompted when she realised the woman was unable to relax or volunteer any information.

'She is with her brother, but I don't know any more than that,' Edith insisted in a spurt. 'I don't know anything at all.'

'Well…please do sit down again, Mrs Vickers.' Elise exchanged a bemused glance with her sister, who'd also noticed their guest's jumpiness.

'Did you have a good journey from London?' Beatrice pleasantly asked.

'Yes…no…I'm not sure…' Edith squeaked and looked about as though wishing to scamper off. She again charged to her feet. 'There is tea in the pot—shall I pour you some?'

'It is cold.' Elise had pulled off the cosy and tested the crockery with a hand.

There was a single reason Elise could think of why her aunt and Edith Vickers would turn up unexpectedly and that was to celebrate her wedding. Her father had not mentioned inviting them and Elise suspected he had not, but Dolly would not let that put her off if she had a mind to be part of it all. Why Mrs Vickers was present, if she felt uneasy at attending the scandalous affair, Elise could not fathom.

'We have been shopping for lace gloves,' Elise blurted, hoping to lighten the atmosphere and still Edith's fluttering hands. Yet a strange sense of foreboding had begun stealing away her happiness as though the older woman's mood was infectious.

Elise unpacked the white, cobwebby articles from their tissue paper and Edith gave them a startled glance. 'I have some similar ones. They are useful for all manner of occasions, not just weddings...' She gasped in relief as Dolly appeared on the threshold.

'Your papa thought he heard you arrive home.' Dolly's brief, defeated shake of the head answered Edith's unspoken question, signalled by her bulging eyes. Dolly gravely turned her attention back to her bewildered nieces. 'Your father would like to speak to you, Elise, my dear.'

Elise plucked the hood of her cloak to shield her cheeks, but the cool breeze buffeting her complexion seemed inconsequential compared to the ice enclosing her heart.

She had been sitting on the bench in the town square for nearly an hour and borne the inquisitiveness of people as they went about their business. Those stares had penetrated her numbness and she knew that she'd been recognised and her behaviour would be talked about.

But she no longer cared about gossip or scandals. All she cared about was to see Alex. Her cold tremulous fingers twisted the heavy diamond on her hand, back and forth, back and forth, while she wondered if soon it would be gone. If there was no case of mistaken identity, and Alex had met his mistress at a tavern, then she could not marry him and would return the ring. She might love him till her dying day, but it was not enough without respect and trust. And how could she respect or trust a man who would betray her so soon after declaring his fidelity and his love?

At first she had giggled in shock when her papa told her that her aunt and Mrs Vickers had witnessed her fiancé kissing a woman at a tavern in Enfield. Once sense had returned she'd registered her father's despair and the reason for the ladies' awkwardness had become apparent. Her father had gone on to say Dolly and Edith had recognised the viscount's companion as Celia Chase. On legs that had felt boneless, Elise had sought her father's wing chair before she collapsed.

Within a moment furious jealousy had torn into her at the thought of Alex kissing and caressing his mistress at a secret location while she had been out buying lace gloves to wear at their wedding.

Now she also felt a stupid, gullible fool and, worse, she realised he must think her one, too, for readily swallowing his lies. On the afternoon he'd promised her the world he might already have had planned an illicit rendezvous with his paramour.

Hot tears again trickled on her cheeks as she clung to a theory that mistaken identity could be to blame. Yet in truth she realised such a forlorn hope was no more likely to save her than grasping at driftwood in a stormy sea when drowning. She must not condemn him yet, her heart argued with her shattered pride, despite all things pointing to his guilt. She must stay here and confront him and watch his eyes.

It was getting dark early beneath the foamy clouds. A faint mist of drizzle was blowing in the breeze, moistening her upturned face. Elise drew her hood again about her hair realising she would soon need to seek sanctuary in the Red Lion. She had gone in there before and asked after Lord Blackthorne. The landlord had told her he'd been gone all day and had travelled out of town. Her stomach had lurched at that damning information, although the fellow was unable to say whether his eminent lodger had headed off towards Enfield that morning.

The rain became heavier, slanting to sting her face, and Elise sprang up, her skirts in her fists, and sprinted to seek the protection of the whitewashed wall of the tavern. She pressed back against it, under the eaves, while trying to pluck up the courage to enter the premises and again face down speculative stares from the innkeeper and his wife.

A stable lad emerged from the adjacent barn with a bale of hay in his arms, closing the creaking door by kicking it to behind him before disappearing. Elise bolted towards the wooden building and grasped the latch, intending to shelter within when she heard the sound of an approaching vehicle. Her breath caught abrasively in her throat. She waited, squinting into the dusk.

The curricle was being driven fast and came to a stop in a spurt of earth in front of the Red Lion. Alex jumped down, tossing the reins to the tiger. The first sight of his tall powerful body caused her a physical ache. It was so easy to understand why women wanted him, why they might not easily let him go. Having waited so long for this moment, Elise now felt frozen to the spot, her tongue welded to the roof of her mouth.

He hadn't seen her, or if he had noticed her bedraggled figure he was ignoring it. And why would he not overlook a lone woman loitering by a barn in the pouring rain? No doubt he considered her what he had on first acquaintance: a soliciting harlot.

Elise knew that if she didn't intercept him he would soon be gone and confronting him inside the inn would be beyond her courage. She must do it here where the wind might whip away her bitter words before they were overheard.

Alex observed his manservant steering the horses into the courtyard, then turned, about to stride into the welcoming warmth of the inn. Instead he hesitated, casting a glance to one side. Despite her shoulders being hunched and a hood protecting her features, there seemed to be something familiar about the willowy woman stationed just inside the barn. With dawning astonishment he crossed the few yards that separated them. His immediate welcoming smile for Elise was quickly followed by a fierce frown.

'This is a very nice surprise, sweetheart. But what on earth are you doing here?' he asked, shielding her from the weather by altering his stance.

'Waiting for you,' Elise replied, gazing up at him through lashes made heavy by mingling rain and tears.

Alex's expression turned shrewd as he sensed an

accusation beneath her cool reserve. This was no impromptu visit because she yearned to see him…as he had longed all day to see her. Neither had she come to find him because he hadn't arrived at the appointed hour to dine at her father's house. But he used that as a prelude to discovering what was wrong.

'I'm sorry I'm late for dinner; I've been out of town. I came back here to make myself presentable before turning up.' He glanced ruefully at his mud-splattered boots and breeches.

'It doesn't matter; it's not important,' Elise said huskily. She was glad that raindrops were masking her watery eyes. Her insides might be wound tight as a spring, but she wanted to appear in control while demanding he tell her what he had done today and whether he needed to change his clothes because they'd been soiled by his mistress's scent as well as dirt.

'Come inside so we can talk. I'll get you something hot to drink while I get changed. You look frozen.' He took her elbow to solicitously steer her towards the Red Lion.

'There's no need for that.' Elise jerked her arm free with a shake of her head. 'I have just one question to ask and I'm hoping…if you feel anything for me at all…that you will dignify me with a truthful answer.'

Alex pivoted slowly towards her, but it seemed she could no longer bear to look at him. He took her sharp chin, silky and wet, in thumb and forefinger, tipping it up so their eyes tangled. 'Ask away,' he invited calmly, yet an inkling of what was troubling her was already in his mind. How she had come by the information, however, eluded him.

'Did you meet your mistress today at a tavern in En-field?' Elise asked in a strong voice that sounded quite unlike her own. He had no need to answer her. She knew from an unbearable silence, from a stony glint between his close black lashes that her aunt and Mrs Vickers had correctly reported what they'd witnessed. She had also been correct in knowing she'd see the truth in his eyes. Still she insisted on having it from his lips. 'A yes or no will do.' Her tone was different now, sarcasm suffocated by the anguish clogging her throat.

This time when Alex touched her arm to take her with him, she slapped at his fingers before swinging that same small hand at his face. The blow was hard enough to snap his head sideways, but she'd stumbled back even before noticing his perilous expression.

Alex jerked her forwards by the arms, lifting her off the ground to slam against his body when her fists began beating at him. When she continued fighting, he slung her over his shoulder. Having regained enough wind to do so, Elise began raining ineffectual punches against the solid breadth of his back. But he was already inside the barn, out of sight of any folk who might come to her aid. Alex slammed the door shut with a foot, so just a small window at high level was left to illuminate the dark interior.

'Put me down…this instant…' Elise screeched in breathless fury.

He dropped her to her feet, barring her immediate attempt to fly to the exit with an arm braced against the wall. She sprang away from him as though scorched, then retreated in time with his slow menacing advance.

Bubbling ire welled up in Elise, suppressing the *fris-*

son of fear that had instinctively made her want to escape him. She held her ground, tossing back her hood. Her loose chignon unwound, descending about her shoulders and her flushed face in a waterfall of honey-coloured waves. 'You are a heartless lying bastard!' Her chest heaved, but he made no comment, simply continued to close the gap between them. 'I told you I loved you and trusted you and you have thrown it all back in my face with your…your vile deceit. You could not even do without your mistress for the short while you were here with me in Hertfordshire, yet you said you had finished with her.'

He was very close now and she could sense a sweetish violet perfume waft in the air between them. Her fists clenched, but she fought down the urge to again lash out in a jealous fury at that proof of his guilt. She took a pace backwards, then another, unwittingly allowing him to trap her against stacks of hay bales.

'Well, I'm glad you and that woman had a sordid tryst because now I know you for what you really are,' Elise flung at him. 'A cheating lecher!' She yanked off the ring on her finger and hurled it at him, making him deflect the missile away from his face with a hand that snatched the diamond before it hit the ground.

She watched him drop the gem into a pocket, then swung her head sideways to use the heel of a hand and smear wet off her cheeks. But she'd not yet finished her tongue-lashing. 'If you think I am grateful that you've patronised me with a marriage proposal you may think again. I don't care about scandal and ostracism. I have my family. I have all I need. I don't need you or any of your grand gestures…' Her voice cracked and she drew in one huge breath. With supreme effort she turned to look directly at him, her eyes settling on his terrifyingly remote expression. But for the muscle jerking rhythmically in his jaw she might have imagined he'd been unmoved by her tirade.

'Have you finished?' His voice was icy and quiet.

Elise jerked a nod, not knowing what else to do.

'Good…it must be my turn to say something. I have not lied to you or betrayed you in any way. Nevertheless, I see now that marrying you would be a mistake.'

'I'm glad we are in agreement,' Elise uttered clearly, while feeling that the wind had been whipped from her sails and the moral high ground, for some reason, was no longer hers. Gathering her skirts in shaking fists, she made to haughtily pass him.

A vice-like clasp on her arm put her back where she'd been. 'I've listened to all you've had to say. You'll return me the courtesy whether you like it or not.'

Elise shoved at him and he pushed back, just hard enough to tip her over on to some hay bales directly behind. Before she could lever herself upright he followed her down, bracing an arm either side of her. Slowly she fell back away from him until her body was supported on her elbows.

'So…where was I?' Alex smoothly enquired, his eyes roving her tear-stained complexion, settling on her soft pink mouth. 'Ah, yes…I remember…reminding you of your manners.'

Elise folded forwards in fury, unwittingly bringing their faces close. *'My manners?'* she hissed at him, eyes sparking golden fire. 'Do you think it is right…or *respectful*…to have a squalid assignation with a woman while your fiancée is shopping for her trousseau on the eve of her wedding?'

'Indeed not,' Alex answered solemnly. 'Had I been guilty of such I would deserve to be castigated by you and horsewhipped by your father.'

Elise blinked and swallowed, then did so again. 'You weren't at the Crown tavern this afternoon with Celia Chase?' she whispered.

'Yes…I was…'

A sob rasped Elise's throat and she lashed out at him for daring to torment her and raise a tiny hope that he might be innocent.

He was ready for her this time. He caught one fist, then the other as they flew at him, forcing them down and pinning them on the hay above her head.

'But the meeting was by accident rather than by design,' he carried on as though there hadn't been a break in his dialogue. 'She was surprised and delighted to see me…I was astonished and angry to see her.'

Elise snorted her disgust. 'I shall not even dignify such rubbish with a response. You were seen kissing her.'

'By whom?'

'It doesn't matter!'

'No, it doesn't. Shall I tell you what matters, Elise?'

'Nothing matters any more; it is all finished with,' she cried, swinging her head to one side, chafing her cheek on her stubbly bed. She was far too aware of one of his knees wedged between her legs, of the vast expanse of his torso looming over her.

'Well, I'll tell you anyway. It matters that you have so readily turned your back on me and doubted everything I've told you without first allowing me to defend myself.'

'You cannot blame me for that!' Elise flared, her tawny eyes springing to his face like talons. 'My aunt and her friend are not blind and neither are they liars. I'm grateful that they arrived unexpectedly bearing the news and saved me from making a dreadful mistake tomorrow.' She flounced her face away from the grim humour slanting his mouth on hearing her betray her source.

'Neither am I a liar,' he said slowly. 'I, too, am grateful that they turned up or I might have remained unaware that you are prepared to condemn me and act like a jealous shrew.'

'Jealous shrew!' Elise gasped, outraged by the description. 'A jealous shrew might have found a gun and shot you. My papa said he would call you out if he were able.' She strained to free a hand to reinforce her argument with a slap.

'I'm sorry your father has been worried unnecessarily,' Alex said, easily thwarting her struggle. 'If he is still interested in having the details, and it will settle his mind, tell him I have a witness to my innocence just as you have people who imagine they observed my guilt.'

'You think I, or my father, would believe a word your doxy says on your behalf?' Elise choked scornfully.

'I doubt she'd defend me,' Alex muttered drily. 'But others who know the truth of the matter would. I stopped at the Crown because one of my horses threw a shoe. I was on my way to do business in Enfield at the time. I did run into Celia Chase there and I also met your friend Mr Chapman.'

Elise whipped her head about to widen astonished eyes on him. 'Mr Chapman also saw you having a rendezvous with your mistress?' She raised despairing eyes to the timbered ceiling. 'God in heaven! How many others have you shocked today with your disgusting behaviour?'

'The only people shocked by my behaviour are those who've jumped to conclusions over it,' Alex answered quietly. 'Anthony Chapman was present when I made Celia Chase turn around and head back towards London in her carriage. She had it in her head to come to Hertfordshire to try to persuade me to resume our affair. Her disappointment at my rejection made her loud and argumentative.' An acid smile twisted his mouth as the first glimmer of uncertainty clouded Elise's eyes. 'Mr Chapman would not only vouch for what he saw, but what he heard. And I have to say, sweet, that being ambushed twice in one day by jealous harpies is more than any man should have to put up with.'

'Don't you *dare* class me with her!' Elise burst out in wrathful indignation. 'I'm not jealous, I'm livid, and have every right to be so!'

'No…you don't, Elise,' Alex contradicted, his voice roughened by bitterness. 'That's why you'll listen to everything I have to say and I'll warrant you'll be haunted by it for the rest of your life.' He shifted their locked fingers, ran the back of his fist over her satiny jaw in a specious caress. 'Just as you'll remember accusing me and rejecting me for no good reason.' He paused. 'After Celia had gone your friends' father had a drink with me at the Crown. He said I had saved him a journey to visit you.'

Elise moistened her parched mouth with a slow circling tongue, unaware of an intense gaze tracking the movement. An awful pang of doubt was making her stomach squirm and she sensed her temper disintegrating, too. She wanted desperately to be able to justify her behaviour, for the thought of losing everything for nothing was too awful to bear. But…if he was right and she was wrong she would deserve his fury and contempt. And he would deserve her humble apology.

She trusted Mr Chapman implicitly and knew he'd never cover up another man's philandering with lies. He would tell the truth, if not to her, then to her father…and Alex knew his version of events could easily be checked.

'Do you not want to know how I saved him a journey?'

Elise mutely moved her head in a small affirmative because regret and humiliation were already closing her throat.

'He was on his way to give you a small packet: a present of lace from his daughters. He asked me to deliver it. It is in the box on my curricle.' A mirthless laugh preceded him concluding his case. 'The family send all best wishes for our future happiness.'

Elise's lashes fluttered down over the stinging heat in her eyes. The appalling irony of him bringing her a wedding gift, coupled with his curtness, had pierced her heart. 'Why did you go to Enfield?' she burst out in despair. 'You said you would be busy with marriage plans today.'

'And so I was…buying you jewellery from a goldsmith,' he replied. 'Now I regret having wasted my time.

It seems there will be no need of wedding rings.' His blackening eyes dropped to her mouth, travelled on to roam her cloaked body.

'Why haven't you asked me to let you up, Elise?' he enquired with sultry mockery.

Chapter Twenty-Three

'Let me up,' she managed hoarsely.

'I don't think you really want me to, sweet.' In a corner of his mind Alex knew he was acting idiotically. But the frustration assaulting him wasn't easy to quash. And neither was the need to punish her for her lack of trust. He'd bared his soul in a way he'd never before done with any woman. He'd pledged eternal love and faithfulness to Elise and meant every word, yet it was as though those solemn vows had meant little to her. He'd done nothing wrong today other than return late to dine with her and her family. And the idea that he might never have a chance to make love to her was a gut-wrenching torment.

'We might not be getting married...but why cancel the wedding night?' Alex purred. 'People already imagine we're lovers...me included in moments of madness despite the painful effect it has on me.'

Elise detected a harsh undercurrent in his voice, but the hand trailing her skin remained featherlight. Her eyelids drooped at the sensation of his long artful fingers brushing against her cheek, curling about her small ear to tantalise the sensitive hollow behind. She flicked her head away from the caress.

'We might have our differences but we're compatible in one very pleasurable way. Shall we enjoy that and forget about the rest?'

Alex dipped his head, touched together their mouths with a tenderness she'd not expected. If he were still furious with her, surely he wouldn't kiss her so courteously. Hope unfurled within Elise that perhaps all might not be lost. Surely he must understand how terribly shocked she'd been to hear such a report from her aunt. Her relatives cared about her, wanted to protect her from harm. *Whereas she hadn't been able to believe her fiancé could do so...*

With wounding insight Elise realised Alex was treating her coldly because of her lack of faith, because he was feeling as ill used as she was.

She parted her lips, inviting in the tongue teasing her, yearning to please him. She was aware that his hands had released hers to flip open the fastenings on her cloak so firm fingers could thrust inside and rove her figure. Elise sensed the familiar heat within kindling beneath his skilful manipulation. Her breasts were tingling in anticipation of being touched and her hips shifting restlessly on hay. He widened her mouth, fusing their lips with bruising pressure. She knew in a few minutes she'd be enslaved by his sensual skill, unable to resist him or whatever he wanted to do. Yet there was so much more that still needed to be said. With a tiny moan she jerked her head aside so his mouth swept moistly across her flushed cheek.

'If we could just talk some more, Alex,' she begged

huskily, her breath coming in short pants that grazed her nipples against his chest. 'I know we are both feeling injured, but I want to trust you…I *do* trust you…' she hastily amended.

'Thank you,' he muttered with obvious sarcasm. 'And do you expect me to trust you?' The taunt was murmured close to her ear.

'Yes!' she keened, scraping her scalp to and fro on hay. 'You must…because I love you…and want to be your wife.' Elise flung her face around, clasped his chin in a small hand. 'You would have been equally suspicious…equally angry…had you heard I'd been seen embracing another man. I know you would, so don't deny it!'

'I've not once imagined you might have another man.'

Elise gulped a laugh. 'You thought me a harlot the minute we met.'

'And you thought me…?' he enquired silkily.

'I thought you…' Her voice tailed off for if she were to be honest no flattering description could emerge from her lips. Her fingers slipped away from the abrasive skin of his jaw.

'…a rake up to no good,' Alex finished for her. 'That's what you thought me. Much as you do now. So why shouldn't I prove you right, Elise? We might not suit as man and wife, but it seems I have a vacancy now for a mistress.'

Elise jerked up her arms, coiled them about his neck, ramming her face into his shoulder so she could no longer see the insolent burning gaze flowing over her, making her feel stripped naked. She was within a heartbeat of willingly allowing him any liberty he wanted to take. And when in a delirium of passion, she might agree to any role he offered her, simply so she might stay close to him.

He loosened her grip and his head lowered, but she whipped up a hand, covering her lips with four quivering fingers before he could touch her. Alex growled a laugh at her tactic to keep him at bay, removing the obstruction with insulting ease before letting their clasped fingers fall aside.

Elise turned her head, staring at eerie straw edifices. Suddenly she flung her face around, eyes blazing. 'You will listen to me,' she insisted, eyes darting to and fro, searching for words in the barn's dusky atmosphere. She'd endured agonies on hearing how his mistress had flown to kiss him in the tavern courtyard. She'd make him admit it must have been harrowing for her to watch tears dripping from the end of her father's nose because he'd had to shatter her dreams and give her that report so soon after celebrating her engagement.

'I'm sorry if I've falsely accused you, but—' Elise began firmly before being interrupted.

'You have falsely accused me, but I'm getting over it, sweetheart,' Alex murmured throatily, undoing with practised ease her bodice buttons and chemise ribbons, then lowering his mouth to tightening pink-tipped breasts.

Instinctively Elise arched to increase the exquisite sensation of his clever tongue circling on her cool pearly flesh. He drew hard on the taut little nubs and she gasped, jerking her hips up to grind against his rock-hard thigh. The arguments forming in her mind scattered as a wild ache streaked to the core of her. She instinctively parted her thighs to the relentless slide of his leg, whimpering his name as the limb scuffed its target.

Alex raised his head at that soft call and looked at her features, blonde head thrown back in tense rapture. From somewhere behind his crazed desire he dragged the realisation that no matter what heights of pleasure he took her to, tomorrow she would hate him. And so would her father. Walter Dewey would have been right to couple him with his uncle: a man who'd wrench apart a family to quench his selfish lust.

But Elise was no passing fancy as Arabella had been to Thomas Venner. In a way Alex realised he wished she were because then it would all be easy; there'd be no inner battle and his body wouldn't feel like a tortured wreck going up in flames. He'd carry on and give them both release.

Elise was naïve, inexperienced in carnality, but instead of cherishing the gift of her innocence he was on the point of using it against her…because he was arrogant and immature enough to put his injured pride above that of the woman he adored.

'What are you doing?'

The murmured question exploded in his head, sent him surging upright because he didn't like the answer he'd found. He dragged together the edges of her cloak, concealing the enticing sight of her perfect body from his hungry eyes, before striding away.

Elise sat up slowly, her eyelids drooping in mortification. She drew up her knees, resting her forehead on them while trying to calm her raw emotions. It seemed even her body was no longer wanted by him and, instead of feeling ashamed of her wantonness, she felt bereft at being so wholly rejected.

She dragged herself to the edge of the hay and stood up. Forcing up her chin, she tidied her clothes and hair with unsteady fingers while taking searching glances here and there to locate him in the shadows. She hadn't heard the barn door creak, but couldn't be sure he hadn't gone away and left her.

The depressing thought of being so absolutely abandoned made a sob well in her chest. And then she saw him as a slanting moonbeam fell from above. He'd hunkered down against the door, his outstretched arms resting on his knees, his head lowered towards them. But it seemed he was aware of her approach.

'I'm sorry…'

'So am I,' Elise whispered in response to his hoarse apology. 'Will you take me home?' She managed to force level civility into her tone.

'Where does your father think you are?'

He hadn't moved, even to raise his face to ask her that question. It seemed so long ago that she had been crying in her room while below the others ate supper. Her sister and her aunt had tried to persuade her to go down, too, but the thought of food had made her feel nauseated. Besides, she'd been determined to confront Alex immediately. She'd not wanted to upset her father again by defying him—and he would have forbidden her meeting the scoundrel, as he'd called him—so she hadn't told anybody she was going out.

Gentlemen had their baser habits, her aunt had confided, patting her hand and trying to console her, and wives had to learn to live with them. Now Elise wished dearly she had acted sensibly, as her aunt had said she must, and rested quietly to put things into perspective. Instead, she'd crept out to beg Mr Francis to take her to town.

Had she not, Alex would by now have arrived to see her, bringing her Verity and Fiona's gift and news of his meeting with Anthony Chapman. The scandalous scene her aunt had witnessed would have been explained away and Elise knew she might have felt privately quite sorry that his mistress had made a fool of herself. Now it was she who'd made a fool of herself and destroyed her chance at happiness into the bargain.

'Where does your father think you are, Elise?' Alex repeated his question, sliding his back up the door so he stood leaning against it, hands in pockets.

'Mr Francis brought me to town on the trap. I sent him home with a message for Papa that you would bring me back after we had talked.' She was glad she'd managed to sound composed. 'Will you do that, please?'

'Of course…in a moment…if you want my company. If not, I'll get my tiger to take you back.'

They both remained quite still while an echoing silence seemed to soar up to the rafters.

'I want you to,' Elise murmured, a catch to her voice. She knew he was feeling guilty for having kept her down on the straw when she'd said she would get up. But he'd known the truth and in temper had taunted her with it. She craved his touch as keenly as he would bestow it. But for her pride and fear of rejection holding her back she'd launch herself at him now and tempt him to do it again.

'I was jealous.' Elise shattered the unbearable tension with the blurted admission, then dropped forwards her head, concealing her shyness. 'I couldn't bear the thought of you kissing her or doing…anything…with her,' she finished lamely, unable to voice the magical way he aroused her…no doubt aroused all the women he fancied.

'I didn't kiss her, or do anything with her. She flung herself at me and kissed me.'

Elise nodded acceptance of his flat declaration, fussing with her cloak fastenings to occupy her quivering fingers. 'I believe you. I know I misjudged you.'

'You didn't misjudge me, Elise,' Alex corrected gently. He waited until she raised her head to look at him before continuing. 'How do you see me?' he asked quietly. 'As a wealthy man, old enough to be respectably married, yet avoiding family life in favour of consorting with women of low principles and lower virtue? That's me…' He claimed his own derogatory description with a sour smile. 'That was me…until the night I went to Vauxhall Gardens and met you.' He walked away from the door to stand before her. 'It's not your fault you sensed my immature failings and thus doubted me. You were right to do so.' He raised a hand as though he would touch her, but his fingers clenched, dropped back to his side. 'Despite what you must think of me after what I just put you through, I swear I'm different now. If I wasn't, I wouldn't have walked away from you a moment ago.'

'I didn't want you to,' Elise whispered, turning her warm face to the cover of darkness.

'I know, sweetheart,' he said tenderly. 'That's why

I had to. You're not some tavern wench to be taken on hay. You're the woman I love.' Again he raised a hand, his unsteady fingers smoothing over her cheek this time, turning her back to face him. It was the first tentative touch from him that Elise had known.

'I know I'm not worthy of you, Elise.'

'You are!' Elise wound her arms about his neck. 'Don't say that! I love you,' she cried. 'You must believe me.'

His fingers speared up into her soft hair, drawing back her head so their eyes could meet. 'This latest fiasco has been my fault, not yours, or your aunt's or your father's. Celia admitted going to Whittiker to find out where to come and pester me. She couldn't accept that I no longer wanted her. I should never have got involved with such a schemer in the first place. But she wasn't the first such character and, but for meeting you, I doubt she would have been the last,' he added truthfully.

'She didn't want to let you go,' Elise responded solemnly. 'I don't suppose the others did either. I can understand why…but I still want to scratch out their eyes.'

Alex chuckled ruefully at the pugnacious sparkle in her steady gaze. A moment later he'd sobered. 'You won't ever need to feel that sort of hurt again. I'm so sorry that I let my stupid pride make me act in that way. I was terrified I'd lost you tonight, and set out to punish you instead of myself.' He rested his forehead against her golden crown of hair. 'Am I forgiven?' It was a husky plea.

'Of course,' Elise cried. 'And you must forgive me for acting like a shrew…I know I did,' she admitted, smiling bashfully. Still she could see a haunted look far back in his eyes. 'You haven't lost me, I promise, Alex.' Elise shook her head, feeling amused and rather awe-struck that the balance of power between them seemed to have shifted so far in her favour. 'Oh, no, you don't get away that easily,' she teased. 'You've got to marry me tomorrow. If you don't, my father might get a gun and shoot you after he finds out where I've been this evening.'

'I'll tell him you've been with your future husband who loves you very much.' Alex's mouth covered hers with passionate urgency, but then was jerked back. 'You're not frightened of your wedding night, are you, because I've acted like an idiot? Forget about what just happened between us, Elise.'

'I'm not sure I want to forget,' Elise said with a gauche honesty that made him burst out laughing.

'On our first wedding anniversary we'll bed down in the barn at Blackthorne Hall, if you require a reminder.' He drove a hand into a pocket and drew out her diamond ring and slid it on to her finger, curling the small digit to lock it there. 'I swear to you I love you and will hon-our every marriage vow we make tomorrow.'

'May I see my wedding ring?' Elise asked with a childish excitement that made Alex smile fondly.

He drew forth from an inside pocket a tiny square box and a longer, oblong casket. He opened the smaller to show her a slender gold band. 'It's inscribed on the inside with our initials.'

Elise made to take it, then quickly withdrew her fingers. 'It's probably tempting fate to touch it yet,' she whispered, widening her eyes on him.

Alex slipped the box back whence it came, then held

out the other one. 'I'd like you to wear this tomorrow. I was going to give it to you this evening when I came for dinner.'

Elise took the gift, lifting the lid to see a gemstone bracelet inside. She moved her hand so a silver moonbeam glanced on the glossy square stones, firing them red. She swallowed, shook her head in awe. 'Rubies… you bought this for me today in Enfield?'

The idea that she'd hit him, shouted at him and generally behaved dreadfully, when his only fault had been to secretly go off and buy her splendid jewellery, made Elise feel bitterly ashamed.

'Do you like it?' he asked.

His boyish eagerness to hear she approved of his choice plucked at her heartstrings. Too emotional to speak, she took his face between her palms and kissed his lips gently, teasing him with just a slide of her silky tongue. 'Tomorrow, Alex, I shall show you just how much I love it, and you, in any way you like.' She ran her fingertips over his stubbly jaw. 'But for now, we must go and see my poor papa and tell him all is well. He was dreadfully upset, you know—' Elise's voice broke at the memory of her father's distress.

'I'll make it up to you all, Elise,' Alex promised gravely. 'I'll prove to your father and to you that I'm nothing like my uncle.'

'It's bad luck, you know for us to be together so late on the eve of our wedding.' Elise sounded faintly concerned by that well-known superstition. 'We should have parted hours ago.'

Alex opened the door of the barn and for a moment

they stood quietly, Elise anchored to his side by a powerful arm about her shoulders.

'It's stopped raining.' He glanced up at the clear, navy-blue sky studded with a moon and stars.

'That bodes well,' Elise said brightly, hugging him about the waist. 'Fine weather on a wedding day is a good omen for a happy marriage.'

'Indeed,' Alex said, bowing to her need to find auspicious signs. 'Thereafter we'll make our own luck, sweetheart; you can trust me on it. I know because I've got you and that makes me the most fortunate man alive…'

* * * * *

ReaderService.com

Manage your account online!

- Review your order history
- Manage your payments
- Update your address

---

*We've designed
the Harlequin® Reader Service
website just for you.*

Enjoy all the features!

- Reader excerpts from any series
- Respond to mailings and special monthly offers
- Discover new series available to you
- Browse the Bonus Bucks catalog
- Share your feedback

Visit us at:
ReaderService.com

RS13

REQUEST YOUR FREE BOOKS!
2 FREE NOVELS PLUS 2 FREE GIFTS!

HARLEQUIN® *Desire*

ALWAYS POWERFUL, PASSIONATE AND PROVOCATIVE

REQUEST YOUR FREE BOOKS!

2 FREE NOVELS PLUS
2 FREE GIFTS!

YES! Please send me 2 FREE Harlequin Presents® novels and my 2 FREE gifts (gifts are worth about $10). After receiving them, if I don't wish to receive any more books, I can return the shipping statement marked "cancel." If I don't cancel, I will receive 6 brand-new novels every month and be billed just $4.30 per book in the U.S. or $4.99 per book in Canada. That's a savings of at least 14% off the cover price! It's quite a bargain! Shipping and handling is just 50¢ per book in the U.S. and 75¢ per book in Canada.* I understand that accepting the 2 free books and gifts places me under no obligation to buy anything. I can always return a shipment and cancel at any time. Even if I never buy another book, the two free books and gifts are mine to keep forever.

106/306 HDN FV3K

Name _____ (PLEASE PRINT)

Address _____ Apt. #

City _____ State/Prov. _____ Zip/Postal Code

Signature (if under 18, a parent or guardian must sign)

Mail to the **Harlequin® Reader Service:**
IN U.S.A.: P.O. Box 1867, Buffalo, NY 14240-1867
IN CANADA: P.O. Box 609, Fort Erie, Ontario L2A 5X3

**Are you a current subscriber to Harlequin Presents books
and want to receive the larger-print edition?
Call 1-800-873-8635 or visit www.ReaderService.com.**

* Terms and prices subject to change without notice. Prices do not include applicable taxes. Sales tax applicable in N.Y. Canadian residents will be charged applicable taxes. Offer not valid in Quebec. This offer is limited to one order per household. Not valid for current subscribers to Harlequin Presents books. All orders subject to credit approval. Credit or debit balances in a customer's account(s) may be offset by any other outstanding balance owed by or to the customer. Please allow 4 to 6 weeks for delivery. Offer available while quantities last.

Your Privacy—The Harlequin® Reader Service is committed to protecting your privacy. Our Privacy Policy is available online at www.ReaderService.com or upon request from the Harlequin Reader Service.

We make a portion of our mailing list available to reputable third parties that offer products we believe may interest you. If you prefer that we not exchange your name with third parties, or if you wish to clarify or modify your communication preferences, please visit us at www.ReaderService.com/consumerchoice or write to us at Harlequin Reader Service Preference Service, P.O. Box 9062, Buffalo, NY 14269. Include your complete name and address.

REQUEST YOUR FREE BOOKS!
2 FREE NOVELS PLUS 2 FREE GIFTS!

◈ HARLEQUIN®

SPECIAL EDITION

Life, Love & Family

YES! Please send me 2 FREE Harlequin® Special Edition novels and my 2 FREE gifts (gifts are worth about $10). After receiving them, if I don't wish to receive any more books, I can return the shipping statement marked "cancel." If I don't cancel, I will receive 6 brand-new novels every month and be billed just $4.74 per book in the U.S. or $5.24 per book in Canada. That's a savings of at least 14% off the cover price! It's quite a bargain! Shipping and handling is just 50¢ per book in the U.S. and 75¢ per book in Canada.* I understand that accepting the 2 free books and gifts places me under no obligation to buy anything. I can always return a shipment and cancel at any time. Even if I never buy another book, the two free books and gifts are mine to keep forever.

235/335 HDN F46C

Name _____ (PLEASE PRINT) _____

Address _____ Apt. # _____

City _____ State/Prov. _____ Zip/Postal Code _____

Signature (if under 18, a parent or guardian must sign)

Mail to the Harlequin® Reader Service:
IN U.S.A.: P.O. Box 1867, Buffalo, NY 14240-1867
IN CANADA: P.O. Box 609, Fort Erie, Ontario L2A 5X3

Want to try two free books from another line?
Call 1-800-873-8635 or visit www.ReaderService.com.

* Terms and prices subject to change without notice. Prices do not include applicable taxes. Sales tax applicable in N.Y. Canadian residents will be charged applicable taxes. Offer not valid in Quebec. This offer is limited to one order per household. Not valid for current subscribers to Harlequin Special Edition books. All orders subject to credit approval. Credit or debit balances in a customer's account(s) may be offset by any other outstanding balance owed by or to the customer. Please allow 4 to 6 weeks for delivery. Offer available while quantities last.

Your Privacy—The Harlequin® Reader Service is committed to protecting your privacy. Our Privacy Policy is available online at www.ReaderService.com or upon request from the Harlequin Reader Service.

We make a portion of our mailing list available to reputable third parties that offer products we believe may interest you. If you prefer that we not exchange your name with third parties, or if you wish to clarify or modify your communication preferences, please visit us at www.ReaderService.com/consumerschoice or write to us at Harlequin Reader Service Preference Service, P.O. Box 9062, Buffalo, NY 14269. Include your complete name and address.

HSEDIR13R

REQUEST YOUR FREE BOOKS!
2 FREE NOVELS PLUS 2 FREE GIFTS!

red-hot reads!

HBDIR13R